The Moaning Lisa

A Paco and Molly Mystery

Rosemary and Larry

MILD

Magic Island Literary Works • Honolulu, Hawaii • 2025

Interior book design by Larry Mild.
Cover design by Larry Mild

Library of Congress Cataloging-in-Publication Data
Mild, Rosemary P.; Mild, Larry M.
The Moaning Lisa, A Paco and Molly Mystery

ISBN 979-8-9863864-1-6
First Edition 2025

10 9 8 7 6 5 4 3 2 1

Dedication

For our wonderful daughters—
Jackie and Myrna

For our beloved grandchildren—
Alena, Craig, Ben, Leah, and Emily

For our precious great-grandchildren—
Kai, Oliver, Luna, and Zora

For our marriage—
Soul mates, partners, lovers

Acknowledgments

We could fill an entire volume with the names of all our readers. You are all precious to us and give us the ultimate push to continue our writing.

Our special thanks and hugs to:

Hawai'i Fiction Writers, for their friendship, encouragement, and advice.

The National League of American Women, Honolulu Branch, for their inspiration and camaraderie.

Disclaimer

The Moaning Lisa, A Paco and Molly Mystery, is a work of fiction. The plots and events therein are of the authors' imagination and invention. All characters therein are fictitious and any resemblance to persons living or dead is purely coincidental, except where noted in the foreword. A few real locations have been altered to accommodate the narrative.

TABLE OF CONTENTS

TABLE OF CONTENTS (Continued)

Foreword

When Larry and I started writing together decades ago, we hadn't even considered writing mysteries—until we visited my father, Dr. Saul K. Pollack, a prominent psychoanalyst in Milwaukee, Wisconsin. That visit set us on a happy new course. My father, a widower in his seventies, had a housekeeper/ gourmet cook named Dorothy. She was sixty-three, with a beach ball figure, waddle walk, taffy-colored curls, and a good-natured, nosy-body personality. She had never gone past the tenth grade, but she was super-smart and keenly observant.

Dorothy also had a unique way of expressing herself. "I have to take my calcium so I don't get osteoferocious." During our visit, my father pulled out a piece of paper from his desk drawer and handed it to us: his secret list of Dorothy's sayings. He thought we could submit it to *Reader's Digest*. Back home in Severna Park, Maryland, we studied the list and decided, "Forget *Reader's Digest*. Dorothy belongs to us." We named her Molly. Her frequent witticisms were "malaprops," but we named them Mollyprops.

The concept of malaprops originated with the character Mrs. Malaprop in a 1775 comedy of manners, *The Rivals,* by Robert B. Sheridan.

Dr. Avi Kepple, the lovable psychoanalyst in *Locks and Cream Cheese*, is patterned after my father, and Dorothy became our Molly. We honor their memories in our four Paco and Molly Mysteries. The plots and first drafts of all four novels were conjured up by Larry.

—Rosemary Mild

* * * *

Our two principal characters have their own history, beginning eighteen years ago. Detective Paco LeSoto, a perennial bachelor, met Molly at the home of psychoanalyst Dr. Avi Kepple, where she worked as his housekeeper/gourmet cook. Soon after, she seduced Paco with her gourmet cooking and eagle-eyed smarts as he stalked villains. She became his sleuthing partner—and more. They fell in love and married, merging their crime-solving skills in our first three mysteries: *Locks and Cream Cheese, Hot Grudge Sunday,* and *Boston Scream Pie.* Paco, now eighty-seven, and Molly, eighty-two, still relish stalking criminals and Molly's antics, while tolerating the aches and pains of advanced age. Their endearing foibles continue here in *The Moaning Lisa* in the year 1998.

—**Rosemary and Larry Mild**

The Dan and Rivka Sherman Mysteries
> Death Goes Postal
> Death Takes A Mistress
> Death Steals A Holy Book
> Death Rules the Night

The Paco and Molly Mysteries
> Locks and Cream Cheese
> Hot Grudge Sunday
> Boston Scream Pie
> The Moaning Lisa

Adventure/Thrillers
> Cry Ohana, Adventure and Suspense in Hawaii
> Honolulu Heat, Between the Mountains and the Great Sea
> On the Rails, The Adventures of Boxcar Bertie
> Kent and Katcha, Espionage, Spycraft, Romance
> Kauai Spies and Big Lies

Short Story Collections
> Murder, Fantasy, and Weird Tales
> The Misadventures of Slim O. Wittz
> Copper and Goldie, 13 Tails of Mystery and Suspense in Hawaii
> Charlie and the Magic Jug and Other Stories

Science-Fiction Novella
> Unto the Third Generation

Also by Rosemary
> Miriam's World—and Mine
> Love! Laugh! Panic! Life with My Mother
> In My Next Life I'll Get It Right

Also by Larry
> No Place To Be But Here, My Life and Times

The Guilded Gates
Assisted Living Community
Approximate Floor Plans
on pages xii and xiii

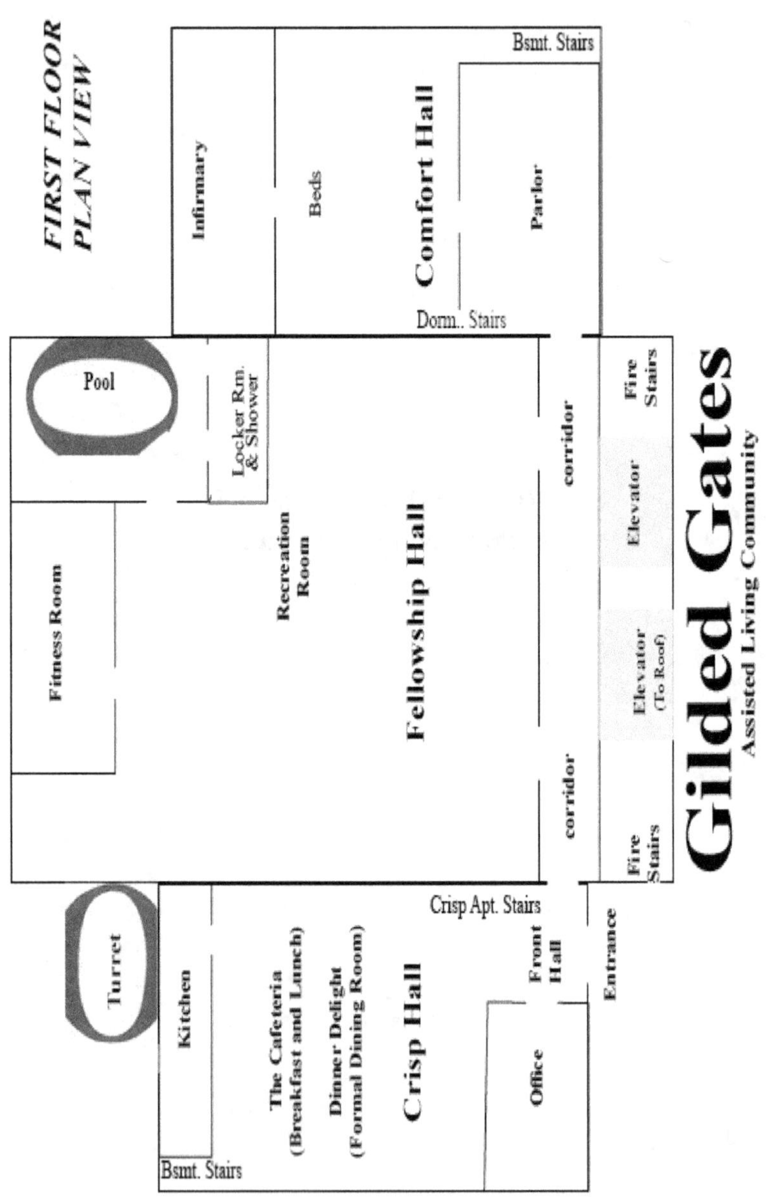
FIRST FLOOR
PLAN VIEW
Infirmary
Beds
Bsmt. Stairs
Comfort Hall
Parlor
Dorm.. Stairs
Pool
Locker Rm. & Shower
Fitness Room
Recreation Room
Fellowship Hall
corridor
corridor
Fire Stairs
Elevator
Elevator (To Roof)
Fire Stairs
Turret
Kitchen
The Cafeteria (Breakfast and Lunch)
Dinner Delight (Formal Dining Room)
Crisp Hall
Crisp Apt. Stairs
Front Hall
Office
Entrance
Bsmt. Stairs
Gilded Gates
Assisted Living Community

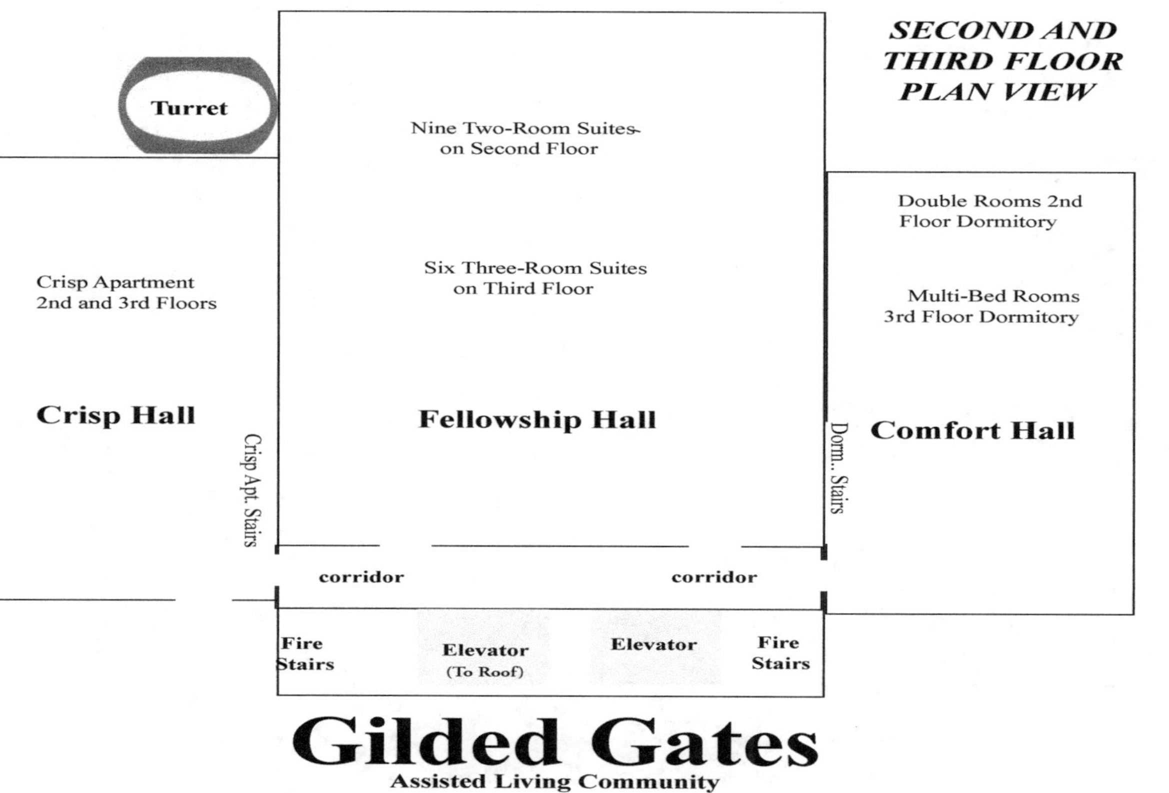
SECOND AND THIRD FLOOR PLAN VIEW
Turret
Nine Two-Room Suites on Second Floor
Six Three-Room Suites on Third Floor
Crisp Apartment 2nd and 3rd Floors
Double Rooms 2nd Floor Dormitory
Multi-Bed Rooms 3rd Floor Dormitory
Crisp Hall
Fellowship Hall
Comfort Hall
Crisp Apt. Stairs
Dorm.. Stairs
corridor
corridor
Fire Stairs
Elevator (To Roof)
Elevator
Fire Stairs
Gilded Gates
Assisted Living Community

Chapter 1
Heart to Hurt
February 1998

On this brisk February day, there should have been nothing scary about the weekly chore of grocery shopping. Ever since their marriage, Paco and Molly LeSoto had driven the twenty-five miles up to the city of Annapolis, Maryland, from their home in Black Rain Corners. They never expected this day at the supermarket to turn out any differently than the hundreds of past Thursday mornings—Seniors Day, when popular items were on sale to those sixty-five and over.

The parking lot at Marabel's Market was crowded, but they found a spot mid-row not too far from the entrance. Molly left her two canes in the car and, instead, hooked her hand into the crook of Paco's strong left arm, content that he would keep her steady and upright until they got through the door. Inside, Molly wedged herself onto one of the store's electric scooters, Paco grabbed a grocery cart, and they headed into the produce department. He began to pick oranges from a bin and drop them in a plastic bag.

Molly shook her frizzled mass of gray curls. "No, not those squeezers. We get the peelers with the belly buttons." She picked one out of the adjacent bin to show him.

"Ah, of course, a navel orange," he acknowledged as his bushy brows shot up and down. "The fruit designed especially for me." His lips made a smacking sound.

She knew Paco liked to peel an orange and pull the sections apart before eating, and he did the same with his grapefruits.

Molly beamed. "I'll get some of those nice nextorines over there beside the peaches." She loved catering to her husband's every need, sometimes overdoing it, and Paco had to gently remind her to stop mothering him so much. After all, he'd lived alone for almost seven decades before he met her.

Maybe she enjoyed fussing over him because they married so late in life, a marriage she never saw coming. What had Molly seen in this five-foot-ten, 160-pound man in his late sixties with the bony-plain face? She liked the natty way he dressed, his expressive eyebrows. His cute tush, too. But especially the kindly way he talked and really listened to her.

And what did Detective Paco see in this five-foot-one older woman with glassy blue eyes, a face round as a full moon, and a beach ball body? Her sugar cookies. Yes, the warm bagful she handed him on the day he came to Dr. Avi Kepple's house to investigate a suspicious death. From then on, Paco simply inhaled her gourmet cooking, respected her shrewd insights, and loved the way she talked—the sound-alike, humorous misuse of words that somehow had other meanings. These choice malaprops became known as Mollyprops among her family and friends. Nobody, not even Dr. Avi, knew whether they were intentional or not.

"Hey, Molly, don't forget Fumble and Bobble."

"I won't," she replied. "I got it right here on my list, a ten-pound bag of Kaytee Gourmet Macaw Food. It's got all the fruits and nuts and seeds they need."

Paco came to their marriage with his two trained macaws. He had bought them after he retired as a detective from the Baltimore Police Department in 1978. In Black Rain Corners, he served part-time on the two-man police force with the honorary title of Inspector.

As a fervent Washington Redskins fan, Paco's hobby was teaching the birds football terms. If he happened to praise Molly effusively for one of her keen observations, Bobble would squawk "Touchdown!"

An hour later they exited the store with Paco pushing the cart down a line of parked cars and Molly following on a store scooter. As supermarket parking lots went, Marabel's was peculiar. Each row was separated by a long island of concrete and grass. Suddenly, Molly braked. "Paco, we're in the wrong row! There's our blue Shovelay in the next row, nosed into the curb." Her voice turned shrill. "You'll have to mosey 'round the corner to the next row to get to our car. You can't get across this island with that heavy cart so full of food and stuff."

"I sure *can* get over it," Paco retorted. "I'm not that old and weak, Mol."

She helplessly watched as Paco pushed the cart into a space until he bumped against the concrete barrier. Leaning down on the cart's handle with all his weight, he tilted the front wheels up onto the island. Next, he bent down, and, with a flushed face, lifted the cart's rear wheels up onto the island. Across the three feet of island grass, he lowered the front and rear wheels back down to the row next to their own car, using his weight to restrain the cart's motion. With the cart safely in an empty stall next to their blue Chevy Malibu, Paco took a deep, painful breath. Both hands flew to his chest as he stood up. Slowly his legs gave way under him, and he sank down to the asphalt surface.

Meanwhile, Molly had scootered all the way around the island to safely reach their car. She let out a screech when she saw her husband lying on the ground in the empty stall beside their car. She wedged herself off the scooter, and knelt at her husband's side. He was writhing in pain.

"Another heart attack," he whispered. His eyelids fluttered. "My TracFone…Call an ambulance."

Molly fumbled around in Paco's left pants pocket for his car key, found it, and unlocked and opened the car door. She saw the Motorola TracFone hooked on the dashboard. He'd used it for his occasional police work in Black Rain Corners. She unhooked it, turned it on, and called 9-1-1. "My husband is serially hurting. It's his ticker. He's already had two hearty attacks. Hurry please. We're at Marabel's Market, corner of Rowe Boulevard and Baylor

Avenue."

She sat down on the asphalt pavement beside Paco and slid his head onto her lap while they waited for the ambulance. As she silently prayed, tears puddled on her cheeks. She tried to wipe at them with her chubby fingers. Meanwhile, onlookers began to gather around. One young man offered to put all her groceries in their car and she accepted. The nice man efficiently loaded their groceries into the trunk.

"You're a goodly gentleman," she told him.

Molly heard the siren, getting louder as it approached—in just six minutes. The Emergency Medical Technicians did a quick examination and transferred Paco to a gurney. To the EMTs' surprise, he sat up. "I'm okay," he mumbled. "Maybe I don't need to go to the hospital." His voice faded as he spoke. He fell back and lost consciousness.

The EMTs whisked him into the back of the ambulance, hooked up a saline solution IV, and sped off to the Anne Arundel Medical Center. Molly couldn't reach the high steps to get in the ambulance and ride along, so she drove to the hospital in their car, following along to the emergency room parking lot. Inside, she was relegated to a waiting room.

Paco woke up on an operating table and was informed that the cardiologists had managed to get his heart rhythm under control, but their attempt to insert a stent had failed. One artery had collapsed; another seemed to be taking over for it. He was out of danger for the time being, but his doctors needed to know how susceptible he would be to future attacks. He agreed to an unusual test, where a chemically induced arrhythmia would determine whether his heart was underfunctioning in a manner known as ventricular tachycardia. The doctors ran the test and proved that, yes, his heart was actually underfunctioning. They applied an external electric defibrillator. It brought him out of that arrhythmia with such a painful shock that he felt—as he told Molly later—like he'd left the operating table by several inches.

"You mean they practically murdered you on purpose?" she asked.

"Something like that," he replied from his hospital bed. "But I'm going to be okay. They tell me I'll be able to go home in three days. I have an appointment with an electrophysiologist next week."

"What's an electrosilliologist, anyway, hon?" asked Molly.

"The way the doctor explained it to me, the cardiologist is the heart's plumber, while the electrophysiologist is the heart's electrician."

"Does the heart have a carpenter, too?" she asked.

"I don't believe it does, sweetie," he answered. "The doctors need to put my own personal defibrillator inside my chest. When my heart misbehaves, it'll shock me back to normal again."

"That doesn't seem right—to punish a part of yourself like that," said Molly.

* * * *

Paco was discharged from the hospital three days later with a regimen of exercise, a heart-friendly diet, a pack of pills, and a raft of behavioral warnings. It took a few days before he felt like himself again. He kept his appointment with the electrophysiologist. Two weeks later, back in the hospital, that doctor performed outpatient surgery. With Paco under anesthesia, he implanted the preprogrammed defibrillator in the left side of Paco's chest. The device was silver-gray titanium metal, two inches square and a half-inch thick, weighing about two and a half ounces, and containing a tiny lithium battery. Two electrical wires from the device were inserted directly into the ventrical portion of the heart.

While he lay in the hospital bed, Molly asked him, "What will it feel like if the device gooses you?"

Paco winced, remembering the shock with which the doctors had brought him back the first time. "I don't want to know," he muttered. He was sent home with instructions not to lift his arm over his shoulder for a month.

Now Molly wasn't exactly the picture of health either. In 1997 she was diagnosed with type two diabetes. Her doctor explained. "In type two diabetes, the pancreas does not produce enough insulin. It's the hormone that regulates how sugar enters the cells to produce energy for the body." Molly half-listened. She already knew she was in big trouble. Her legs were continually swollen, her toes had a burning sensation, and her fingers were always cold. She could walk with two canes, but not far, and stand in place, but not for long.

It was all life-changing. She had to rely on her Rollator, a three-wheeled walker, to get around in and out of the house. She called it "Roly." Her gourmet meals were reduced to plain grub. No more of her rich sauces and cupcakes with buttercream frosting. And the dust bunnies propagated much faster than they used to. Around their charming Cape Cod cottage, it became a matter of who would be today's caregiver. The LeSotos loved where they lived and put off the inevitable, but a decision was slowly being forced upon them. The care they gave each other consumed most of the effort needed to take care of their home and grounds. In short, it wasn't long before they realized they had to make a choice: constant outside help or new living accommodations.

Molly suddenly remembered a quote by her favorite movie actress, Bette Davis: "Getting old is not for sissies."

Chapter 2

Decision Time

Six Months Later

On a Sunday morning in August, Molly pushed her Roly into *her* kitchen—it was always *he*r kitchen—to find Paco standing at *her* stove, tending a frying pan containing five sunny-side up eggs. An electric coffeemaker gurgled to make its presence known. On the counter a layer of paper towels sapped four strips of crisp bacon of their excess fat. The kitchen table held two of everything—plates, mugs, napkins, and silverware.

"Paco, are you out of your noggins—cooking here in *my* kitchen?"

Thinking her protest was totally about him and his surgical implant, he responded, "Don't worry, Molly, it's been six months since my defib surgery. I'm fine now to do almost anything."

"I agree, but I wasn't talking about your defibber. One, you're taking over my job in the kitchen. And two, the doctor didn't inlaw bacon in your heart diet, sweetie."

He waited for her to park Roly and plop down in a kitchen chair, their custom-made ones with castors and a thick booster cushion on Molly's.

"Darlin', I have no intention of taking away any of your daily activities. I just thought you'd be pleased to have someone wait on *you* for a change. And it's been so long since you made me bacon that I thought a single time wouldn't hurt us."

Molly didn't say anything at first as she rolled her chair to the stove, turned off the burner, and took hold of the frying pan handle. She rolled back to the table and spooned three well-done eggs with their yolks intact onto Paco's plate and two more onto her own. After setting the pan back on the counter, she returned to the table, balancing the bacon strips on paper towels, and distributing them equally.

"Sweetiekins," she said hesitantly, "our doctors are looking out for our well-beans, and I agree with their look-outs. They've told us bacon is not good for either one of us. I need to lose a lotta weight and you need to stay away from all those no-no foods that are bad for your heart. We want to live healthy, so we can be together for a long time."

"I concur, Molly dear," said Paco, pushing the bacon to the edge of his plate. "But there's something more that we have to think about concerning our health. I can no longer keep up with many of my chores around the house, and I can't mow the lawn. I notice where you've simplified your menus and dropped gourmet items from them. That's all good." Paco softened his voice. "But you've been avoiding a good deal of your usual housework."

"Well," said Molly, her voice huffy, "toodling my tush around on Roly makes it kinda tough to do anything anymore."

"I know, and I'm not complaining, Mol. Let's face it. I know I should be helping you more. What's stopping me from pushing the vacuum cleaner around? And don't tell anyone, but the toilet brush and I don't see eye to eye. Bottom line: I think we've come to that ripe old age where we need help. A lot of help."

"Because we both have misabilities now, you mean hire someone to come in to clean and cook for us? What would we do with ourselves all day instead?"

"That's not what I meant. I saw a feature article in the evening crab-wrapper about a modern assisted living facility halfway between Black Rains Corner and Annapolis. That would be nice and convenient for us."

"You mean one of those smelly places where everybody sits around and stares at the three walls all day?" Molly screwed up her flushed cheeks. "And I don't want to be commented to a place with crazies for the rest of my life."

"No, no, no, it's not a mental hospital. Quite the opposite," Paco said. "The place is called Gilded Gates. It has individual furnished mini-apartments, where you can choose communal or private meals. Two dining rooms. They have an indoor swimming pool, a recreation room, and all sorts of sporting and social activities suited for the advanced in age. Residents have to be at least seventy to be accepted. They even have a facility for the infirm."

"How do you know all this about the place?" she asked.

"Uh, well, after I read the article in the newspaper, I emailed them for this brochure." He slid the glossy trifold in front of her and waited as she perused each of the six sides.

"It looks okay," she admitted. "But, as the saying goes, lookers can be disbelieving."

"Mol, we can fix that by going to visit the place. If you agree, I'll make an appointment with them, and we can go have a look for ourselves."

"Aren't those sorts of places kind of suspensive?"

"I believe they are, but I have a plan, Molly dear. My double-dipper pensions, my life's savings, and what we'd get from the sale of the house should be enough for as long as either of us lives."

"It can't hurt to look, Paco, but do you really want to sell your house? You've had it since you retired, and it is so, so *you*, dear."

Paco shook his head, eyes downcast. "I don't think we could swing it otherwise. That's another call I have to make—to get an estimate on the house."

"You mean, call the real mistake people?"

"Yes, Molly, we'll need a real estate agent to sell the house."

"What about all our furniture and clothes, honeybunches?"

"The apartments are furnished, and there's a little kitchen with a fridge and microwave. Maybe they'd let us fit some small pieces of furniture in, but I doubt it. As for the clothes, we'll have to draw the limit at what will fit in the closet space."

"What about all my cooking and cleaning vitals?"

"You won't need most of them anymore," he assured her. "They do all the cooking and housecleaning for us."

"No stove in the kitchen? I won't be allowed to cook anything?" She sighed. "I s'pose they think we old ladies will burn the place down. Well, as long as we're just looking, I give my reproval."

* * * *

On the following Wednesday, a fortyish woman climbed the three steps out front and rang the doorbell at 62 Willow Way, the LeSotos' white Cape Cod cottage in Black Rain Corners.

"The doorbell tinkled," called Molly from their bedroom.

"I'll get it," said Paco, who was feeding Fumble and Bobble in the dining room where their cage stood.

He put the scoop of bird food down on the dining room table, hustled to the front door, and swung it open.

"Mr. LeSoto?

"Yes."

"I'm Judy Maxwell," said the trim woman in the gray business suit standing there. "I'm the real estate agent, sir. I believe you called Sherwood & Maxwell for a home evaluation? I'm Norm Sherwood's partner."

"Yes I did," said Paco. "Come in. My wife will join us." Turning toward the first-floor bedroom, he called, "Hon! It's the real estate lady."

Molly showed up immediately maneuvering Roly.

"Hello, Mrs. LeSoto. I'm Judy Maxwell."

"You must be the real mistake person," Molly said with a straight face.

Thinking she must have mis-heard, Judy merely smiled.

"Let's all sit down in the sitting room," Paco said, leading the way.

Seating herself in a wing chair, Judy waited until her prospects had settled themselves on the couch. Setting her briefcase on the floor beside her, she said, "I'm fully licensed and capable, Mr. and

Mrs. LeSoto. I'm sure you'll be pleased with the efficient and timely way I'll handle the sale of your home."

"I'll assume you're all you say you are, Ms. Maxwell," said Paco.

"You may call me Judy."

"You can call me Paco, and this is my wife, Molly. We're definitely looking to sell the house. You see, we're both having a problem managing the stairs, and taking care of the house has become a hassle."

"I do see and quite understand. This is a charming house. Tell me about it."

"We have four rooms and a bath on this floor," Paco replied. "A kitchen, sitting room, dining room, and a den that we've turned into a bedroom. There are two bedrooms and a bath on the second floor. No basement."

He led her into the dining room where the macaws' cage stood. While she stared in amazement at the two beautiful blue and yellow birds, Paco opened the cage door and slid a bowl of pellets, nuts, and dried fruit inside. As was his routine with his buddies, he rattled off "Redskins third down and seven. Hike!"

"Screen pass," squawked Fumble.

"Crossing pattern over center," screeched Bobble.

"Shoestring catch, still running," squawked Fumble.

"Into the end zone!" screeched Bobble.

Judy's jaw dropped. "Marvelous. You've taught them to speak. And the complicated NFL vocabulary!" she said, trying to ingratiate herself. Then back to business. "Do you have a floor plan by any chance?"

"Sorry, no."

"Then I'll just take some measurements and a few photos, if you don't mind."

Judy took a steel tape measure from her purse and proceeded through each of the first-floor rooms, stretching and retracting the tape while recording the measurements on a clipboard.

"You should have no trouble selling our house. We're neatniks," said Molly. "You should get a goodly price for her."

"Price will depend on a number of things," said Judy. "I'll go back to the office and compute a selling estimate based on location, layout, size, overall condition, and the neighborhood comparables."

"Compatibles?" asked Molly. "What are compatibles?"

"Comparables," Judy corrected. "The average going price for a similar home in your neighborhood."

"Can you give us a rough guesstimate off the top of your brain?" asked Molly.

"Good question, Mol," said Paco. "We'll need at least a ballpark estimate when we talk to the assisted living facility."

"Of course. This is such a charming little love nest," said Judy. "It should list somewhere between a hundred-thirty and a hundred-eighty thousand. I might even have a buyer in mind. We'll see."

"What about all our furniture, Judy?" asked Paco. "Does it sell with the house?"

Judy straightened her shoulders as she prepared to answer the touchy question.

"Unfortunately, your furniture will most likely not sell with the house. Buyers prefer to bring their own. But I'm happy to tell you your home is pleasantly furnished and in good taste. When the house is shown, your furnishings will help buyers visualize living here. Some buyers might want to purchase an individual piece or two. So...if you decide to move into an assisted living facility, you'll most likely be selling almost all your furniture." Judy took a breath before continuing to be sure her audience was still with her. "I'm happy to tell you I know a highly respected man who sells and auctions off used furniture out of a storefront. He'll give you a single figure for the lot of it. I'm sure it'll be a fair price. If you agree, he'll empty the house and haul everything away for you." She wrote the name and number down in her notebook, tore the page out, and handed it to Paco.

"Thank you, Judy," he said. "You seem to have all the answers. So, Mol, should we sign on with this lady and her company?"

Molly nodded. "Okay. Judy, you know your stuff. It's as plain as the nose on your head."

"Thank you, that's nice to hear," she replied, suppressing a smile. She removed a tiny camera from her purse and snapped a picture or two in each room on both floors. When she finished, she put away the measuring tape, camera, and notebook. Paco ushered her to the front door. Outside, she took a few more pictures before getting in her car and driving off.

Afterward, the LeSotos stood looking at each other in silence, trying to absorb the impact of their decision. Their silence was broken by a piercing squawk from Bobble: "Extra point is good."

Suddenly Molly noticed Paco's expression turn sad. "What's wrong, honeybunches?"

"I'm worried about my birds," he replied. "What if the assisted living place won't let me bring them?"

"What can we do about the birds, then, Paco, honey?" asked Molly. "Do they have an Old Birds' Home for macaws?"

"They're not really old, actually. Some macaws live more than sixty years in captivity. Maybe the zoo in Baltimore or the National Zoo in Washington will take them in. I've had them for over twenty years. They're family to me—all I had until I met you, buttercup."

"Maybe Caitlin Neuman can make a home for them. At least they know her, and she lives close by."

"That would be just wonderful," said Paco. "We could come by and visit with them as often as we pleased."

"I'll phone her," said Molly. "I just can't remember Caitlin's marriage name. Maybe we should take her to lunch at Bubba's Deli. You know—fatten her up for the killer question."

"Don't pressure the woman, Mol," he cautioned. "Be gentle."

* * * *

The next morning Molly slipped into a sweater and grabbed her three-wheeled Rollator walker. Her destination was Locust Lane, one street away, where Dr. Avi Kepple had lived and where she worked for the beloved doctor as housekeeper and cook for twenty-four years. The ivy-covered colonial next door had been owned by Olivia Raphael, Avi's devoted lady friend. She died less than a year ago and bequeathed the house to her adoring granddaughter, Caitlin. Olivia had raised Caitlin from the age of seven after her parents died in a car accident.

Molly put her hand out to ring the doorbell, when she saw two name plates just above it: Wallace Yellen and Caitlin Neuman. She rang and a few minutes later Caitlin opened the door. When she saw who was standing there, she rushed into Molly's arms for a huge hug.

"Molly LeSoto, just the person I wanted to see," said Caitlin. "I've been working on an oil painting I'd like to show you. Come in, come in."

"I see by the doorbell you kept your maiden name," said Molly.

"I'm part of the new generation of modern women," said Caitlin with a wink.

Five-foot-eight and long-limbed, Caitlin exuded confidence and snuggly warmth all rolled into one. She had fair skin, intense green eyes set off by long dark lashes, and tortoise-shell glasses propped on a straight nose. She looked comfortable in the same hairdo since her teens: chestnut-brown curls smothering her high forehead and a single glossy braid flopping down her back all the way to the waist of her khaki pants. Her plaid cotton shirt with rolled up cuffs had a few paint spatters decorating it. "May I help you with your chariot, Molly? I'll lift it over the step."

"Goodly job, girl, Roly here takes a bit of nudging," Molly said, already slightly out of breath. Pushing her walker, she followed Caitlin through the house to what had been Olivia's spacious veranda, now a glassed-in artist's studio. Propped up on the floor, half a dozen watercolor landscapes leaned against one wall. An easel stood at the far end of the room, where the sun's rays were most intense.

Caitlin stood next to the large canvas on the easel. "Anyone you know, Molly?"

"Oh, Lordy me, it's like Dr. Avi Kepple come alive. You're truly a protectional artist now. I'm so proud of you I could bust. Where's it going to hang up anyway?"

"It was commissioned by the Marche House Museum committee to hang in the front room between the two staircases. It's so nice you came over to visit and be my first critic for this work."

Molly's blue eyes turned intense. "I gotta shamely admit that I didn't just come for a visit, Caitlin. "I have a reversive motive in popping up to see you."

"I'm glad to see you in any case," said Caitlin. "But what's this other reason for coming?"

"You see, my Paco and I are planning to move to a retiring home, a resisted-live-in place. We've gotten too darned old to take care of our house any more. We gotta sell, or give away or throw out most things, but there's two items we're worried about. And shame on me, they're not items. They're our buddies."

"Your buddies??"

"Fumble and Bobble."

"The macaws!"

"Yeah. They're like family, and we can't take them with us. Paco would have to leave them with a zoo as a last resort. They could live another forty years."

"I see."

"Wouldn't *you* like some company in the house while you paint?" asked Molly.

"I probably would," said Caitlin. "I've even thought of painting the two colorful birds, but adopting two new members of the family is something else again. I'll have to talk it over with my husband. Wally does have some allergies." Caitlin cocked her head. "Can people get allergies from birds?"

Molly's flushed face scrunched up in distress. "I do hope not. That would surely throw a monkey's wrench in our plans for our birdies' new home."

"I hope not too, Molly. Can I let you know in a day or two?"

"Of course."

"By the way, which assisted living facility did you select?"

"None yet, but we're going to look over a place called Gilded Gates."

"Gilded Gates. That's where Grandma Olivia spent her last

days." As Caitlin helped Molly and her walker down the single step to the front walk, she spoke with a sad note in her voice. "Grandma was fairly fit for a woman her age, but her memory got so bad she had to be watched every minute. She didn't even recognize us anymore. It was heartbreaking. She was ninety-two when she died. Well, good luck in your search."

We're surely gonna need it, Molly thought.

Chapter 3
Gilded Gates

A week later, the LeSotos were on the way to meet the director and his wife at Gilded Gates, located midway between Black Rain Corners and Annapolis. They were dressed in their finest to make a good impression. Paco in his navy-blue suit, sky-blue dress shirt, and striped tie. Molly in her beige and aqua flowered dress.

Paco pulled their Chevy Malibu to an abrupt stop just outside the gates and stared. The twelve-foot-tall gates were painted a glistening gold and crafted with gilded wrought-iron flowers and graceful curlicues. Wide open, the gates beckoned residents and visitors alike to freely come and go. The imposing sign over the front entrance, "Gilded Gates," loomed in elegant gold letters.

The entire complex sat on a rolling knoll, with a manicured green lawn, despite the parching 90-degree August heat. Surrounding the lawn and the entire facility was a black five-foot-high wrought-iron fence—dark and sinister, even Gothic-looking, in contrast to the welcoming gilded gates.

Paco struggled to understand their meaning. *There are a couple of implications here*, he thought. *Either the place is so good that it's approaching the Pearly Gates, like we might say about a luxury tropical resort. Or it's the last stop before we die. Maybe both.*

"Wow!" gasped Molly, echoing Paco's reaction. "Look at them

fancy golden gates. We must really be on our way to heaven, sweetie pie. I don't know if I'm ready for this."

"Don't worry, Mol, we don't have to agree to do anything we don't want to. Let's just give the place a fair chance."

The early afternoon sun flashed a blinding light as Paco turned into the asphalt-surfaced driveway. What they saw through the windshield was an expansive three-story modern white brick building, flanked on the left and right by two stately Victorian-style homes, all mutually conjoined. Little arrow signs led them around the left to the visitor parking spaces.

Paco opened the trunk, removed Molly's Rollator, and they followed a sign directing them toward the office. The entry door glowed from backlit stained glass. Inside and to their left, they saw the open office door, where a man in a white smock sat behind a large oak desk. He was busy writing something. Behind him were three arched Gothic-style windows. Paco knocked. The man looked up and laid his pen down.

"Come on in," he said. "How can I help you?"

"I'm Paco LeSoto and this is my wife, Molly. We have an appointment with the director at one o'clock."

"Yes, yes, welcome, you've come to the right place. I'm Dr. Phelix Crisp, and I'm the director." The fiftyish gentleman with steel-gray coiffed hair stood several inches over six feet as he rose to greet them. Leaning over the desk, he shook hands with them both, then pointed to the two tufted leather armchairs in front of the desk. Sitting down in his own high-backed chair, he asked, "Now, how can I be of assistance?"

Molly plunged in. "Are you a doctor-doctor or a doctor-dentist or a pet vet?"

Dr. Crisp flashed a confident salesman smile. "I'm a licensed physician with specialties in both internal medicine and psychiatry. And my wife, Irma, is a licensed physician's assistant."

Molly piped up, "My former employer was also a psycho doctor, Dr. Avi Kepple. He's passed up now. Did you know him?"

"Of course," Phelix answered. "He was my mentor and a friend."

Paco launched into their situation. "I'm a retired Baltimore police detective and the former head of the Black Rain Corners police force. I'm eighty-seven and I recently had my second heart attack. There's not much I can do anymore to take care of our house. I can barely take care of myself. Molly here is eighty-two. She's diabetic and confined to her walker, so she can't maneuver the steps anymore, nor can she clean and cook as much as she used to. We'd like a tour of your facility to see if we would actually fit in here. Oh, one other thing—we're in the process of putting our house up for sale."

Dr. Crisp laced his fingers together, leaned forward, and began his business spiel. "Our basic entry fee is $100,000, nonrefundable." He paused to test their emotional temperatures. Some prospects at this point abruptly stood and departed. The LeSotos didn't.

Adjusting his rimless glasses, Dr. Crisp continued his rehearsed pitch. "We have some suitability requirements, of course, and there's also the question of available space in your selection of accommodations. Meals are included—private or communal, your choice in any case. I assume you're looking to move into one of our furnished two-room suites—a sitting room/kitchenette, and one bedroom with bath. The two-room one goes for twenty-two-hundred a month, and the larger, three-room, furnished suite with the extra bedroom and bath goes for thirty-one-hundred a month." Dr. Crisp deliberately softened the steep fees by avoiding the words *thousand* and *dollars*. "If you don't move in right away, there is also an upfront two-month administrative fee and a two-month security deposit. Should you become infirm once you are residents, there is a prorated fee, dependent upon the length of time you've been with us. Should you both need to move directly into our Infirmary facility now, that would involve another two-month fee up front. Do these requirements meet with your approval?"

The LeSotos sat without speaking for several minutes. They had no intention of spelling out their financial worth for this guy. Before even making the appointment, they had sat down at their kitchen table, and with paper and pencil, Paco had gone over their financial details. He figured the sale of their house would clear about $150,000. His two pensions totaled $2,100 a month. Most of his savings were in stocks—market value about $30,000, yielding dividends of $150 to $200 per month. And Molly had added, "Paco honey, don't forget—Dr. Avi left me $50,000. And I have my savings—I banked $200 a month for thirty years." Paco scribbled the calculations. "We're in good shape, hon."

Dr. Crisp waited, knowing better than to force a response. He decided to assume, since they hadn't jumped up and fled, that they were financially secure. "Mr. and Mrs. LeSoto, why don't we see if we can match you up with your desired accommodations. I'll have the larger suite available in a matter of days, the smaller one should be available possibly in weeks."

"I don't want you to push anybody out of her bed or even out of this world," said Molly with a shudder.

"Of course not," said Dr. Crisp. "There's absolutely no pushing of any kind. It's just that sometimes we are able to see the handwriting on the wall, so to speak."

Molly stared at him and began buttoning up her beige sweater, as if to shield herself from any more of this gruesome talk.

"Don't you have any other kind of accommodations?" asked Paco.

"Well, yes, we also have single-room quarters and four-to-a-room dormitories, if that's what you mean," sniffed Dr. Crisp, revealing his distaste for the less affluent.

"Is it possible to see inside the two-room suites, so we can make an intelligent decision?" asked Paco."

"Of course," said Dr. Crisp, mentally rubbing his hands together. "Why don't I have someone special take you on a tour of our entire community? Perhaps one or two of our residents will be kind enough to show you inside their suites. You'll get to meet some of our staff as well—first of all, my wife." He reached over and pressed an intercom button. "Irma, would you come to my office, please? We have visitors I'd like you to meet."

A tall woman in a gray pants suit and white smock appeared in the doorway. "Hello, I'm Irma Crisp, physician's assistant and head of nursing at Gilded Gates." Her body language exuded a touch of sternness. The woman's smile came from a hard, sculptured face, and her professionally friendly voice carried a slight scrape with it.

"Irma, I'd like you to meet the LeSotos, Paco and Molly," said Phelix. "They've shown an interest in joining our little community and would like a tour of the facility. Would you please take them around?"

"What's a physical assistant?" Molly whispered to Paco.

"It's an almost-doctor, requiring more schooling than a registered nurse," murmured Paco in her ear.

"I'd be delighted," said Irma. "Please follow me." First, she turned to them and explained, "There are three buildings here at Gilded Gates. We're in Crisp Hall—this lovely Victorian-style structure so-named because my husband and I make our home on the second and third floors. It actually served as a family home for almost a century." Adjusting her friendly tone to blunt, Irma said, "As you might expect, the residents are not permitted above the first floor in this building unless invited. Just so there's no misunderstanding, Dr. Crisp and I keep this door, the stairway to our apartment, locked at all times."

The upper half of the polished cherrywood door had graceful carved flowers in a wreath design. In his detective's mindset, Paco wryly wondered, *Broadcasting affluence upstairs, a perfect target for a thief.*

Irma shifted back to her professional-friendly tone. "The first floor is for Administration and our two large dining rooms. This is our cafeteria where you will enjoy your breakfast and lunch." The LeSotos noted Formica tables in different colors and matching vinyl chairs, vinyl-tile flooring, and colonial lighting. Irma then led them into a spacious formal dining room—white tablecloths, royal blue wall-to-wall carpeting, and Tiffany-style, multicolored glass fixtures over each table. "We call this our Dinner Delight, elegant dining for all our residents. Four menu choices, and formal seating with waitresses. As you might expect, our kitchen is equipped with the most up-to-date appliances."

Leading the LeSotos down a carpeted corridor, she ushered them into the facility's largest, most modern, building. "Welcome to Fellowship Hall and its excellent amenities, always buzzing with activity," gushed Irma. A sweep of her hand with its clear-polished nails pointed. "Here we have the recreation room, a playroom of sorts."

Paco thought, *A playroom, huh? Does Gilded Gates think of retirees as old fogies regressing to their childhood?* He surveyed the tall windows and beige tweed carpet. Along the walls were two sofas, three recliners, and a number of upholstered wing chairs, all in friendly plaids. At the pool table covered in green felt, two men were slowly wielding their cues, ball knocking against ball, none falling into the pockets. The men were chatting and enjoying themselves, not caring a whit about their goofed attempts.

"The man hunched over is Mark," said Irma, "and the one with the chubby gut is Ed."

Paco and Molly watched a perky couple playing Ping-Pong, the click-clopping of the little ball slapping against the paddles.

"They're Jeff and Maryanne. He's okay, but she's a tattletale."

Irma couldn't resist spilling details, her misguided way of show-ing she actually knew the residents. At one of the four card tables, a woman with glasses perched on her nose sat arranging the corners of a barely begun jigsaw puzzle. "That's Alice. She's a recluse—in-sists on keeping to herself." At another table, four men, unsmil-ing and intent, played out a hand of bridge. A canasta game was in play at the third table. Irma pointed out, "That's Geraldine, in the wheelchair. She was an off-Broadway actress. She tries to insert lines from her plays into conversation. Ruth, with the blue hair, changes unmatched outfits several times a day. Wanda, the one with the braids, likes to sneak around and eavesdrop. And Mitzie, the bottle blonde, tells us over and over that she was a big-time fashion model."

A poker-chip dispenser sat atop the empty fourth table. Paco took note of it, thinking, *I wouldn't mind some penny ante games.*

Nodding toward a man dozing off in a recliner, Irma said, "He's Peter. He drools a lot." In the far-right corner stood an ultra-large TV set. Nobody was watching the cooking show with its sound turned off.

"Follow me, folks," said Irma. Pushing Roly behind her, Molly scowled and whispered to Paco, "For an almost doctor she doesn't have a goodly opinion of her patients." Paco nodded his agreement, thinking he wouldn't count on Irma for professional confidential advice.

Irma led them to an open door off to the left. "Here we have the Fitness Room, but I like to call it fitness fun! Less intimidating, don't you think?" she asked, not expecting an answer. Currently unoccupied, it held two stationary bicycles, a treadmill, and a metal rack holding an array of weights from one to five pounds. Irma fairly warbled. "We have a daily exercise class, nice and easy, after breakfast five days a week—Sunny Silver Workouts. Our residents can even sit in a chair while they're doing the exercises. Also, a special teacher comes in twice a week for Tai Chi class, beginners welcome. And, Mr. and Mrs. LeSoto," Irma's voice rose as if speaking to first graders, "please remember that while you live here you should never exercise alone."

Crossing to the right side of the room, they came to two doors marked Gents and Ladies. "Locker rooms and restrooms," she said. She opened a door where they felt an immediate swoosh of chlorine and humidity—a heated swimming pool about twenty-five feet long. A woman in a one-piece bathing suit was swimming laps.

"She looks in fine fetus for a woman her age," declared Molly.

When Irma stopped in her tracks and gave Molly a puzzled look, Paco hurried to explain. "She meant fettle, in fine fettle. It's an expression she overheard."

"Your wife speaks kind of strangely, doesn't she?" Irma asked Paco. "Does she talk like that all the time?"

Molly's eyes turned an icy blue. "You can say what you have to say about me directly at me. I'm not a horsefly on the wall, you know."

"I apologize," said Irma. "I meant no harm."

"That's okay," said Molly. "I wouldn't hold it under you."

This time Irma merely smiled and led them into the corridor leading to the Victorian-style building to the right of Fellowship Hall. In decades past, it had been a stately home with high ceilings. "Ahead of us is Comfort Hall." But she stopped midway in the corridor at the elevator doors.

"Aren't we going to tour Comfort Hall?" asked Paco.

"Well," pouted Irma, "on the first floor of Comfort Hall we have our medical wing—our Infirmary and special needs spaces. Oh, and straight ahead of us through those doors, is our parlor, decorated in its original period fashion. The second and third floors are the dormitory levels. There isn't much to see up there except the sleeping arrangements. The beds are two, or four, to a room. Plus a few single rooms." She shrugged, betraying a slight distaste.

"I'd much prefer to take you upstairs to see the two-room suites, which are on the second floor and the three-room suites, which are on the third floor of Fellowship Hall. "You did say you were interested in our two-room and three-room suites, didn't you?"

"Sure we're interested, Ms. Irma. I never turn down anything sweet," declared Molly. "I'd like to see everything, though. I don't like snipping off any part of the tour."

"Oh, very well," said Irma, realizing she'd better shift gears and do a proper selling job. She led them through a set of etched-glass doors. "Here we have the parlor. We retained the charming décor from when Comfort Hall was a private home. The furniture and paintings are all reproductions, of course."

The LeSotos noted a pleasant room with pastel floral carpeting; two maroon velvet sofas framed in curved mahogany; brocade side chairs with graceful cherrywood legs; and on the far wall, a tapestry of a medieval forest scene with a heroic leaping lion.

Pretty and richly, but not very cozy, thought Molly. *Maybe that's why nobody's in here.*

Moving into the hall, she pushed open a pair of double doors to a large, fluorescent-lit expanse that emanated a sterile, alcohol smell.

"We are now in our Medical Wing. This is the Infirmary."

The first room revealed four bedridden residents hooked up to IVs and monitoring machines. A stocky nurse in green scrubs bent over one of the beds, taking a patient's blood pressure. Irma murmured, "We have three full-time registered nurses here. That's Penny Summers. I'd introduce you, but she's busy, as you can see." Irma pointed. "Here we have a few examining rooms. The original master bedroom has been partitioned into private rooms for the chronically infirm. That room off to the rear is our Dispensary, where we keep medications and dressings on the shelves, and, of course, in the refrigerator, which contains medications requiring cool or cold."

"Very nice," said Paco. "Glad we stopped. Molly was right, Ms. Irma. Looking at the entire range of accommodations is the best way to determine the quality of your facility. So now we'd like a good sampling of the dormitories."

Irma suppressed her annoyance with silent teeth gnashing. *Most prospective residents weren't as intellectually sharp and persistent.* She led them back down into the corridor to the elevators and took one to the second floor, then led them back into Comfort Hall to poke their heads into the dormitory rooms.

No amenities for the less well-heeled, Paco observed.

The dorm-room beds had a low-budget look, including severe vinyl headboards. However, each bed did have a uniquely patterned comforter and vertical six-drawer dresser, each one painted to match the comforter colors so the residents could remember which bed and dresser was theirs.

At the other end of the next room, two women sat at a small table arguing politics, their voices reaching the strident level. When they saw the visitors they abruptly stopped. Irma defused the situation nicely, introducing them to the LeSotos.

Irma whizzed past the next open door, but the LeSotos foiled her attempt to avoid it. They stopped to peek into a heavily draped sitting room. Five men and women sat slumped in upholstered armchairs. Four of the residents stared out into eternity, while the fifth stared at the oriental carpeting with a hang-dog look.

"These are the ambulatory, yet functionally incapacitated," said Irma as she hurried them past.

The group poked their heads into several more of the dormitory rooms and found them mostly empty.

"Where are all the inmates?" asked Molly. "There's a heap of beds in this outfit, but no one in the rooms."

"Residents, *not* inmates, Mrs. LeSoto," corrected Irma. "Most are at activities, some here at the facility, and others off-site. There are seniors' classes at the university and at the local community center. We have Gilded Gates shuttles that take them to and from. On Sundays, a number of them are on home visits with their families. You see, we have an open-door policy here. That's what's so special about Gilded Gates. Almost everyone can come and go as they please.

"Now—I think it's time to leave Comfort Hall and have a look at what you came for, the suites. We'll need to head back to the corridor and cross over to the second floor of Fellowship Hall."

The door to the corridor, at the second two-room suite they encountered, had been left wide open.

"Hello, Gordon," Irma said to the man inside.

A bald man with fringes of white hair, round owlish glasses, and a thin white mustache was seated in a rocker reading a John Grisham novel. He looked up. Molly waved to him. He raised his left hand in a tentative wave, and buried his head back in his book.

"Gordon is ninety-six, our oldest resident, a compulsive reader—always has a book in his hands," said Irma, sounding almost as if there was something wrong with being an avid reader. "He spent his whole career as an undertaker, in a small town in Virginia, I believe."

Molly wasn't surprised. She thought he looked quite formal in his black suit and open-collared white shirt.

"I love sweets, especially fudge. How many are there?"

"Here on the second floor we have nine two-room suites," parroted Irma. "The six three-room suites are on the third floor."

Paco and Molly noticed that most of the doors were shut. They stopped at one open door where they saw a man with neatly clipped hair and an intelligent face sitting cross-legged in an armchair, reading *The Saturday Evening Post*.

"Good morning, Zane. Would you mind if I showed our guests your apartment?"

"Go ahead," he replied. "But no snide remarks about my bachelor housekeeping."

"Mum's the word, Zane," chirped Irma. "I'd like you to meet Molly and Paco LeSoto."

"We just want to nosy around a bit, Mr. Zane," said Molly. "Looks like you keep house just fine."

"Why thank you, Ms. Molly, but the real credit goes to the housekeeping staff."

His cheerful two-room suite consisted of royal blue carpeting, a large bedroom, and a sitting room with a sofa, a recliner, a puffy armchair, side chairs, and a TV. The bedroom had a queen-size bed with a headboard of flowered chintz, two night tables, two dressers, and a blue-tiled bathroom. The double-wide window in the bedroom had a louvered shade.

Paco surveyed it all moodily. *This is going to take some getting used to. Our whole life crunched into these two rooms.*

Molly stared at the alcove off the sitting room. A small porcelain sink, Formica countertop, two overhead cabinets, a modest-sized fridge, a microwave oven, and a small round table with two vinyl chairs. "But where's the real kitchen?"

Irma tried to suppress her condescending voice. "This is what we call the kitchenette, Mrs. LeSoto. All the suites have one."

Molly gave her a glassy look. "But where's the stove?" she asked, already knowing the answer but hoping there were exceptions.

"Actually," said Irma, "we discourage our residents from cooking. We much prefer that they take their meals in our excellent dining rooms. That way we're assured that no accidents can happen. Do you think you'll need to see the third-floor suites? They're top-of-the-line and the highest priced. And the most comfortable." Irma thanked Zane and waved.

"Not necessary, Ms. Irma. The two-room is more likely what we'd need," said Paco, regretfully.

They took the elevator down to the first floor. As soon as they got off, a gaunt-looking, stooped man with hollow eyes and sharp chin approached them in the corridor. In his gray sweatsuit he planted himself squarely in front of them, intentionally blocking their way. He shifted from foot to foot silently for several moments before speaking.

"Don't move in here," he warned in a cackly just-audible voice. "The place is evil. She is evil."

"Vince, go to your dormitory room right now," said Irma in a do-not-disobey-me voice.

Vince sucked in his breath to say something more, but gave up, dejected, and tottered back down the corridor.

"Who was that?" asked Paco.

"That was an unfortunate and inflammatory outburst from a disturbed yet harmless resident," said Irma. "It's time for his meds."

"He sure was all mental muddled," offered Molly.

They resumed their walk down the corridor to Crisp Hall.

Back in the office, Dr. Crisp asked, "Well, have you two reached a decision yet?"

"We will deform you about the two-room suite for sure in maybe three or four days," said Molly after looking over at Paco for his approval.

Dr. Crisp couldn't stop himself from his pushy behavior. "Normally we would require two months' rent to save a suite any longer than that."

From the LeSotos' viewpoint, the atmosphere had noticeably chilled.

Chapter 4
Coming or Going?

The September sun broke through the billowing clouds to flood the LeSotos' kitchen with bright light. Paco sat reading the morning paper between bites of a buttered English muffin and sips of coffee. Molly spooned up Oatmeal Squares, sopping with milk and artificial sweetener. She picked up the Gilded Gates brochure and read through it for the third time. Then she spoke to Paco through his newspaper barrier.

"Sweetie, did you remember to send a save-me check to Dr. Crisp?"

"Honeybunches, I wrote that check to him last Wednesday— right after we made the big decision."

"I just wanted to be sure. What if we sell the house early? Won't we need a place to plop our tushes until our two-room sweet is ready?"

"Don't worry about that, Mol. There's always the Inn at Gander Pointe. We can stay there for a piece."

"Ooh! That would be so romancy," said Molly, with a girlish grin. "Like another honeymoon maybe."

"Not as adventurous as our first one," said Paco. "We had a great time touring the National Parks out West. Didn't we?"

"Sure did, Mr. Detective."

They were still at the breakfast table when the doorbell

screamed. Molly gripped her walker and trudged to the front door. She opened it to their real estate agent, Judy Maxwell, dressed in her usual business-gray suit.

"You won't believe the news I have for you!" gushed Judy. Without being invited in, she barreled past Molly and strode all the way to the kitchen, fairly bouncing up and down as she waited for Molly to catch up.

"Good morning, Judy," said Paco, having no choice but to fold his newspaper and set it on the table.

"Good morning! Good morning!"

Paco motioned to the third captain's chair. "Why don't you sit down and catch your breath?"

"Yeah, Judy," said Molly, settling back into her own chair. "You're just about popping out of your skin. Now tell us already. The suspects are killing me."

"I've got you a buyer for the house, even a good-faith deposit," Judy said. "Do you remember last Tuesday, when I asked you to leave while I showed a couple through the house?"

"Yes," they both answered.

"At first, I didn't think they were interested. But they came to the office with their check late yesterday afternoon. How do you like that?"

"Fine," said Paco. "But when do they want to move in?"

"I can arrange a closing by the end of October, mid-November at the latest. After that, your home is theirs." Blunt as always, she said, "You'll have to clear out of here some time before then."

"Does this mean these buyers already have their loan approval?" asked Paco.

"Even better," said Judy. "The gentleman has retired from the law profession, and they've sold their home in D.C., so they have ready cash. Apparently, the Thornberrys—the buyers—have had some connection to Black Rain Corners before this."

"Felix Thornberry?" asked Paco.

"Why yes," said Judy. "You know the Thornberrys?"

"Marti and Felix," said Molly. "She was Martha Marche before she got hitched up. Her family donated their big fat mansion to Black Rain Corners. You must be 'quainted with the Marche House Museum here."

"Of course. Then you are friends?" asked Judy.

"Not exactly," replied Molly. "They were sometimes guests in Dr. Avi's home, where I worked."

"And I knew them through my police work here in town," said Paco.

"I heard you were chief of police here in Black Rain Corners," said Judy.

"Not quite, I was their police inspector," said Paco. "If I'd been a real chief, they would have had to pay me more. You see, the town has limited funding."

"I got to help him sometimes with his sleuthing," offered Molly.

Paco smiled. "More than sometimes. So, Judy, just what happens before settlement?"

"The buyers will pay for an official house inspection to determine if anything needs fixing, and everything must be out of the house by settlement—furniture, clothes, drapes, curtains, and food. You'll also need the deed or some proof of ownership for the actual closing."

"What if we can't get rid of everything before then?" asked Molly in a stressed voice. "What do we do?"

"Did you call Sol Kramer?" asked Judy. "I gave you his number earlier."

Molly's brow furrowed as she tried to remember.

Judy took note and helped her out. "Sol has a storefront in Annapolis where he sells estate goods from home sales."

"Oh. I forgot. Okay," Molly said, her brow relaxing. "I'll call him today. But what do we do to prepare for him?"

"You start by making four piles," said Judy. "One, the things you want to keep. Two, the items in good enough condition to sell. Three, the items you wish to give away. Four, the trash headed for the dump. If you wish, I can also give you the name of someone who can haul off the trash for you."

"Yes, please do," said Paco.

No-nonsense Judy wrote down the number for them and jumped up from her chair. "I'd better get moving. I'm showing a house at eleven. I just wanted to give you the good news." She gathered her purse and notebook and headed for the door.

Molly swished her spoon in the now-soggy bowl of Oatmeal Squares. Swallowing the last one, she looked up at her husband. A broad milky coating painted her upper lip, and a sad expression took hold of her face. A lone tear crossed her cheek.

"What's wrong, Mol. You look as though you're about to cry."

"I'm scared of all the big changes coming down on us. There's so much for me to do. They're overwhelping. Are we doing the kosher thing, moving to that Guilty Gates place? Is it the right place for you and me?"

"Gilded Gates, dear," he corrected. "Why are you suddenly having such doubts?" asked Paco. "Do you regret selling the house and moving? Or is Gilded Gates what's bothering you?"

Molly blinked back a tear. "I may be having repercussings from a dream I had last night. Oh, Paco, in it I saw that awful man, Vince, warning us not to move in. I know he was all mental, but he scared me. And Olivia died there."

Paco stood and came behind her chair. Leaning down, he wrapped his arms around her shoulders. "There, there, Molly. I don't think we want the ravings of a deranged man to dictate what we should or shouldn't do. And Olivia was ninety-two. She died of dementia and old age. I'm pretty sure we're making the right move." He kissed her on the right cheek to seal the deal.

"You make all the right moves, sweetie."

* * * *

By the sixth of October almost every major item in the LeSoto home had a color-coded Post-it attached, Molly's way of making piles. It was also the day Dr. Crisp notified them that a two-room suite, number 225, would become available for them on Monday, the second of November. So, on the fourteenth of October, Sol Kramer came and collected the furniture, wall hangings, small appliances, and excess clothing and toted them to his storefront. That Saturday the house was emptied of every last thing.

Except Bobble and Fumble. With pangs of sadness, Paco petted them and said goodbye. He was transporting them to Caitlin's house. *Easy enough*, he thought, as he wheeled them out to the car. The tall, domed cage had an elegance to it: black wrought iron, resting on a matching stand with curved legs and wheels. But Paco hadn't counted on the weight. He lifted the cage from its stand and groaned. He'd bought the birds when he was in his sixties and hadn't moved their cage since. His chest heaved as he struggled to prop it up on the back seat of the Chevy. Next, he wheeled the stand to the open trunk and wriggled it in sideways. Settling into the driver's seat, breathing hard, he sat for a few minutes and waited to calm down—not just his body, but his emotions, too. The macaws cocked their heads in silence, knowing something strange was happening.

Paco pulled into Caitlin's driveway, wondering how he would find the strength to bring the birds into the house, but he needn't have worried. Wallace was right there to do the honors.

At first Caitlin had been apprehensive. How would the bird guests go over with her husband? He was in his first job as an attorney at a firm in Annapolis. Turned out, Wallace was a kindly, cheerful guy and actually welcomed Bobble and Fumble. With a gleam in his eye, he said, "Well, sir, since they already have a football vocabulary, maybe I'll teach 'em a little legalese." Paco chuckled with relief. And Caitlin assured him he had permanent visiting rights any time, day or night.

The next day the LeSotos moved into the Inn at Gander Pointe, the sole hotel in Black Rain Corners. They went to settlement on the twentieth of the same month. That evening, the Thornberrys treated Paco and Molly to a celebratory dinner in the hotel's Chandelier Room.

* * * *

Their two-week-plus stay at the inn started out enjoyable—fine dining, comfortable third-floor room overlooking the Chesapeake

Bay, and no responsibilities. When boredom set in, they drove over to the nation's capital to see the sights. Starting at the Lincoln Memorial, Paco had to push Molly in her transport wheelchair wherever they went and he tired quickly. They spent more time in the car than sightseeing. Molly wondered aloud, "Are we coming or going?" So, it was back to the hotel to watch daytime television or drive up to Annapolis to see a movie. Finally, on the second day of November, their assigned date to move into Gilded Gates arrived.

They drove through the elegant golden gates and up the winding drive to a residents' parking spot. The Chevy Malibu was jam-packed with clothes and personal items. Molly and her walker chugged up the sloping walkway. "How come it's not nice and flat? That's not very considerational of them."

"That's for sure," grunted Paco, pulling a large wheeled suitcase in each hand behind him. In the front hall, Dr. Crisp met them with their keys. Arriving at their new suite, number 225, Molly unlocked the door and swung it wide for Paco to deposit the luggage. After struggling to set the suitcases inside, he saw Molly still standing in the doorway. "My love," he said, "if you think I'm going to carry you over the threshold, forget it—those days are over, sad to say."

"Of course they are, sweetiekins. I was thinking about our honeymood, the time you *did* carry me."

"Yeah, the Mile-High Sportsman's Inn, room 1023, in Denver."

"You've got a good remembry, dear."

"Thank God for that," he said. "I guess I'd better go down for another load." Before he could leave, he heard a knock at the door. He opened it to a short, buxom woman with salt-and-pepper pigtails.

"Bertha, Bertha Bubbaschlufsky!" shouted Molly. "My good friend, what are you doing here? Come in."

"Welcome to Gilded Gates. I'm in suite 223," replied Bertha. "I came over to welcome my new next-door neighbors. I didn't know it was you and Paco."

While the two ladies engaged in a bear hug, Paco sat down on the sofa to watch and listen.

"I'm so glad you're here and next door to us," said Molly, wishing she too could have a girly look with piggy tails. "It's been five years since I've seen you."

"Yes, I know—since Schlemule and I sold Bubba's Deli. We got too old to run it anymore. And Schlem's health wasn't too great. So we moved into this assisted living place."

"Why didn't you tell me where you were?" asked Molly. "I would've come to see you, and we coulda visited like old times. And you know what? The new people at the deli aren't friendly like you and Schlem. They don't carry any of the homemade especialties that you used to make."

"That doesn't surprise me," said Bertha. "Nothing stays the same. But we were happy here—until the worst happened. Five months ago I lost Schlem, may he rest in peace. We were together over sixty years, you know."

Molly's eyes teared up. "Oh my goodness gracious. I'm so sorry, Bertha."

"Me too," said Paco, shaking his head.

"You know, life here is so complete you don't look back at your past, at least I'm trying not to," Bertha murmured. She noticed the luggage nearby. "I see you folks are still moving in, so I'll let you be. So happy you're here. See you." She disappeared into her suite as quickly as she appeared.

Paco got to his feet, leaving Molly to start putting things away. He trudged back to the elevator and took it to the first floor. When the elevator doors opened into the lobby, he discovered a tall gentleman in a smoking jacket and ascot, pushing a bellhop luggage trolley toward him. "Hello, old chap. The name's Parker, Chester Parker." He offered his hand for a shake. "I saw you come in a bit ago hauling a load. I guessed you might be moving in and thought maybe this would be of help."

Paco, a full head shorter than the man and the cart, grabbed hold of it and said, "Thanks a whole lot, Chester. I can sure use this. I'm Paco LeSoto. Yeah, my wife and I are just moving in. And frankly, I'm getting too old for this kind of stuff."

"Happy to meet you, Paco. You don't happen to play bridge, by any chance?"

Paco shook his head. "Sorry, I never learned." He noted the man's crestfallen face. "Needing a fourth, are you?"

"To be sure," said Chester. "My long-time partner up and croaked on me." He spun around and walked off.

Paco took a few seconds to digest this response. *Was he kidding? Maybe not. Typical Englishman.* "Thanks again," he called out. Chester raised a hand in acknowledgment and kept going.

Paco pushed the hotel cart out to the car, and lifted out carton after carton, piling them up almost as high as he was tall. *I should've divided the load and made two trips, but I want this damn moving business to be over.* Panting, he struggled to push the heavy cart up the walk and inside the lobby. Maneuvering it into the elevator, he pulled it out on the second floor, wondering whether he was going to make it down the hall.

Just outside the door of suite 225, he felt a jolt, a violent thud on the left side of his chest, as if he'd been slugged by a prizefighter. *What the hell? Am I having another heart attack?* And then, through the painful haze, he realized…he remembered…the device protecting his heart, his defibrillator, had sent him a dire warning. His knees collapsed under him and he slid to the floor behind the cart, crying out, "Mollyyy…"

Chapter 5
Disheartened

Monday, November 2nd

Paco had fallen against the luggage cart. His weight gave it one extra push against their door, which he had purposely left ajar for his return trip. Molly heard the door bang open and his desperate plea for her help. She pushed her Roly to the front hall, but set it aside to muscle the luggage cart all the way into the sitting room in order to reach her husband. He lay collapsed across the threshold. She knelt down beside the unconscious Paco.

"Oh God," she shrieked, cradling his face, "he's having another heart attack. Someone call Dr. Crisp!" She looked up to see if anyone had heard her.

Luckily, Nurse Penny Summers had just left suite 224 across the hall on her way to the elevator. She spun around, hurried to the patient, and dropped to one knee. She unhooked her stethoscope and listened to Paco's chest in several places for a few moments. then used her fold-out cell phone to call the office.

"Dr. Crisp," said Penny. "We have a patient with a dire heart problem outside 225. Come quickly."

The nurse took a large pill from a bottle in her breast pocket, crushed it between her fingers, and waved it under Paco's nose several times until he shook his head back and forth as if saying No to avoid the acrid smell of ammonia.

Slowly his eyelids opened. "I'm sorry, Molly," Paco whispered. "I tried to make it all in one load, and it was just too much for me."

Minutes later, Dr. Phelix Crisp arrived and pushed both Penny and Molly aside to listen with his own stethoscope. He spoke at long last after searching Paco's eyes with a penlight and taking his pulse. "I've called for an ambulance. They should be on the way by now."

"Doctor, is he going to die?" asked Molly.

"I don't think so," said Phelix. "His vital signs are a little on the high side, but still within the normal range. I believe something triggered his defibrillator, and the shock knocked him for a loop. What was he doing beforehand?"

"He was exerted, pushing this heavy luggage cart all the way here from the parking space," replied Molly.

"Ah, no wonder," said Phelix. "Well, a trip to the hospital will do him some good. They'll check him over and make sure he's okay."

Paco weakly asked, "If everything's normal, why do I have to go to the hospital?"

"It's procedure when the defibrillator alarm goes off," replied Phelix. "I highly recommend a full day of bed rest as a minimum."

Just then the elevator doors opened and two EMTs emerged, pushing a collapsed gurney. They collected their own set of vital signs and came to the same conclusion. They unfolded the gurney and transported Paco to the ambulance and then to the county medical center's cardiac unit.

* * * *

Paco was under the care of Dr. Mason Mejiro, a fortyish man of medium build with black hair, a fair complexion, and an air of confidence yet kindness. Paco spent the rest of that day and two nights in the cardiac care unit. He got his required bed rest, and his meds were carefully supplemented.

Molly spent every available visiting hour in his room, casting a critical eye at every meal tray a nurse's aide brought him. *No filet minnion and scalped potatoes? No Hundred Island salad dressing?*

And at breakfast, just a hard-foiled egg and toast? Molly knew why, and had a pang of regret. She had preacheed the new rules to Paco and tried to comply, but years of her "heart-hefty" cooking had contributed to where they were now. She didn't dare imagine what the Gilded Gates dining room menus would offer.

The cardiac unit was equipped with state-of-the-art equipment designed to monitor a patient's defibrillator and how well it was functioning. The unit provided a two-way WiFi—a wireless network that was able to connect the defibrillator implanted in Paco's chest to an external programming and recording instrument.

A brisk young man wearing a hospital badge entered Paco's room. "Hello, Mr. LeSoto. I'm Jason, a medical engineer trained to check out your device." He selected a round object resembling a hockey puck attached to a black cord and draped it across Paco's shoulders. The puck rested on the left side of Paco's chest, directly over the internal defibrillator. The electromagnetic connection extracted a history of Paco's past cardiac behavioral data and the efficiency of the defibrillator, transmitting all of this to the instrument itself. The results appeared on a monitor display and printouts for the cardiologist to interpret and analyze.

Paco's anxiety kicked in. "So, Jason, how's my ticker performing with my defib?"

Jason deftly skirted the question. "Your doctor will give you all the results, Mr. LeSoto." He quickly left the room.

During the second day in the hospital, Dr. Mejiro came in to examine him, and that's when Paco's sharp mind and logic shifted into overdrive. Sitting up in bed, his dark eyes alert, he said to Dr. Mejiro, "I know I overexerted during our moving. Too much heavy stuff all at once. But Doctor, I don't get it. Why did my defib give me that awful jolt?"

Dr. Mejiro gave his patient a shrewd look. From Paco's admission record, he knew his patient's background in law enforcement, and chose to be straight-out blunt. "Your defibrillator kicked off unexpectedly, telling me it needs adjustment—some fine-tuning. The battery is still strong. I instructed the engineer to make the programmed adjustments. Mr. LeSoto, this is a remarkably smart device. It's guiding me in assessing your daily care and your medications, and most important, your heart function." The cardiologist paused for effect. "And even your lifestyle." The gentle scolding came next for seriously overdoing his activities "at your age."

Paco listened, thanked him for his care. But later he brooded. *What am I supposed to do all day?*

* * * *

Molly arrived at the hospital early the next morning to be sure her Paco was given the best care during his discharge. A nurse wheelchaired him out the front door with Molly pushing her Roly close behind to the waiting van from Gilded Gates. It delivered them to their new home just before noon. When Molly opened the door to their suite, it occurred to Paco to ask, "What happened to the cart full of our clothes and things?"

Molly's round face flushed with importance. "I had nothing to do when I came home from the hospital that first night. I couldn't sleep, so I put all the clothes on their hang-ups and the other stuff away in their proper cubbies. Then I pushed the empty wagon out into the hall. The next morning it was gone."

Paco stifled a laugh. "You're amazing, Mol."

"And you're gonna rehave yourself from now on," she scolded. "No more pushing your weight around."

"Okay, okay. Isn't it lunchtime in this establishment?"

"Sure, it's noonish," she replied. "The dining rooms are on the first floor of Crisp Hall, take a right at what's-his-name's office. We take the elevator down and walk over there."

They entered the cafeteria, eager for their first meal at Gilded Gates. Already the room resounded with clinking and clanking noises amid the conversational din. They stood in line, sliding their trays along as they made their selections. Paco picked up his tray, ready to go to a table. But he stepped back, realizing that Molly had a dilemma. She depended on her walker. How could she carry a full tray at the same time? She surprised him. She set her tray on top of the handlebars, gripping it and the handlebars at the same time, with her thumbs on top of the tray to steady it. She was able to move away from the line into the seating area, slowly and precariously, but she did it. Paco watched her with admiration.

The round Formica tables seated six and the rectangular ones seated eight. Molly started toward one where only three places were occupied. Paco gruffly spoke up. "No, not there Mol, that's Chester Parker, an English fellow. He was nice and gave me the big luggage cart, but then he snubbed me when I told him I didn't play bridge."

"That's his losing," said Molly. "How about over there?" She nodded to a rectangular table of six with two people sitting at one end and a lone person at the other.

"Those two were playing Ping-Pong when we got our tour," noted Paco. "Irma told us their names, but I can't recall them."

"I guess we'll have to reduce ourselves all under again," said Molly.

"Mind if we join you?" asked Paco.

"Oh, please do." The woman returned her half-eaten sandwich to her plate. "I'm Maryanne Amati and this is my husband, Jeff." They wore matching blue sweat suits with a Nike Swoosh on the jackets.

"I'm Molly LeSoto, and the cutie here is my husband, Paco." Molly slid her tray onto the table, collapsed Roly slightly, and sat down. Paco made sure she was comfortable before he shuffled his chair and slid in close to the table.

"You're new here, aren't you?" asked Jeff, pulling the paper top off a container of pudding. "And yet you look vaguely familiar."

"Yes, we *are* new to the place," replied Paco. He took a bite of his turkey sandwich, chewed slowly, and swallowed. The couple waited patiently for him to continue. "If you've lived anywhere in the vicinity of either Baltimore or Black Rain Corners, we might have come across each other. I was a police detective in both places."

"Well, that puts Maryanne and me smack in the middle of both places—in Annapolis," declared Jeff, plunging a spoon into his chocolate pudding. "We ran a stationery store on Maryland Avenue just off of State Circle and the Capitol. We called it The Red

Balloon. Did well for a lotta years. Then the foot traffic fell off and it got to be too much, long hours and all. We sold it three years ago. It was the right move. I was seventy-two. Maryanne could've kept at it. She was still a kid."

His wife laughed. "Some kid. I was sixty-nine." Paco noted that she did look quite a bit younger than Jeff. In fact, she looked younger than most of the other residents in the lunchroom, with her pert nose and cocoa-brown hair in a boyish bob.

"Paco, now I remember you," said Maryanne. "You were that nice police inspector that gave us instructions on how to get to the Marche House Museum, at least four years ago."

"I'm glad I was of service," said Paco. "Small world."

"Sure is," agreed Maryanne, who turned her head toward Molly as though expecting her to tell her story next.

Molly had been savoring her vegetable-barley soup, but took the hint. "I was a homekeeper and cook to Dr. Avi Kepple," she said, putting her spoon down, but wishing she didn't have to, so the soup wouldn't get cold.

"Oh, what kind of doctor was he?" asked Maryanne.

"He was a renowned psychiatrist and psychoanalyst," Paco said.

Molly's curls bobbed up and down as she nodded vigorously, crumbling a Saltine cracker into her bowl.

"Jeff!" interjected Maryanne. "Maybe you should consult a psychiatrist. That's the kind of doctor who might be able to help you with your somnambulism problem."

"Snobulism?" Molly tried to repeat. "What's that?"

"Somnambulism is a medical term for sleepwalking," said Maryanne.

Jeff made a sour face. Even at age seventy-five, he had a physically large presence and the rugged complexion of an outdoorsman. His entire head was crowned by a halo of thick white hair that descended over his ears to form a luxurious beard flowing down in front of his neck. A generous white mustache covered his upper lip. At this moment, his intense blue eyes behind black-framed glasses sent daggers to his wife.

"You don't have to air our dirty laundry in front of friends we just met, do you, Maryanne?"

"Do you have any better ideas?" snapped his wife. "You need to face up to your sleepwalking sooner or later. I can't take much more of this. Every blessed night you're gone from our bed three or four hours and the next morning you don't even know where you've been. I worry that you might fall down some stairs or something."

"I do know where I've been," declared Jeff. "I'm pretty sure I wander the halls of this establishment and I swear I hear weird sounds like voices. I don't know where they're coming from or exactly what they are. But the next morning I definitely remember hearing them."

"What kind of sounds are you talking about?" asked Paco.

"A kind of wailing or moaning, a female voice, like someone in trouble," replied Jeff, calming down a bit. "I think my sleepwalking has to do with searching for the source of these sounds."

"Do you think that if you did find the source, it would cure your sleepwalking?" asked Paco.

"I believe it would," said Jeff, "but there's no way to be sure."

"How do we get in touch with this Dr. Kepple?" asked Maryanne.

"You can't," replied Molly. "Dr. Avi passed up a number of years ago."

"Damn!" said Jeff, slapping the table with the flat of his hand. "Now I'm really sorry you brought all of this up, Maryanne."

In a trembly voice, she said, "Don't get angry, dear, I was only trying to help you."

"Well, you're doing just the opposite," Jeff growled.

"You don't have to worry about us," offered Molly. "We know how to keep your beans from spilling."

"She's right," assured Paco. "We will, obviously, exercise the utmost discretion. However, If you don't mind, I believe that you might benefit from some of my detective skills. Free of charge, of course."

"No, Paco," interrupted Molly, poking him in the ribs with a finger. "I don't think they want you revolved."

"On second thought," returned Jeff. "Maybe you have something we haven't tried. What exactly did you have in mind?"

Paco took a long slug of water as he constructed his idea. "Maybe if I wait outside your apartment and follow you at a distance for a few nights, at a minimum we'll know where you've been, and if you're following a pattern. And if we're lucky, I might hear or even locate the moaning sound."

"Sounds like a great plan," said Jeff. "Are you sure you want to do this? I don't want to put you out, my friend."

Molly broke in. "Paco, honey, it's your first day home from the hospital. The doctors told you to rest. You need to sleep at night. Besides, this will be our very first night together in this place."

"Are you sick?" asked Jeff.

Molly blurted out, "His refriberator misbehaved."

Jeff squinted in confusion. He couldn't imagine how to respond.

"Not to worry, Jeff," said Paco. "Molly's trying to say my defibrillator misbehaved. I've been doing nothing but sleeping for two days in the hospital. Besides, I can nap in the daytime now that I don't have to go to work."

Jeff took a deep breath of relief. "Then you agree to be my shadow tonight? Oh, wait a minute. That's damned pushy of me. I'm sure you need a few days to recover from the hospital and get organized, this being your new home and all."

"You're right," said Paco. "It's a bit too soon. I will be your shadow three times starting next week—only you won't know which nights they are. That way, my presence won't affect the outcome. Do you agree?"

"I do," said Jeff. "I'm anxious to get to the bottom of this as soon as I can. It's friggin' embarrassing."

"Then I'll need two things from you, Jeff," said Paco. "First, your suite number, and second, the time you fall asleep each night."

"We're on the third floor in 309. I usually fall asleep somewhere between eleven and eleven forty-five each night."

"Maryanne, what time does your husband start roaming the

halls?" asked Paco.

"He—"

Jeff scowled. "How the devil would you know that, Maryanne? Aren't you asleep?"

Maryanne's wide mouth pouted. "Jeff, you know perfectly well I'm a light sleeper. Your slightest move can wake me. Each time you wake up I think you're just going to the bathroom. You do a lot of that these days—I mean nighttime." She turned to Paco. "It varies from night to night. My best estimate would be that he takes off anywhere between one and two-thirty. He's always back by daylight, but sometimes much earlier. He's unpredictable."

Jeff lapsed into silence as he scraped the last of his pudding from the plastic dish. Clearing his throat, he said, "Thanks a lot, Paco. Nice to meet you folks. Sorry to hit you so hard with my crazy situation."

"No problemski," chirped Molly.

The Amatis finished their lunches first. They excused themselves—Maryanne to watch *General Hospital* and Jeff for a swim. With their trays in hand they headed for the Drop-off counter.

Molly watched the Amatis cross the room and disappear through the doorway. "Nice people," she said, but her troubled face reflected what she was really thinking. *I wonder what my Paco's gotten himself into.*

For the first time, she observed the lone woman in a dull brown dress at the opposite end of their long table. The woman seemed to be eating in slow-motion-replay while reading her *Reader's Digest*.

In a chipper voice, Molly called out, "Hi, I'm Molly."

The woman looked up, then over at Molly. "Were you talking to me?"

"Yes. We're new here and I just wanted to interduce ourselves. I'm Molly and my mister is Paco."

"Alice Mayport." She immediately returned to her reading.

"Oh, I remember now," whispered Molly to Paco. "She's the one Irma called a shecluse."

Paco suppressed a grin. He stood ready to leave, with his empty tray and Molly's piled on top. She followed him to the Drop-off counter. They each had the same thought. The first few hours in their new home had been miserable.

Chapter 6
Revelations in Broad Daylight

Molly convinced Paco that another night's sleep and a day of relaxation would do him a world of good. So Paco rested for the remainder of Monday, and made no attempt to follow Jeff that first night. Instead, right after a hot oatmeal breakfast the next morning, he and Molly set out to reconnoiter the layout of the entire assisted living home under daylight conditions. His main purpose was to use the daylight tour to create a complete mental map of Gilded Gates. Visual rather than written down. Such a map would be essential while trailing Jeff under less-than-ideal lighting conditions in the dead of night. He had no idea where Jeff would lead him, or what Jeff could have possibly learned or experienced during a journey sometimes taking more than three hours in a single night's walk.

The reconnoitering task began at the cafeteria's Drop-off counter. This was to be Molly's show. Paco sauntered back to a small table with a cup of decaf coffee. Molly asked to speak with the cook on the kitchen side of the counter. She sweet-talked her way in by convincing Carla Dobbs, the head cook, that she also was a professional "homekeeper and gourmet cook." A few swapped recipes later, Carla gave Molly a half-hour tour of the kitchen, pantries, and equipment. Afterward, she gave Carla a great big hug in gratitude and Carla returned the embrace, cementing a newfound friendship. Back in the dining room, Molly described what she had seen to the waiting Paco, who was pleased and grudgingly happy for extra resting time.

On their way out of Crisp Hall, Paco sidled up to the door blocking the private stairwell to the Crisp residence. He glanced around to make sure nobody was watching before trying the door. Locked, just as he expected. *The Crisps wouldn't want anyone else wandering through their home and personal things.*

Examining the recreation room was tricky, as it was constantly occupied by residents making use of the facilities, or just relaxing and chatting. The LeSotos wanted to keep their exploring discreet. Any truthful explanation would violate the Amatis' trust. The first set of doors off the recreation room led to a sports-gear cabinet full of Ping-Pong paddles, tennis and badminton racquets, pool cues, softballs, baseball bats, and bases.

The next set of doors opened to an exercise room with its stationary bikes, treadmill, and rack full of assorted hand weights and stretch bands. Coming out, they spied Bertha Bubbashlufsky sitting at a card table reading a letter. The short, heavyset woman with white hair tied back in a bun made her unmistakable.

"Her face looks too tragical," said Molly. "I wonder what's cooking in her oven."

"Let's go over and find out," said Paco.

"What's wrong, Bertha?" asked Molly, shoving Roly aside to place a sympathetic arm around her shoulder.

"After five years here, I'm being evicted," Bertha sputtered. She handed the letter to Paco. Behind horn-rimmed glasses he studied the large-print notice.

"You're getting kicked out of Gilded Gates?" asked Molly. "That's terrible."

"No, no," said Paco. "You're just being moved. This letter says you and your belongings are being moved from your suite to a group living arrangement in Comfort Hall at your convenience anytime between Friday, the sixth and Monday, the ninth of this month. That's not much notice, is it?"

"Who's the letter from?" asked Molly.

"Angular Properties Management Associates," replied Paco after perusing the letter once more.

"But why?" asked Molly. "They would have no raisins to do that to you."

"I'm afraid they do, Molly," replied Bertha. "All my money is used up. I'm living longer than I'm supposed to. When we came here five years ago, we didn't have enough assets to sign a monthly rental lease. Schlem and I had to turn over all our assets in return for a lifetime care agreement. This morning I complained to Dr. Crisp about being forced out of my suite. He pointed out that our original agreement doesn't specify the particular living arrangements after the money runs out."

"But the deli, Bertha," reminded Molly. "You must have sold Bubba's Deli for a goodly amount."

"Not as much as you'd think," said Bertha. "We made a decent living, but we poured so much of what we made right back into the business that there was very little left over for savings. The deli's selling price was dictated by a small, really pathetic, list of available customers in Black Rain Corners. The new owners practically stole the store from us. They weren't nice people, taking advantage of a decrepit couple like us. Schlem was so aggravated, it wasn't good for his heart."

"Don't worry, Bertha," said Molly. "You're not going to Siberie. We'll still be friends. We'll see each other in the cafeteria and dining room every day now."

"Cafeteria," repeated Paco. "It's lunchtime already. We'd better get over there before they stop serving."

"Bertha, come with us and munch a lunch," said Molly. "It'll do you up."

"I'll come," she answered, relieved not to have to eat alone. What she'd avoided revealing was the embarrassing fact that Schlem had never taken out a life insurance policy, leaving her high and dry.

They found empty seats together at a table for six, where Gordon H. Lowe III sat alone, his lean body with erect posture. Paco sat down at the head of the table. Molly and Bertha took seats across from Gordon. Beyond the introductions, he chose not to converse. The shortage of exchange was not for the lack of trying. Jabbing her fork into her Waldorf salad, Molly began munching the tasty apples, seedless red grapes, and walnuts. Between bites she tried several times to start a conversation, but a curt word or two was all she received in return. While cutting up her lettuce and chomping on celery bits, she recalled Irma saying he'd been an undertaker in Virginia. *A tad creepy. Unfriendly in his dark suit and black tie.* He had a thin mustache above turned-down lips decorating his angular face. His tiny eyes seemed to stare at something off in the distance. *Hah. He needs no one but hisself—and dead people.*

After lunch Paco and Molly said goodbye to Bertha and resumed their reconnoitering, starting with a walk through the locker and restrooms, showers, and pool. Some doors led them to new territory, others to storage, linen, and janitorial spaces. They explored stairwells, halls, and rooms they hadn't even noticed before.

In the first-floor parlor of Comfort Hall they stopped to chat with Nadine Chasdane. Paco's eyes flicked over her. *Fairly young looking, considering the general population in this place.* Nadine's abundant blonde curls, tickling her shoulders, bore nary a trace of gray. She stood about five-four in a purple cardigan sweater over a flowered blouse and matching purple pants. But her smart appearance was betrayed by teary eyes.

Molly, yearning for conversation from anyone at all, gave her a loud, friendly hello. "Hi, we're Paco and Molly LeSoto. I'm Molly," she said with a giggle.

Nadine perked up on the tenor of the introduction. "So glad to meet you folks. I'm lonely. I miss my good friend."

"We had to leave lots of good friends when *we* moved here," said Molly.

"No, you don't understand," protested Nadine. "Lisa Howard and I were roommates here until a week ago. When I woke up on that Tuesday, she wasn't in her bed across the room. She just disappeared! We're so close. She wouldn't have just up and left without letting me know why. No one will tell me anything—not even Dr. Crisp or Ms. Irma. All they said was that I would be getting a new roommate next week. It was terribly frustrating."

"Is your good friend in questionable health?" asked Paco.

"Could she have passed up?" added Molly. "Maybe it was her time."

"Oh, no, she's a picture of good health," said Nadine, warming up to their sincere interest. "She swims laps in the pool several times a week. She's eighty-four, two years younger than me, but she looks *ten years younger* than me."

Paco's bushy eyebrows shot north. "You're eighty-six?"

Nadine smiled for the first time and fluffed a few curls with two fingers. "I get help from my friend Winnie the Wig. The rest of me is real, though."

"Those curlicues look pretty naturelle to me," Molly said.

"How long have you lived in Gilded Gates?" asked Paco.

"Let me see now. Seven years in the suites and five months here in Comfort Hall. It's one of two tiny double rooms, but it's ours, and we get along so well."

"Were you asked to move from the suites?" asked Paco.

"You sure ask a lot of questions," said Nadine. "But yes, we received an eviction letter from the management firm. Frankly, I still can't believe they call it eviction."

"Well, let me say that you're satisfying the curiosity of a retired police detective."

Nadine's eyes widened, no longer teary. "Wow! That's good news—I think."

"Are you and Lisa gay ladies?" Molly blurted out.

"Molly!" scolded Paco. "That's personal—none of your damn business."

"I don't mind answering," said Nadine. "No, we're just close companions. Before our husbands died, the four of us traveled together a lot—leaving us with wonderful shared memories. And by the way, I hope you get it that I still speak of Lisa in the present tense. I'm praying she'll come home soon."

"Of course," said Paco. "One more question. During your seven years here, did you ever know of anyone else in good health disappearing like your friend?"

Nadine's eyes brightened behind her rhinestone-framed glasses. "Now that you mention it, there are at least two other missing residents. Rumor had it that Mindy Norton was locked in a closet for two whole weeks. Then it was also rumored that Bruce Jameson had fallen and hit his head in the cellar of Crisp Hall. But you know what? That's the weird thing. None of us have seen hide nor hair of Mindy or Bruce since. Dr. Crisp generally announces all those who have passed on over the public address system. He usually ends with some little nondenominational prayer. But nothing about Mindy or Bruce."

"Frankly, Nadine, all that sounds a bit on the preposterous side," said Paco, "but a missing person is still a missing person."

"There were many others who died, but they were obviously the sick, the aged, or had some kind of accident." Nadine pulled her sweater tightly around her chest and added in a trembling voice. "And now Lisa's missing."

"Thank you, Nadine, for sharing with us," said Paco. "You've stirred up my detective juices."

"Does this mean you'll look into Lisa's disappearance?"

"Yes, but I can't promise you anything," said Paco with a glance at his watch. "Take care," he added as he and Molly left the parlor. They spent two more hours exploring the intricacies of Comfort Hall before returning to their suite for their afternoon naps.

* * * *

Back in their suite after dinner, Molly noticed that her husband seemed restless. Her instinct proved right. "Sweetiekins, you told Jeff you would wait 'til next week to do your detectivating."

"Yeah, I did," Paco admitted. "But I'm already getting bored in this place. Can't resist the challenge."

"Well, be careful, honeybunches. I don't want to lose you to some ghost."

"You won't, sweets, I promise I'll be careful."

In the past few days, reality had struck Paco in more ways than one. He and Molly had entered a new phase of their lives much more dramatically than they'd expected. He would never again be able to drive his Chevy Malibu, or any car. In one year, his driver's license would be up for renewal and he knew his cardiologist would not allow him to renew it. Not at his age and with his heart condition. Luckily, Judy, the LeSotos' real estate agent, jumped at the chance to help. She bought the Chevy for her own use and sent Paco the check. When it arrived, Molly breathed a monumental sigh of relief.

And now he was ready for his new escapade—tracking Jeff's sleepwalking.

Chapter 7
Stalking

At 1:30 a.m. Paco placed a folding chair in a janitorial closet across the dimly lit hall, two doors down from suite 309. With the closet door left just enough ajar, he had a perfect view. He slipped his Walkman headset on and listened to FM music while he waited for Jeff to appear, knowing there was a chance he might not. At 1:45 he was rewarded. The door to the Amati suite swung open, and the sleepwalker stepped out into the hall in his navy-blue plaid pajamas and brown leather bedroom slippers. He left the door slightly ajar. Paco unplugged the headset and slid it down around his neck as he stood to follow his quarry. After Jeff passed by the closet, Paco waited a moment, slipped out into the hall, and followed some fifteen feet behind.

Jeff's eyes are open, but is he actually asleep? Paco wondered. *He's standing straight and stiff, and his steps are annoyingly slow, but regular and unhesitatingly constant, the perfect automaton—surely the indicators of a sleepwalker.*

To Paco's surprise, Jeff knew exactly where he was going. He took the stairs all the way to the first floor and crossed the corridor into Crisp Hall. Paco did the same, past the offices, through the moonlit dining rooms, to a pair of louvered double doors that led into the immense kitchen. As the nightwalker entered, Paco wondered why the kitchen doors weren't locked. Jeff began rattling cabinet doorknobs, apparently seeking one in particular. He managed to open four tall doors to pantries, stocked with abundant supplies of foodstuffs or cooking equipment. Impatiently shutting each one, he made a circuitous spin around the kitchen to the steel door at the back, the one he sought. This one opened to a deep stairwell going down. Jeff's fluid legs took these stairs so smoothly he never lingered on any step. Gripping the railing, Paco trailed at a safe distance into the semidarkness of the cellar below. He was glad he'd worn his favorite motley sweat suit, and sneakers that made his own footsteps silent. But he also wondered how much energy he had left to continue this insane quest.

Half a minute passed before Paco's eyes adjusted to the meager light given off by the green pilot light above Crisp Hall's electric power panel. But Jeff was nowhere to be seen. *Where the hell is he?* Paco faced stacks of wooden crates and cardboard cartons sitting on pallets—forming a kind of maze, defying any sort of aisle. *No doubt these are supplies needed by the facility, but in such disorganized fashion,* Paco thought. He halted and held his breath to listen, thinking he was hearing steps ahead and to his left. But no. It was the scraping, pattering of little feet—mice? rats? scrambling off to his right. Weaving his way around three randomly situated pallets, he found himself in a rudimentary sort of aisle.

A loud hissing sound caused Paco to stop suddenly. Something darted out of the shadows and leaped up toward his face, its almond eyes glowing. Paco's still-quick reflexes brought both hands up to protect himself and deflect the creature, sending it to the concrete floor. A tabby cat landed on its feet with a thud and retreated immediately. *How come it's not going after the mice?* he wondered. *Or did it already have its dinner?* Paco took a deep breath and felt a sharp pain in his upper chest. Three normal breaths later, the pain—more like a shock—went away altogether, making him wonder whether his defibrillator alarm had been the shock he felt. He put it out of his mind and set his eyes and ears to the search once more.

Paco thought he saw Jeff's shadow moving along one wall, but in the blink of an eye it was gone. *Have I lost him altogether? What to do now?* The makeshift aisle was his best move, so he took off in pursuit. The aisle ended at an open door leading to a much larger cellar space, giving Paco the idea that he was now under the corridor of Fellowship Hall. That was a given when he saw the two elevator motor enclosures to his right. Just past the second enclosure, he saw another open door and perceived some motion—the sleepwalker! Paco watched as Jeff trudged up the concrete stairs to a door secured by two spring-loaded arm and slot latches, one two feet above the other at mid-door. Jeff lifted up the arm of both latches at the same time and opened the door, exposing the back of a large wall-hanging tapestry. He pushed it aside and stepped into the room beyond. The tapestry hid this secret door leading from the basement to the first-floor room above.

Jeff knew it existed. He's done this before! thought Paco.

He waited several more seconds not to reveal himself, stole up the steps, and followed Jeff by unlocking the door in the same manner, opening it, and pushing the tapestry aside for himself. As soon as he stepped inside the room, he realized it was the same Leaping Lion tapestry he and Molly had seen on their tour. Paco was astonished to find himself in Comfort Hall's Victorian-style parlor.

He watched Jeff halt between the two sofas as though he were unsure where to go next. Paco waited until his quarry began to move again—this time up the public stairs leading to the second floor of Comfort Hall. As Jeff passed each room of sleeping residents, he hesitated, leaned in and appeared to be listening as though he actually wanted to hear the infernal snoring and weird sleep noises that ordinary people make. Apparently not hearing what he expected, he returned to the front of the building and entered Fellowship Hall, where the two-room suites were.

Jeff headed for the nearest suite door, stopped abruptly, and leaned in, pressing his left ear to it. A few seconds later, he straightened up and shook his head. At the next suite door, Paco witnessed the nightwalker's identical motions with the same result, shoulders drooping in disappointment. Jeff made his way past many more suites with the same action and result.

It suddenly occurred to Paco: *Maybe Jeff is searching for the person who made the moaning sounds he'd heard on one of his earlier sleepwalks—the peculiar moaning sound he described to Molly and me at lunch.* Snapping out of his reverie, Paco slipped into a nearby alcove to hide when Jeff reversed himself and headed back toward the UP staircase. Out of breath, a weary Paco tailed the nightwalker up to the third floor, where he repeated his listening actions at a number of additional doors—all in vain.

The nightwalker gave up in despair. He walked slowly to his own suite, 309, and shouldered through the barely open door, just as he had left it. Exhausted, Paco trudged downstairs to suite 225, and flopped into bed next to Molly.

Chapter 8
Fallout

The next morning Molly could hardly wait for Paco to wake up. She wanted to know what mischief had occurred while she slept. Rising at their usual hour of seven, she showered and dressed and rattled around in the innocent hope of rousing her husband, but he slept on for another two hours. He called to her as soon as he opened his eyes and sat up in bed. She sat down on the edge of the queen bed and kissed him straight on. Then leaning back, she said, "Well?"

"Can't I even brush my teeth and wash my face and have a cup of coffee before I tell you everything?"

"Of course," she replied. "But I've got the heebie-jeebies waiting for you."

Ten minutes later, he moseyed into the kitchenette and sat down at the round bistro table for two. "Okay, where's my coffee?"

"I made a fresh pot from Mrs. Coffee," said Molly, as she poured two cups and joined him. She was so eager to listen that she didn't even complain, as she usually did, about the tiny kitchenette. "Cozy," Irma had described it. *Cozy my foot, crampled is more like it*, Molly thought. She missed the freedom of creating lavish meals, even though she couldn't stand on her feet long enough to make one—and Paco wasn't allowed to eat them anyway. She actually liked the bistro table with its white marble top and decorative black metal base.

Paco took his first sip and sighed contentedly. "Thanks, Mol. So here goes. I waited in the closet across the hall for Jeff to come out, and when he did, I had to satisfy myself that he was actually asleep."

"Was he?"

"I'm pretty damn sure he *was*, but he did some amazing things while sleepwalking, things that I didn't think one could accomplish while asleep."

"Like what?"

"Oh, like manage so many stairs, or even navigate such a complicated journey as the one he took in the middle of the night."

"So how do you explain it?" asked Molly.

"From what I've read and heard previously, our brain doesn't shut down when we go to sleep. For example, we continue to breathe and pump blood throughout our bodies. When someone sleepwalks, a few pieces of the brain and the body functions they govern actually shut down. The sense of sight, hearing, and smell, as well as motor skills like walking, may still be in use, even though our sense of awareness has gone to sleep. And our subconscious produces dreams, whether we like them or not."

"I'll take your word for it, sweetie," replied Molly. "All that goes under my head."

"Haven't you ever been awakened by a sound or a smell?"

"Oh, yeah. But tell me about Jeff."

Paco's detecting skills and memory for detail were intact, even at the age of eighty-seven. He precisely described Jeff's path down the kitchen steps, across the long basement floor and up more steps into the parlor of Comfort Hall, all the way to the end when Jeff finally returned to his suite on the third floor of Fellowship Hall.

"I never heard of any sleepy walker doing tricks like that," said Molly.

"You might be right. Usually a sleepwalker travels a well-known path—not like the nightmarish journey through a dark basement full of obstacles that he took me on. There has to be some explanation."

"Wait, Paco. You said it looked like Jeff didn't hear any moaning or wailing. How about you? What did you hear?"

"I didn't hear anything. But I didn't have my ear up to the doors like Jeff did."

"Are you going to report everything to the Amatis?" asked Molly.

"Not everything just yet," said Paco. "I want to follow Jeff at least one more time before I draw any conclusions."

"I'm hungry," said Molly. "Let's go to breakfast before they stop serving."

"It's too late already, hon. They stopped at nine. It's 9:15."

"I can rustle up some Oatmeal Squares and milk," said Molly. "Sorry, no fruit."

"I guess I can make do," said Paco, reaching up into the cabinet for the cereal box.

* * * *

At noon the LeSotos headed for the cafeteria. Molly chose the beef stew and biscuits, while Paco opted for the salad plate. They didn't see anyone they knew or needed to know, so they sat down at an empty table. They'd eaten most of their lunch when they heard their names being called. Looking up, they saw both the Amatis hurrying forward and flopping their trays down on the table.

"Well!" said Jeff without even a hello. "A couple days have passed, and we haven't heard from you. Have you had a chance to observe my sleepwalking yet?"

"I followed you just once," said Paco. "But I'd like to reserve any conclusions I might make until I've had a chance to follow you one or more times."

"Hey, you can't fault me for being anxious, can you?" asked Jeff.

"Of course not. You dropped out of my sight down there in the semi-dark basement from time to time," said Paco.

A frown line creased Jeff's high bald forehead. "Basement? You gotta be kidding. What the hell was I doing in the basement? Boy, I must be losing it."

"Perhaps you were doing a little bargain-basement shopping," said Molly with a grin.

"I have to admit, the basement was full of goodies," said Jeff.

"Yeah, he's always looking for a steal, buy something cheap," chimed in Maryanne.

"What more do you expect to learn from another night of trailing me?" asked Jeff. "Why can't you just tell me the whole story now?"

"If you insist."

Paco began elaborating on the route Jeff had sleepwalked, but when he got to the part where Jeff entered the parlor from the basement, Jeff interrupted.

"Hold on! Maryanne and I have been in the parlor a thousand times. I don't remember seeing any door that leads to the basement. How would I know it was there?"

"Jeff, when I followed you in the basement I saw you," said Paco. "There's a second set of basement stairs. At the top of them there's a small door. You went up that staircase, undid the two latches, and pushed the door open. A tapestry wall hanging was in front of the door. You pushed it aside and went into the room. It turned out to be the parlor. You must have known about it in advance somehow. When Molly and I were given the tour, including the parlor, we saw the tapestry of the Leaping Lion on the far wall, but we had no idea it was hiding a secret door. What troubles me is how you found that secret stairway to the basement in the first place. It has to be off-limits to the residents."

"Ooh! I love secret passages," said Maryanne. "How mysterious."

"Sounds pretty spookified to me," said Molly. "Maybe I should have come along."

"I don't remember any of this," said Jeff, stroking his thick white beard.

Paco continued his narrative of the sleepwalk until he reached the part where the sleepwalker stopped to listen at doors to most of the dormitories in Comfort Hall and suites in Fellowship Hall.

"I must have heard the moaning in one of those rooms," said Jeff.

"You didn't appear to have heard it last night because you kept shaking your head and moving on to the next room," said Paco.

"You looked frustrated. From there you went back to your suite without incident."

"I take it you didn't hear anything either?" asked Jeff.

"No. By the way, was the person moaning a man or a woman?"

Jeff said, "That's a good question. I have no idea, even though I remember the moaning quite clearly. Someone was in great distress and I desperately wanted to help whoever it was. Was it all a part of some dream or nightmare?"

"We live in an assisted living facility," explained Paco. "The place is full of old, aching, and infirm people likely to call out—wailing or groaning or moaning on occasion. Whether the moans you heard were real or not is unimportant. What does matter is that there's a medical staff here to help someone when help is needed. You are under no obligation to render assistance."

"I see. When will you follow me again?" asked Jeff.

"More than likely, one of the next three nights," replied Paco. "But you're not going to know which one."

"Paco, I'll ask you again. What more do you expect to learn from another night of trailing me?"

"I need to know if there are any patterns. Like, do you go to all the same places in the same order each night, and do you react the same way in each place? In other words, are you a consistent sleepwalker? Knowing what you know *now* might alter or even deter your sleepwalking habits altogether."

"That would be a definite bonus," said Maryanne standing up with her empty lunch tray.

"Yeah, I'd love to wake up feeling refreshed for a change," said Jeff, getting to his feet.

As the Amatis left their table, Paco said, "I guess it's time for us to get a move on, too."

"Honeybunches, would you mind if I join you later?" asked Molly.

"Of course not. What did you have in mind?"

"I haven't been outside in days," she replied. "I need some refreshed air. I'll see you in half an hour or so."

Paco nodded, and the two parted in the lobby of Crisp Hall—Paco to their suite to read his morning *Washington Post* in peace, and Molly outdoors, with her three-wheeled Roly, on the paths edging the green lawns surrounding Gilded Gates. She decided to follow the narrow cement path circling the facility, rather than risk following the steep knoll path to the front gate. She encountered forest-green benches on concrete bases every fifty feet along this path, each one facing the building. The second bench appeared just in time for a short rest. Panting, she parked the walker and sat down hard.

Looking straight in front of her, she saw an architectural structure she hadn't noticed before: a round stone turret, a kind of medieval tower, rising from the ground at the rear of Crisp Hall to well above the reaches of that Victorian structure. A single tiny window near the top of the turret reminded her of the Rapunzel fairy tale. The only thing missing was her long golden hair hanging out the window.

A snapping breeze blew out of nowhere, chilling Molly, and she buttoned up her wool cardigan sweater. It was time to move on. Despite the chill, she chose to continue on the path rather than retrace her steps. Molly was bound and determined to complete the circle. She passed another two benches, and as the third one came into view, she noticed someone sitting there. Her legs told her she needed another rest stop.

Twenty feet later she recognized Alice Mayport sitting at the far end of her targeted bench. Alice was bundled tightly in a navy-blue coat and matching cap pulled snug over her ears. Molly parked Roly and plopped down at the near end of the bench. She took a few deep breaths and said, "Good morning."

Alice slowly turned toward her with a cold, unfriendly expression and nodded. In passing seconds, that expression seemed to melt away with recognition. "Oh!" she said, peering at Molly through rimless glasses and slightly bulging eyes. "You're that nice lady that introduced herself the other day at lunch."

"Yes, I'm Molly LeSoto. We're new here, and I just wanted to make friends with you."

"That's so good of you," said Alice. "Most people ignore me. It seems like my reputation as a recluse has always preceded me. I'm not *known* as a happy person, but I would very much like to have you as a friend. In fact, I admit, I *am* sad and lonely. I'm only seventy-one, but I feel like ninety. I suppose everybody can tell, which makes me kind of an outsider. Nobody likes a sad sack."

"You know, friends share their miseries as well as their happinesses," said Molly. "Maybe you'd want to cornfide in me."

"I can't burden a new friend with my problems," said Alice.

"I'm a goodly listener," returned Molly. "And what else could I be doing in this joint?"

"I don't know," said Alice.

"How else are you gonna get that terrible frown off your face?" teased Molly. "You'd be a pretty woman if you smiled."

Alice's thin unlipsticked lips widened into a smile that creaked a bit, as if her smile muscles hadn't been exercised in a long time. "You think so? Well, now, Molly, you're gonna get an earful. Don't say I didn't warn you."

Molly grinned. "My earfuls are ready."

Alice's posture perked up and her cheeks took on a tinge of blush. She had a friend!

"Seven years ago, I was still married to Albert Mayport. An arranged marriage, followed by forty-three years of loveless, miserable living. Albert was a grumpy old man from the get-go. He was a salesman, away most of every week. We didn't even get along when he was home. We didn't talk beyond one or two words at a time. So I began to treasure the time he was away. I learned he was unfaithful and played around a lot, but so long as he stayed away from me, I tolerated his nonsense. He was generous, sort of. I always had plenty to run the house, groceries, that kind of thing. But not nice new clothes."

"Why didn't you end the marriage if it was such a contrastrophe?" asked Molly.

"I couldn't," said Alice. "My religion doesn't permit divorce."

"So what did you do?"

"Do? I kept house and taught myself to live alone. Mostly, I did a lot of reading and listening to the radio."

"What about TV?"

"Oh, no, Albert wouldn't have one in the house."

"Didn't you make friends with the neighbors or the people at church?" asked Molly.

"We had no neighbors way out in the country like we were. And Albert hustled us in and out of church in a hurry. We never got a chance to talk with anyone. Not even a word. I eventually lost all my social skills."

"Couldn't you at least have driven into the city to meet friends?" asked Molly.

"Oh no. Albert always left the car at the railroad station when he commuted to the city," said Alice. "Besides, I never learned to drive. He refused to teach me."

"So what happened then?"

"Seven years ago, Albert developed Alzheimer's, and over the next two years, it got so bad that we moved here. The doctor's recommendation, which was fine by me. We lived in a suite for two years, and he was almost docile and livable. No talking then either, though, and he threw a fit when I wanted to buy a TV. Then one night he wandered off and I never heard from him again. First Dr. Crisp, and then the police, searched for him. They were both baffled. Two months later I was moved to the dormitories. To this day I do not understand why. The one nice thing Albert did for me early in our miserable marriage was to take out a life insurance policy with me as the beneficiary. But I've never seen a penny of it. It may have been enough for me to stay in my suite. Can you see anything in all I've said to be happy about?"

"Oh, yessee, lady," consoled Molly. "Your new life begins now with a new friend. Me. Don't you feel a little better now?"

Alice nodded vigorously and broke into a genuine smile.

The two women chatted for a while until the breeze whipped up enough to give them the chills. They walked back to the entrance together.

Molly couldn't stop thinking—*All the years no TV? No talking? No driving? If I was her, I'd be celebrationing that he disappeared.*

Chapter 9
The List

Late that afternoon Molly burst into the suite to find Paco in his Barcalounger doing a football-themed crossword puzzle. She called his name twice, and he responded with a wave of the hand to signify that he knew the answer to another clue: the winner of Super Bowl XXII. She waited patiently while he penciled in "Redskins." Smiling, he stuck the pencil behind his ear and looked straight up at her.

"You must have had a nice long walk. You were gone for quite a while."

"Oh yeah. It was real pleasant and chockful of surprises," said Molly. "I saw Alice Mayport. Remember when we sat with the Amatis in the cafeteria for the first time? Alice was at the other end of the table by herself."

"I remember. On our tour Ms. Irma called her a poor recluse."

"That's the one. Well, I just had a mind-to-mind talk with her. Sweetiekins, Alice is not a shecluse at all. Inside, she's just one sad but nice people with a big load on her noggin."

"Where did you meet up with Alice, and how did you find out so much about her?"

"You know that crackly cement path that goes all around this place? There's bunches of resting benches for my old tired feet in all the right places. Anyway, we shared one of those benches around back of the buildings. Alice was already sitting there when I came over to her. She opened up to me because I broke the ice at lunch the other day when I introduced us. The poor woman has led a tough life—forty-three years with this tyranntical husband who wouldn't allow her to be friendly with anyone but him. She told me he traveled a lot, but always took the car with him and left her alone in their house, way out in the sticks. She didn't even have a television to watch. It didn't take long before she lost all her socialite behavior."

"Why didn't Alice divorce the scoundrel?" asked Paco.

"Alice told me her religion didn't believe in it. She took her vows serially, so she learned how to be a permanent hermit."

"If that's the case, how did she wind up in this place?"

"Her husband got Alfredheimer's disease and got so bad he forgot how to bully her, but she needed help taking care of him. So they came to Gilded Gates and lived here in a suite for five years. One night he wandered off, and nobody ever heard from him again."

"Is that the end of your story?" asked Paco.

"Not yet. They moved Alice into the dormitories three months later. Sweetie, I haven't told you the biggest thing—the one nice thing Albert did. He had a life insurance policy for her. But—and here's the biggest part—Alice never saw a penny of it!"

Molly sat down on the sofa across from him to rest, but Paco could see there was more spinning around in her head. After several minutes of nothing but the sounds of their breathing, he asked, "What else?"

"Don't you think it's strange that so many people disappear around here?"

"Nadine Chasdane asked me to look into the disappearance of Lisa Howard, but who else did you have in mind?" asked Paco.

"Alice's missing husband. And didn't Nadine mention two more names?"

"I don't remember. I'll have to look in my notes." He hoisted himself out of the recliner and over to the Early American pine desk, pleased to see his little spiral notebook sitting right where he'd left it. The notebook was a carryover from his full-time detective days. He kept it with him whenever they went out, tucked in his right-hand chinos pocket. Flipping the cover open, he stopped at the two names Nadine had given him. "It's Mindy Norton and Bruce Jameson."

"That's four people already, but we don't know how many more," said Molly.

"Are you suggesting there's some kind of conspiracy going on here?" Paco asked. "We live in an old folks' home and everyone living here faces their ultimate mortality sooner or later. It's not necessarily a conspiracy—it's expected."

"But most of 'em were in seasonable health when they disappeared," Molly protested. "Lisa Howard and Albert Mayport, anyway. Their good health is what they had in common."

"You've got a point there, hon. On the other hand, we don't know that for sure. Bertha did *not* say anything about Bubba's death being premature. He had a heart condition aggravated by the sale of the deli. There must be a record of all the residents' demises somewhere, especially if they were natural deaths. A doctor's death certificate, a funeral service log, even a morgue posting. I think the two of us should do a little sleuthing and put this conspiracy theory to bed once and for all."

"Ooh, yeah, let's tuck it in. It'll be just like old times."

"Let's see," said Paco. "Hoover's Funeral Home handles most of the deaths in our county. There's one in Annapolis and one in Glen Burnie."

"I wonder which one Dr. Crisp prefers," said Molly.

"I don't think he makes the choice," replied Paco. "I remember, on our application forms, the spaces asking for a funeral provider and interment preferences. I know we indicated Hoover Funeral Home and Hillcrest Memorial Park for our preferences. I sure would like to look into the files and the applications for each of our missing persons."

"Since Crisp is a medical doctor, wouldn't he have a medical file on each of our missing persons?" asked Molly.

"You'd think so," he replied. "But getting to look at even one of them would be a major hurdle. We're dealing with an individual's privacy here and there are laws against breaching it."

Molly's cheeks crinkled into a smile. She looked down at her left hand, and with her right hand's thumb and index finger, she began twirling her gold wedding band around her chubby ring finger. Round and round.

Paco recognized the gesture. Molly did it automatically when she was thinking up her next impish thought or brainstorm.

Her pale blue eyes turned bright as crystal. "We could sneak into the doctor's office one night after he goes to bed and get all the suspicional information."

Paco shook his head and ran his fingers through his still-thick salt-and-pepper hair. "No, no, Molly. A break-in—that would be illegal. I've been an honest lawman most of my adult life and I'm not going to start breaking the law now."

"We wouldn't be taking anything," she pouted.

"Sure we would. We'd be invading someone else's privacy and stealing their personal information. I've got a better idea. Why don't I call the Medical Examiner's Office in Baltimore? Maybe they'll do a retired homicide detective the courtesy of checking out our missing people. Later I'll call Hoover Funeral Home and see what Gary Hoover can do for me."

Paco sat down at his desk and pulled the corded phone close. He flipped through the pages of his little spiral-bound notebook until he found what he was looking for—the number of the Balti- more morgue. Leaving that page open, he dialed the number.

"Morgue, Kruger here!"

"Not my old partner Sargent Mickey Kruger by any chance?" asked Paco.

"Sure is," replied the voice. "Who's asking?"

"It's Paco LeSoto, you old goat."

"Not Detective First-Class LeSoto?" asked Kruger. "I heard you retired and got your own police force down in Black Rain Corners."

"Two men are hardly a force," corrected Paco, "but otherwise, all true. Listen, Mickey, I need a favor."

"Anything, buddy," said Mickey. "I'm running a special on old partners this week. What can I do for you?"

"I've got a list of names here that I'd like you to run through your computer," said Paco. "I would like to know if any of them passed through your facility and their official cause of death. You can limit the search to the last five years."

"I've got the keyboard in front of me," said Mickey. "And I've set the boundaries. Now let's have your names."

Paco read the list of names to him and, shortly, he had his answer—none of the names appeared in their records.

"Hey, Mickey, thanks for the favor," said Paco. "By the way, partner, how'd you wind up in this job?"

"I took a slug in the back that's too risky to remove," said Mickey. "So they gave me early retirement. The check amount didn't quite make it, so I went to work here for the state of Maryland."

"Thanks again," offered Paco. "And keep in touch, partner." He hung up and flipped to another page in his little notebook for another number. He dialed it.

"Hoover Funeral Home," said the soft tenor voice. "How may I assist you?"

"Gary?" asked Paco.

"Yes."

"It's Paco LeSoto."

"Ah, Inspector Paco," said Gary. "How are you? I hope all is well and you're not seeking my professional services."

"No, no," Paco asserted. "We're both okay. I just have a few questions for you and maybe a small favor."

"I do have a service in ten minutes," said Gary, "and I'm booked for the rest of today. Could you call me back around ten tomorrow morning?"

"I have a better idea," replied Paco. "Suppose Molly and I stop by for a chat about that time?"

"Excellent. See you then."

Paco put the phone down, and was about to flop back down in his recliner when Molly came in from the bedroom. "Paco honey, you're not going to waste the whole day snoozing, are you?"

"I hope not. Know what I miss most living in this joint?" asked Paco.

"You're not talking about upturning your retirement, are you?"

"No, no sweetie," he replied. "I'm talking about Fumble and Bobble. I miss them terribly."

"You've got visiting rights, honeybunny. Caitlin said you can visit them any time."

"I guess I could give her a call and see if today would be a good time. I wonder if they miss me as much as I miss them. Do we have her phone number?"

"My address book is on the desk, in the corner. Caitlin's last name is still Neuman and her husband is Wallace Yellen. I've re-memberized both their names."

Paco dialed and Caitlin answered on the third ring.

"Caitlin?"

"Yes."

"Paco LeSoto here."

"Paco! How nice to hear your voice."

"Thank you, Caitlin. I wonder if sometime today would an optimal time for Molly and me to come for a little visit with you—and my birds, of course."

"That would be wonderful," Caitlin bubbled. "I'm free all day. I can't wait to see you and hear all about your new life. We miss Molly and you already. What time did you have in mind?"

"How about around noon? I'll stop in at Bubba's Deli and bring lunch for all of us."

"Are you sure? I could fix something."

"No, no, we don't want you to go to any trouble," said Paco. "It'll be our treat for being so nice and adopting Fumble and Bobble."

"Hey, that was an offer I couldn't refuse," said Caitlin. "Bobble's so talkative I think he's going to ask me for a cell phone."

Paco laughed. "So…What should I bring you for lunch?"

"Corned beef on rye and a dill pickle would be nice. And coleslaw, please."

"Got it. See you near noon."

After hanging up, he turned to Molly. "Well, sweets, how about a round of Scrabble before we take off for Bubba's?"

"Sure 'nough," she said. "But tomorrow morning, could we go down to the recreation room for a game of Ping-Pong?"

"Great idea, hon." He loved watching her grip a handlebar of her Roly with her left hand and bat the balls with her right. She managed to last about twenty minutes, and he was grateful for that.

Chapter 10
From Fun to Funeral Home

The next morning, Paco and Molly stepped off the elevator feeling chipper for a change. The recreation room at Gilded Gates and the adjacent exercise rooms were a hive of activity. They had to wait their turn for the Ping-Pong table and, even then, Paco had to beat Rudy Shuster 21 to 18 in order to keep possession of the paddles. Rudy was a good loser. He shook Paco's hand, complimented him on his play, and headed for the nearby sofa.

Molly waddled up to the table, gripping Roly with her left hand and returning shots as best she could. No matter how gently Paco played, resisting all temptation to "put away" the ball, wifey always lost the game, this time 21 to 11. Still, she was proud of herself for being able to play at all. Paco then defeated two other women residents decisively before taking on Rudy once more. This time the game went into overtime with Rudy winning 27 to 25. However, Rudy gave up the table and joined Paco and Molly at a grouping of chairs in a corner next to a window looking out onto the rear of the facility. They exchanged names and a few pleasantries.

Dropping easily into an upholstered armchair, Rudy crossed one leg over the other knee. The short lively man looked quite spritely in his green and black plaid flannel shirt and black chinos. Rudy had a shiny bald head bounded by a tiny monks' fringe and a perpetual smile.

"Wow!" he said when they had settled. "I haven't had competition like that since Dora left this place."

"Left this place?" parroted Paco. "Who is this Dora and where did she go?"

"That's just it," replied Rudy. "I don't know. One day Dora Ferarri was living here, and the next day she wasn't. I can't explain it, nor can anyone else around here. No one seems to care enough about her."

"Sounds like you've got another name for your list, Paco," said Molly.

"What list is that?" asked Rudy.

"It's our ever-growing list of unexplained missing persons from Gilded Gates," offered Paco.

"I didn't think it was as bad as all that," said Rudy. "Why are you making this list? Wait, LeSoto...aren't you that detective from Black Rain Corners?"

"None other," said Paco. "Rudy, do you mind answering a few questions?"

"Fire away," said Rudy.

"When did Dora disappear?"

"Oh, maybe six months ago."

"To the best of your knowledge, was she in good health?"

"I'd say robust health. We even took long walks together when the weather permitted. She was quite frisky, I might add."

"Did you have a romantic interest in Dora?" asked Molly.

"We were good friends, but she was more interested in Happy Harry Lightfoot," replied Rudy. "He was wining and dining her right and left. I don't know whether they were sharing a bed or not. You had better ask him for those romantic details. He's sitting over there reading his newspaper, the guy in a yellow jersey."

"Do you know of anyone else we should add to the list?" asked Paco.

"No, not really."

Paco thanked him and shuffled across the room to where Happy Harry sat with his legs crossed. Paco stood just opposite him. He noticed that Harry had a full head of red hair flecked with streaks of gray and a cowlick that fell carelessly over his broad forehead. Paco extended his hand in greeting.

"Hi, I'm Paco LeSoto and I'm new here."

The two men shook hands. "Hi yourself. I'm Happy Harry Lightfoot. Pleased to meet you."

"Likewise, I'm sure, said Paco, sitting down across from him. "Mind my asking, why do you call yourself *Happy* Harry?"

"I try to be friendly and I smile a lot. My dad tagged me with the nickname when I was a kid and it stuck."

"I'm trying to locate Dora Ferarri. Rudy told me that you and Dora were quite the item a few months back. Can you tell me anything about her?"

"When Dora's husband walked out on her, I tried to comfort her, cheer her up. But Dora told me she was actually relieved when the sonofabitch left—so much so, that she went on a buying spree for a whole new wardrobe. At first she appeared to be pleased with my company and somehow she slowly became romantic. When I told her that I wasn't interested in marriage, she disappeared. I just assumed she got pissed and moved elsewhere to get away from me."

"Do you happen to know the husband's name?" asked Paco, noting no change in Harry's body language.

"I'm afraid not," said Harry. "I might have known it at one time, but I can't recall it now."

"Thanks, Harry, we'll get together again real soon, I'm sure."

"Great!" replied Harry with a cordial smile.

Paco returned to where Molly sat reading *People* magazine. He explained what he had learned.

"Without a name, there's not much we can besearch."

"Not so, Molly. We could look up Dora Ferarri's marriage at the Bureau of Vital Statistics and find his name and age."

"Look at the time, Paco. If we're gonna pick up food for lunch at Caitlin's, we'd better get on our horseys and giddyup before we're late."

"You're right, Mol," agreed Paco. They headed to the corridor and the elevator.

* * * *

Paco had already called for the cab to arrive at 11:15 and now he waited while Molly changed. She appeared in a four-button, brown coat with a fur-trimmed collar. She took one look at her husband and protested.

"Paco LeSoto, you go and put on a coat," she scolded. "The weatherman said it's 40 degrees outside. You'll catch your life out there in just a sweater."

Without saying a word, Paco relented and fetched his Redskins jacket. They arrived downstairs at the entrance just as the cab pulled to a stop out front. Paco opened the rear door for Molly and while he scooted around to the opposite side to climb in, the driver folded and stored Roly in the trunk.

"Bubba's Deli in Black Rain Corners," he told the driver.

In ten minutes they arrived at the corner of Shore Lane and Maple Run. The driver stopped in front of the blue clapboard store. Its yellow gingerbread trim added a Hansel and Gretel charm to the place. From the front door one could see both the Chesapeake Bay on the right and Black Rain Creek dead ahead. On the opposite corner stood the Town Hall, where Paco's former office, the police station, occupied the whole second floor.

"It still looks the same," said Paco, as he paid the driver, who then pulled into the parking lot behind the store in order to get lunch for himself.

"Oh look," declared Molly. "The sign still says Bubba's Deli and General Store. I guess the new owners wanted to cash in on Schlem and Bertha's repartation."

"It's good business," said Paco as he held the entrance door for her and Roly.

"The tables are gone from the front," said Molly. "I see a new room full of tables out back—full of people eating. So that's why they've been closed for six months. They must have reinvented the inside of the deli."

"Looks like there's a few people in front of us," said Paco. "Let's get in line."

"What'll you have?" asked the man behind the counter as soon as they got close enough.

Molly took a deep breath and ordered lunch for four. "Three corny-beef on rye with yellow mustard, three pastramis on pumpernickel with brown mustard, a pound of cold slaw, a pound of potato salad, a half-pound of soured kraut, six mund rugelach, and a liter of rooty beer. Oh, and three dilly pickles."

"Got it," said the counterman. He was efficient and everything was bagged and ready in just over five minutes. Paco paid and picked up two of the bags and Molly tucked the rest and the soda bottle into the canvas basket in front of her Roly walker. They headed out the door and trudged along the short, tree-lined road from Maple Run to Locust Lane and Caitlin Neuman's house. With Molly pushing her loaded Roly, it was slow going, with frequent stops to rest. It was 12:20 when they arrived.

Caitlin, in a red cable-knit sweater and red-plaid pants, heard them before they could press the doorbell and swung the door wide. After hearty hugs, she took their jackets and led them into the sunroom with a bay window overlooking evergreen shrubs and several elm and poplar trees.

Seated on the rattan couch with knees crossed was a woman in a gray knit dress. She looked up and sprang to her feet.

As soon as Molly saw the strong resemblance to Caitlin, she screeched, "Oh, my goodiness, Laura!" She let go of her walker long enough for a firm embrace. "It must be at least ten years since we laid eyeballs on you. You're all filled up and prettied out now."

"Thank you, I think," said Laura. "When Sister said you were coming over to visit those two crazy macaws, I told her I wanted to be here, too."

"It's wonderful to see you again," said Paco. "You're looking more like twins than I remembered. Most attractive twins, I might add."

"Thank you, Paco," she replied. "You are both so dear to me."

Caitlin glowed with happiness at the impromptu reunion, and

said, "Okay, everybody, come into the kitchen and sit down so we can eat all this delicious deli food." A bustle of pulling out captain's chairs followed as they settled themselves around the large table.

Caitlin had designed the spacious, sunlit kitchen. She was an artist, and her college graduation gift from Grandma Olivia Neuman was a trip to France. A highlight of her trip was a visit outside Paris to Giverny, home of the world's most famous Impressionist painter, Claude Monet. Inside his charming house, the kitchen had blown Caitlin away. The table, chairs, and cabinets were painted bright blue and yellow, so fresh looking that she felt rapturous, as if Monet himself had just gone out for a walk. Now in her own kitchen, she had duplicated the furniture and colors as closely as she could, always feeling surrounded by Monet's inspiration.

Paco set the deli bags and soda bottle in the center of the table, already set for four. Caitlin cut all the sandwiches and pickles in half, so everyone could sample whatever they wanted. At first it was "Pass this" and "Pass that," then they ate silently for a few minutes. The treat of deli foods simply sated their senses and squelched their speech.

Paco's detecting brain did a few silent calculations. The identical twins were now eleven years older, making them twenty-eight. Strong, appealing looks. Chestnut-brown hair, oval faces, hazel eyes that looked at you forthrightly; slightly turned up noses, and well-shaped lips with only a hint of lipstick. Caitlin, a professional graphic artist, seemed to express more freedom in her red outfit; Laura was more subdued, in business gray. Laura had abandoned the curly bangs; hair cut straight to shoulder length. The youthfulness in both women's faces was broken by stress creases emanating from the outer corners of their eyes, evidence of a trauma eleven years ago. A car accident during a blizzard—when they had defied their father and stayed too long at a holiday party.

Paco eventually broke the silence. "Laura, what's your life like now? Where are you living and what are you doing?"

Laura swallowed a savory mouthful of corned beef. "I'm living in Washington, D.C. and working as a third-year trial lawyer for a

Chestertown law firm."

"I just knew you would be a whipping success," said Molly.

"Oh, Molly, I owe it all to you," said Laura. "How can I ever thank you enough?"

"Your rosy confection is plenty thanks for me, and look at the way you've become a big-time mousepiece in a fancy law firm. You've got life down to a séance."

"Molly, you actually gave me my life back," said Laura. "I was just coming out of the coma caused by the car crash when evil Nurse Britta decided to stick me with that poisoned syringe. I'll never forget how you wrestled with her until she fell on the needle and killed herself. So you see? I wouldn't be here now if it hadn't been for you."

"Wauk! Mol-liiii!" screeched Bobble from a far corner of the kitchen.

"She recognized your voice, Molly," said Caitlin. "They must have missed you folks terribly."

"Pah-ko! Pah-ko!"

Paco laughed. "I've missed them, too. I need to spend some time with both of them. They were my only family until I married Molly. "So, if you'll excuse me."

He strode over to the tall double-wide wire cage, which stood in front of two windows. The matching birds wore brilliant red feathers on their crowns and breasts, extending halfway down their backs to yellow and blue feathers, and blue-green tails, with white patches around their eyes and bills.

"Awauk! Pah-kohoh!" squawked Fumble.

"I'd love to see them, too," said Molly, as she got up and pushed her walker toward the cage.

"Who's gonna win?" yelled Paco.

"The Skins, who else?" squawked Bobble.

"Time out, time out!" screeched Fumble.

"Third and long," yelled Paco.

"Pass play, pass play," returned Bobble.

"It's a run off tackle!" yelled Paco.

"Block 'em, block 'em," returned Fumble.

Caitlin stepped next to Paco, laughing. She called out "Hi, guys."

"Hi, guys," echoed Bobble. "Hello there!"

"I see you've been busy educating the birds," said Paco.

"Of course. A little avian etiquette never hurts," grinned Caitlin. "It's become a hobby for my Wally."

"Got a present? Got a present?" squawked Bobble.

Molly said, "They'll keep asking and squawking like crazy if we don't bring them a goodie. Just like little kids."

Paco reached into his pocket, pulled out a handful of chopped walnuts, and placed them inside the cage. The birds noisily devoured the treats.

Caitlin poured fresh coffee and the foursome sat around the kitchen table eating the rugelach, small rolled pastries stuffed with ground poppyseed, cinnamon, and chopped nuts—then sprinkled with powdered sugar. "Don't you worry about your birdies, Paco. Wally has kept their Redskins' loyalty intact. But don't be surprised if you hear something new."

As if on cue, Fumble squawked, "Order in the court!"

Paco burst out laughing. "I love it. Thanks for giving them such a great home."

Accompanied by a sharp nudge in his ribs, Molly whispered, "Paco, it wouldn't be hurting her to ask."

"On another subject," started Paco. "It may seem a little unusual to ask this question now, but I'm unofficially looking into an unnatural trend of missing folks at Gilded Gates. We were wondering whether there was anything strange about your grandmother's demise. Did Olivia go missing or anything strange like that just beforehand?"

"I know you two were on your honeymoon at the time of the funeral," recalled Caitlin. "But no, with the exception of her growing dementia beforehand, everything went as expected. After all, she was ninety-two."

"You mean she showed up to her own funeral?" asked Molly

with a deadpan face.

"Of course," replied Caitlin.

Around three o'clock, Paco mentioned his appointment and was about to call another cab, when Caitlin offered to drop them off at the funeral home.

Paco waved to the macaws. "Goodbye, sweethearts, see you soon."

"Come again! Come again!" they squawked.

* * * *

The Hoover Funeral Home, a Georgian-style white building, appeared quite stately because of its four-columned facade. A thin young lady in a demure black suit met them at the entrance and led them to Gary Hoover's office. Gary, a fiftyish man in a pin-striped charcoal suit, stood behind his desk and came forward to greet them. The two men shook hands, and Paco introduced his wife. A few minutes passed as Paco and Gary reminisced about their professional connection as police inspector and funeral director.

"So, what brings you here today, Inspector?" asked Gary.

"I have a bit of a conundrum that I believe you can help me unwind," replied Paco.

"I thought you retired," said Gary.

"I *have* retired. This one is kind of personal, a favor for a friend."

"Well, let's have it then."

"I assume you're acquainted with the Gilded Gates Assisted Living Community."

"Of course. We do quite a bit of business with them," said Gary. "In fact, whenever someone passes without specific funeral arrangements, Dr. Phelix Crisp is kind enough to send the business our way."

"I have a list here of five people who have apparently gone missing from Gilded Gates. They are Lisa Howard, Dora Ferarri, Albert Mayport, Bruce Jameson, and Mindy Norton," said Paco, after taking the list from his pocket. "According to close friends there, Lisa and Dora were reasonably healthy at the time of their disappearance. I'm wondering if any of them passed through the Hoover

Funeral Home. And, if so, whether any official cause of death was noted."

"If their demise took place in recent years, our computer records should certainly reveal all of what you are looking for." Gary took the list from Paco, sat down at his desk, and pulled the keyboard closer to him. "How far back should I limit the records search?" he asked.

"No more than five years," said Paco. "By the way, does the computer here have the records for both of your funeral establishments?"

"Of course," said Gary.

Paco asked, "Any death certificates in the last five years for the Gilded Gates people?"

"Of course. I have a death certificate and interment permit for Albert Mayport. Kidney failure, and it looks like Dr. Phelix Crisp signed off on this one."

Paco frowned and his dark eyes squinted. "Now that's extremely odd. His wife, Alice, told my wife that Albert had Alzheimer's and he disappeared one day and was never heard from again. She apparently has no knowledge of his so-called kidney failure and death certificate. Alice also said he had a life insurance policy for her, but not a cent of it ever came to her."

Gary looked up from his computer. "I can't imagine what went on there." He continued typing and brought up a legitimate death certificate for Mindy Norton. "Age 96. Cause of death: dehydration and old-age malnutrition."

Paco frowned. *The death certificate may be legitimate, but the cause of her death is highly suspect. My guess is she was locked in the electrical closet against her will. More than likely, she was cruelly murdered.*

Gary continued. "And a death certificate for Bruce Jameson, age 92. Cause of death: head injury from a fall. Signed off by Dr. Crisp." The computer held nothing on either Dora or Lisa Howard. He printed out all those certificates he could and handed the copies to Paco.

"Excellent. Thank you, Gary. From your inspection of the cadavers, did you ever have any reason to doubt the cause of death?"

"Our routine is to embalm, wash, dress, and apply makeup to our patrons," said Gary. "After all, they've reached their natural optimum ages. So there's hardly any reason to inspect them any closer. They appear to be natural deaths. It seems to me that Mindy Norton was especially thin, wrinkled, and shriveled, and that's to be expected with dehydration cases. Besides, we're not in the business of suspecting foul play."

"What about Bruce Jameson?" asked Paco.

"Wait!" said Gary. "Now I remember Jameson. There was head trauma and a broken leg bone we had to set."

"Indeed, I'm told he had a pretty big fall. What about the other names—Dora Ferarri and Lisa Howard?" asked Paco.

"I can check other funeral homes in the area and let you know what I find. It may take a few days."

"I'd appreciate that," said Paco. "And thank you for the hospitality and data. If you'll let me call a cab, we won't take up any more of your precious time."

The three shook hands. The LeSotos left the Hoover Funeral Home and took a cab back to Gilded Gates.

Chapter 11
A Telling Trace

Molly turned over in their queen-sized bed and discovered that Paco had already gotten up. All that was left was a slight impression on his pillow. She knew him to be an early riser, so there was scant cause for concern. Or was there? The darkened sitting room meant that he had also left their suite. *But what if he's gone missing like those on the list?* She felt discombobulated, stranded. *We've only been here a week and it feels like a year, so much is going on in this place.* She shook her shoulders and fluffed her curls. *I better get a gripper on myself.*

One glance at the wall clock and Molly realized, at ten o'clock, that she had been at fault for missing her husband. Too late for the cafeteria. She slipped into a print housecoat and retrieved a box of Raisin Bran and a bowl from the cabinet, along with a carton of milk from the fridge. Sitting at the little table a half-dozen spoonfuls later, she heard the door to their suite rattle, then swing open.

"Hi, sweet stuff," Paco said, tossing his cap on the sofa and flopping down on the chair next to her.

As soon as he sat, the phone rang. Paco picked up and said, "Hello," a long string of "uh-huhs," "thanks a lot, buddy," and "bye" before hanging up.

"Who was that?" asked Molly.

"Gary Hoover. He made those phone calls he promised us and

learned who interred Dora Ferarri. It was the J.H. Lamante Funeral Parlor. Dora died of dehydration and malnutrition. The same as Mindy Norton, would you believe. And Crisp signed off on both of them."

"Wow!" said Molly. "So where've you been galabanting around so early this Monday morning? You didn't even bother to wake me up."

"I thought you needed the extra sleep after all that walking you did yesterday. I took the bus up to Annapolis at 5:30 this morning. I stopped in at the Bureau of Vital Statistics on Rowe Boulevard to learn a bit more about Dora Ferarri. Got there just as the office opened. Had a quick look at her marriage license. Then I grabbed the next bus back."

"So what did you find out?"

"Dora Minnetti, age twenty-seven, married Anthony (Tony) Ferarri, age twenty-nine, in May of 1945," he read aloud from his little spiral notebook. "Dora would now be eighty. Rudy told us her husband left her two years ago, so the husband doesn't count."

"Maybe so," said Molly. "Anyway, you do have another name for your list. That leaves three suspicious names now: Mindy, Dora, and possibly Lisa."

"True enough," said Paco. "And at least the others appear to have died of natural causes. I don't have enough to assume there's been any foul play there. Let's face it, apparently healthy people die all the time of old age."

"Then what about all that wailing and moaning shenanigans that Jeff claims he heard?" asked Molly. "Is he making all that up?"

"Good question. I'm thinking Jeff believes they're real enough, but is he actually hearing them or imagining them? That remains to be seen. I can't even link one thing to another—the missing people to the moaning."

"Don't we owe Jeff another sleepwalk?"

Paco blinked hard. "*We?*"

"Well, *you* are not going alone, mister," insisted Molly. "Jeff's gonna be a birdy with two tails. I'm not going to miss all the fun."

"There's no fun involved. It could actually be dangerous," Paco said. "There are lots of stairs and obstacles in the way and a good portion of where he went was hardly lit at all. Are you sure you want to come along?"

"I'm coming with my two canes, sweetie. I promise to be careful on the stairs. You'll help me. Besides, Roly would make too much noise and Jeff would discover us."

Paco frowned. "Your canes are not nearly as safe for you as Roly. You could fall. If I find that you're having too hard a time I'll abort our mission and bring you back up here. Is it a deal?"

Molly sighed with resignation. "Yes, honeybunches."

"Good. I have to first find out if Jeff is still sleepwalking—after everything I told him about my last experience following him. It could have had a beneficial effect on him. Meaning maybe he's stopped it."

"We could meet them for lunch and find out," suggested Molly. "It's only an hour and a half from now."

* * * *

The LeSotos decided to kill time in the recreation room. They randomly chose a pair of upright armchairs opposite the exercise room door. From a side table, Paco picked up a year-old *Sports Illustrated* swimsuit issue and began to thumb through it. Gorgeous, voluptuous young women, with breasts so perfect they hardly looked real.

Molly's gaze drifted out the tall, wide windows. "Paco, the sun is shining. Maybe we should go for a walk this afternoon."

"Uh, walk?" he responded distractedly. "Sure."

Her attention drifted toward the exercise room. Through the open door, she saw Paula Mertz doing repeated toe touches. "Look over there, honeybunch. Paula's doing those exercises to strengthen her abominables. Wow, touch my toes? I can't even see 'em," she giggled.

"Toes?" he responded.

"Paco, you're not paying attention to me."

"What? Yes, dear. Is it time to go in for lunch yet?"

"No!"

"Then what?"

"Paco, do you still love me?"

"Of course. What kind of question is that?"

"I don't know. It's just that this place is aboundant with so many shapely ladies here. I figure I'm not down to snuff."

Paco's bushy eyebrows shot north. "So many shapely ladies? You gotta be kidding."

Molly didn't let on that she saw him thumbing through the *Sports Illustrated* swimsuit issue.

He jerked himself into reality and recovered nicely. "Molly, sweetie, I've got four good reasons to love you. One, you're the kindest, most considerate person I know. Two, you're clever and creative enough to help me with my detective work. Three, you're the only one that knows how to put up with me. And four, there's so much more of you to love." By the time he'd finished his words, Paco was out of his chair and behind hers, squeezing her shoulders and kissing the curls at the top of her head. "You know, sweetie, we have something most marriages never achieve. We're a team!"

A shiver ran down Molly's back. She looked around to see if anyone was watching their personal antics. Nobody was. "Time to go in now," she said.

They were among the first few residents entering the cafeteria. They selected a centrally located empty table to save room for the Amatis and started pulling out their chairs.

"I want to sit facing the door so I can yoo-hoo them over to our table," declared Molly.

"Can't we get in line for our food before it gets too long?" answered Paco.

"Not yet, sweetiekins. There they are, coming in the door. Yoo-hoo! Yoo-hoo! Maryanne! Jeff!" she yelled, waving one hand over her head

Oh-oh, Paco thought, *they look surprised and embarrassed. And a bunch of heads have turned around, but okay, the Amatis are heading for our table.* "Please join us," he said when they arrived.

Maryanne blurted out, "Paco, dear, do you have any more to tell us? We're most anxious."

"Not really," he said. "I haven't made that second excursion yet."

"Hey, don't sit down," said Jeff. "They're serving pizza for lunch."

"Let's all get in line then," suggested Molly. They tilted their chairs forward to reserve their places.

Jeff shifted from sneaker to sneaker while they were in line with their trays. "Paco, what are you waiting for?"

"Well, for one thing I need to know whether you're still sleep-walking."

"I'm not sure, It's like an out-of-body experience. I remember things, but they don't make sense. Maybe they're simply my stay-ing-in-bed dreams."

"Good grief, Jeff!" Maryanne blurted out, standing behind him. "You *are* still sleepwalking." She turned to Paco. "I can vouch for that. I wake up whenever he comes and goes."

"If you're awaked, why don't you stop him and bring him back to wake up?" asked Molly, as she picked out her flatware and a nap-kin. "It would save a lot of mileage on your husband's feet."

"I heard that could be dangerous to the sleepwalker," replied Maryanne. "It could be a tremendous shock."

"Where did you hear about that?" asked Molly. "Is it medical or theresay?"

"I don't really remember," replied Maryanne. "But I'm pretty sure it was a reliable source."

They picked up their pizza slices, salads, and oatmeal-raisin cookies, and returned to where the leaning chairs marked their places at the table. The pizza was cold and flat to the taste and the salad had gone limp and soggy, but they ate the fare anyway.

"Paco, now that you know I'm still sleepwalking, when will you tail me again?" asked Jeff.

"Probably tomorrow night. Or maybe the next night. I haven't decided yet, and besides, you shouldn't know exactly when."

"You can't blame me for trying, old man," admitted Jeff. "And, Molly, I never considered the mileage on my feet before. I never knew how far I'd gone until Paco explained it to me. I always thought of it as lost sleep, but that's not right, because I'm asleep while walking. I guess it all comes down to the missing bed rest and the toll on my legs and feet, like you said."

"I'm not sure you *are* completely asleep, Jeff," said Paco. "Some part of your brain must be awake enough to navigate so precisely over such a lengthy and complicated course. What's missing is the communication between your sleepwalking state and your present state."

"Ooh! I wish Dr. Avi could hear you say all that," declared Molly. "I love it when you speak mental."

"Who's Dr. Avi?" asked Maryanne.

"Oh, he was the psycho doctor I used to work for."

"What?" The dumbfounded Amatis responded in unison.

"A psychoanalyst," Paco clarified. Sometimes he couldn't decide whether Molly was serious or pulling someone's chain.

"Oh," giggled an embarrassed Maryanne. "You did tell us, on the day we met. I'm sorry, my memory deserted me." With her straw, she slurped up the last of her iced tea. "Time for us to go, or I'll miss my afternoon soaps."

"Molly, you talked about a walk this afternoon," said Paco. "Let's do it."

"Sure. The sun's shining, but it's November. We need coats, hon," said Molly, as the two couples got up and went their separate ways. "Let's go upstairs and get 'em."

As the LeSotos returned to their suite, they encountered Bertha leaving her suite next door. Her squat, heavy body seemed to sag and her cheeks were damp with spent tears. She pulled a small two-wheeled overnighter suitcase in one hand and carried a cloth tote in the other.

"Bertha!" Molly piped up. "Where're you going"

"I'm on my way to the dormitories in Comfort Hall for good—all moved out. Not because I want to. When my Schlem and I escaped from Poland, bought our home, and started the business in Black Rain Corners, we never dreamed of having to leave there.

After we moved in here I foolishly thought our suite would be our last move. Now look where I'm going. My next move will be to a plain pine wood box in the ground."

"Hey, Bertha, that's no way to talk." Molly wrapped both arms around her friend. "You have to look at the shiny side of life. You're a tough old broad. You'll make it, girl." She kissed Bertha on the forehead.

"Good luck," said Paco.

"Thank you both." Fresh tears squeezed out, forcing Bertha to turn away and trudge to the elevators.

Minutes later, in their warm jackets, they found themselves downstairs at the main entrance steps with a decision to make.

"I went around to the right the last time," said Molly.

"How about we go around to the left this time?" Paco answered.

"Maybe I'll get to see what's new over on this side," she said, pushing Roly.

"You hit the nail on the head when you called Bertha a tough old broad," said Paco. "She's a survivor. Gary provided us with proof of Schlem's death. Bertha did tell us he had heart trouble, so I'm assuming it was all kosher."

"The cause of death was coordinary trombones. That's why we took him off our list."

"You're right," said Paco. "That leaves three. Lisa is still unaccounted for. But you know what? I really think of Albert Mayport as missing, even though there's the death certificate at Hoover's for him. Because Alice said he just 'wandered off' and next thing she knew there was the death certificate and she insists he did not have kidney problems. And there's something else I've noticed in the paperwork accompanying the three death certificates that we *did* find at Hoover."

"What was that?" asked Molly.

"There was no next of kin listed for any of the three we have death certificates for—Mindy, Bruce, and Alice's husband, Albert. That's why we thought they were missing. And of course, Olivia never made our 'missing' list in the first place."

"What about Jeff and the moaning sounds," asked Molly. "Are they connected to any of the missing?"

"There's nothing yet to connect them," replied Paco. "I think tonight might be a good night to check on Jeff's sleepwalking ventures. Are you still game?" Paco held his breath, hoping she'd have changed her mind.

"You bet your bippy I'm game. I love games."

Oh boy, he thought.

Chapter 12
A Stroll in the Dark

At 1:15 a.m., Paco placed a folding chair in the same janitorial closet across the dimly lit hall just as he had done the first time. Only now he stood behind the chair with Molly sitting in it while they waited for Jeff to come out—or not. With the closet door ajar, they had an excellent view of suite 309. At 1:40 the door slowly opened, and the sleepwalker, his burly body in blue and white striped pajamas and brown leather slippers, stepped out into the hall.

Molly stood up and grabbed her canes. As soon as Jeff passed by their lair, they slipped out into the hall and fell into step some two dozen feet behind him.

"Paco, his eyes are wide open," whispered Molly.

"I know," Paco whispered back.

When the nightwalker hesitated at the DOWN staircase, Paco held up one finger for Molly to see. She waddled into the elevator and rode to the first floor. Paco followed Jeff down two flights of stairs to the first floor, into Crisp Hall, and through the formal dining room. From the doorway between the dining rooms they watched the sleepwalker hesitate, shuffle a few steps, and then continue until he located the kitchen door. Opening it, he stepped inside. Paco and Molly waited a few feet away, before following him into the kitchen, so they wouldn't be discovered.

In the shadows of the kitchen, lit only by moonlight leaking in through its two windows, Jeff tried one locked door and then another. Finding the third door unlocked, he opened it and started down a flight to the basement. Paco waited to give him a head start. He was about to follow, but realized he needed to help Molly, fearing she couldn't possibly manage fourteen stairs. With a determined look on her flushed face, she handed Paco her two canes. Clutching the railing on the right wall with one hand, and Paco's shoulder with the other, she followed him carefully down each step to the basement floor. Paco held his breath, praying she would make it safely, and yet hoping they hadn't lost Jeff's trail. Oddly enough, they didn't. Paco handed Molly her canes.

Jeff had migrated around to the left, a wall some ten feet away. He stood still for several minutes, tilting his head, lending his ear toward a pair of utility shelves as though they were capable of sound. The shelf units, each one eight feet high and six feet wide, were loaded with cardboard boxes, ludicrously innocent of sound quality.

The elevator motor at the far end of the basement began to hum as someone on the levels above them had decided to change floors in the middle of the night. This sound didn't startle the nightwalker. He straightened up to walk deeper into the poorly lit basement, weaving among the cartons and barrels, in the LeSotos' line of sight only for a few seconds, and then gone for a time.

Paco and Molly moved forward, huddling close each time the sleepwalker reappeared. Then they lost track of their quarry. Suddenly, a strange face popped out of the darkness in front of them.

Molly gasped, whispering in a choked voice, "It's a poltergoose!" The hum of the elevator going up drowned out whatever frightened sounds she emitted.

"You who invade my lair are evil," declared the contorted face now fully illuminated by the beam coming from Paco's penlight. "No one's allowed down here. It's plain wickedness and you shall pay for it." The eerie voice had an improvised scratch to it.

"Vince Eden!" Paco cried out. "Are you crazy? You frightened the hell out of my wife. That's a terrible thing to do."

"Sorry," cackled Vince, clutching his gray pajama top. "It was only a prank. Nobody got hurt, did they?"

"What in red blazing hell are you doing in this basement?"

"I could ask you the same question," retorted the hollow-eyed Vince. "I was in the kitchen sneaking a snack from the fridge and I saw you folks going down the stairs. I don't sleep much nights, so I followed you. When you stopped to watch Mr. Amati, I snuck around in front of you."

"In the kitchen?" asked Paco. "Why didn't we see you there?"

"I didn't want you to see me, so I hid behind the pantry door."

"But why would you want to scare us like that?" asked Paco.

"No reason." Vince grinned with satisfaction, opening his thin lips wide to show the front two teeth missing in his upper jaw. "Maybe I just like to play pranks on folks. It's the only way I get them to talk to me, even if it is a scolding most of the time."

"Okay, you've had your fun. Now get yourself upstairs and back to bed before I report you to Dr. Crisp," said Paco.

"Oh, he won't care none," said Vince. "It's that damnable Ms. Irma that'll come down hard on me."

Vince started to leave in the wrong direction. Paco turned him around and sent him back the way he had come, watching to make sure Vince left them, then feeling a bit guilty for talking so harshly to him. Molly shuffled ahead to pick up Jeff's trail. She had reached the end of the Crisp Hall basement and passed through the door at the left into the Fellowship Hall basement. Paco caught up with her. Just past the second elevator enclosure, he thought he saw movement, so he rushed ahead to the door in front of them. As soon as they passed into the basement under Comfort Hall, she looked up and saw a flash of light.

"I just saw Jeff at the top of those stairs," said Molly, "but only for a second."

Paco knew those stairs led to the secret door into the parlor. He watched as Molly stubbornly insisted on taking herself up. She handed him her canes and gripped the railing in both hands, hoisting herself up one painful step at a time. Paco snuggled up one step behind her in case she started to fall. But she made it to the top landing all by herself, then took the canes back from him. On tiptoe, Paco reached around her and lifted up the double-latch, door-lock handles. Moving to the right, he pushed the door open and out of their way, holding the Leaping Lion tapestry aside so they could both enter the parlor. Out of breath but smiling triumphantly, Molly watched while Paco pushed the door shut behind him and made sure the tapestry was properly back in place. Now, to pick up the nightwalker's trail, they stepped out of the parlor and into the Comfort Hall corridor. He felt a pang of frustration and regret that Molly was slowing him down, but she trudged doggedly along, leaning on her canes, refusing to be left behind.

Stepping into the long hallway leading into the Infirmary, they saw a tall shadow—the nightwalker stopping to listen at one of the patient's rooms. Then he moved from one room to the next, stubbornly pressing an ear to each door down one side, then turned and started back toward Paco and Molly. They had to slip back into the parlor to keep from being seen.

While the sleepwalker took the stairs up to the second floor of Comfort Hall, Molly and her canes made use of the elevator. Paco stayed with their quarry, following a half-dozen steps behind. On each of the second and third dormitory floors, Jeff repeatedly stopped and listened at the door of every room. On the second floor he crossed over into Fellowship Hall and listened at each of the suite doors. Then he returned to the third floor, putting an ear to each of the suite doors there. When there were no more doors to listen at, the nightwalker returned to 309, his own suite, where the door was slightly ajar, as he had left it, and slipped inside, closing the door behind him.

Paco and Molly congregated outside the Amati suite. "His listens were tuned to all the dormitory rooms and the suites, too," whispered Molly. "Where else can he look?"

"That's a good question," said Paco. "But I haven't the least idea how to answer it."

"Maybe we should head back to our place and sleep on that condom," said Molly.

"I think you mean conundrum, hon," corrected Paco with a slight snicker.

"Yeah, that's what I meant."

* * * *

The LeSotos slept late the next morning, again missing breakfast in the cafeteria. They shared what was left of the Oatmeal Squares. Until lunchtime Molly tidied up and watched *The Price Is Right*, while Paco scoured his two newspapers, the *Washington Post* and *Annapolis Journal-Gazette*.

They reached the cafeteria ten minutes early and settled at a table. Minutes later Molly felt a hand on her shoulder and turned to see Nadine Chasdane standing behind her.

"Join us, please," said Paco. "I'd like to learn a little more about your missing friend."

"Does this mean you haven't found Lisa Howard yet?" asked Nadine.

"Yes. Sorry," said Paco. "I'm afraid we have no information yet on Lisa. Why don't we pick up our food first and then we can tell you about the progress we *did* make."

"Yeah, let's do that" agreed Molly. "I just wish that lunch was sit-down service like it is at dinnertime. Then we could eat like real fine mensches."

"You and me both, Molly," said Nadine. "I'm always afraid I'm going to drop my tray."

The round trip to the food counter and back yielded lukewarm cream of celery soup, an assortment of sandwiches, coleslaw and potato salad, a glass of juice, strawberry Jello, and an apple. When Paco saw that Nadine was through eating, he began to explain.

"We did make some inquiries at a local funeral home—one that this facility uses when the person hasn't designated any other. I was able to account for three of the missing persons on our list there."

"List?" questioned Nadine. "I don't understand."

"Just asking around, we discovered there were more people that were missed by some of our residents."

"You mean like a conspiracy?" asked Nadine.

"Nothing that conclusive, but it is a possibility," replied Paco. "We were checking area funeral homes for five likely victims, including your Lisa. We now know about the other four, but nothing on your Lisa. Three of the four were handled by the Hoover Funeral Home. Dora was handled elsewhere."

"How did they die?" asked Nadine. "I hope nothing terrible has happened to all those people."

"I hesitate to tell you how two of the missing actually died for fear that you might project the same fate for Lisa," cautioned Paco.

"Please, I need to know this, Paco," said Nadine.

"We believe two of them died of malnutrition and dehydration, but this could be a natural thing with elderly folks," said Paco.

"That's simply horrible!" said Nadine. "Ghastly even."

"Now don't go blowing things out of preposterous," said Molly. "We don't know enough about any of these people's fates yet."

"I think she means proportion," corrected Paco.

"Yeah, that's it," said Molly.

"And the other four names—the ones you previously accounted for?" asked Nadine.

"They were the same two names you gave us earlier—That is, Mindy Norton and Bruce Jameson, plus Dora Ferarri, and Albert Mayport," replied Paco. "Now, can you tell us anything more useful about Lisa?"

"Of course." Nadine adjusted her rhinestone-studded glasses on the bridge of her nose and leaned forward. "Like I told you before, we were just companions who grew used to each other after our husbands died. Not intimately close, but we've lived together as roommates for over seven years. I also told you about her swimming and tennis, so you know she was in good health. She was quite an athlete. I couldn't keep up with her—I've always been a total klutz when it comes to sports. I don't know what else to tell you, except it's totally not like her to go off and not tell me about it. She just wouldn't do that."

"Did Lisa have any friends or relatives she might have wanted to visit?" asked Paco.

"There were maybe one or two friends we shared—mostly acquaintances, and I think she once mentioned a niece somewhere in California. But even if Lisa did contact her recently, she would have told me about it."

"Did she have any other activities that didn't include you, either here or elsewhere?" asked Paco.

"Well, occasionally, she did sit in for someone at bridge," replied Nadine.

"Betcha I can guess who was in that foursome," said Molly.

"Really, Molly?" asked Paco.

Nadine chimed in. "The usual four were Chester Parker, Paula Mertz, Gordon Lowe, and Happy Harry Lightfoot. She'd fill in once in a while, when one of them couldn't make it."

"She see any of them socially?"

"Not that I know of. She wasn't particularly fond of any of them."

"Okay, Nadine," said Paco. "Let's shift gears now and talk about Mindy Norton. You told us that she supposedly locked herself in a closet for two weeks. Frankly, the idea that she locked herself in is preposterous. Do you know which closet it was?"

"We were told Mindy was found in terrible condition inside an electrical closet," said Nadine. "The one across the front corridor from the recreation room. I highly doubt she was suicidal."

"I agree," said Paco. "If it was suicide, it would be a difficult and gruesome way to choose death. If it were accidental, her pleas for help would surely have drawn help in that high traffic area. I saw an electrician working in there just yesterday. The room is full of circuit breaker switches, power meters, and steel conduits running every which way. You even need a special key to open that particular steel door. I can't imagine how she got in there."

"Maybe she had a little help," said Molly.

"Then there's that third possibility," agreed Paco. "Foul play."

"Could someone else have locked her in that closet?" asked Molly. "Either accidentally or on repurpose?"

"Someone could have," replied Nadine. "I don't see why anyone would want to harm her. She wasn't a bad person."

"Maybe the door was accidentally left unshut," suggested Molly.

"Even if it was open, why would she want to enter such a place willingly?" asked Nadine.

"Curiostipy killed the cat," offered Molly.

"Molly!!" scolded Paco.

"It's a postibility, Paco."

"From what you've already told me, Nadine," Paco said, "it doesn't look like she was suicidal or addled, so I have to suspect foul play, How about a motive? Was she wealthy?"

"Not really," said Nadine. "I'd say she was comfortable."

"Who discovered the body?" asked Paco.

"I was told an electrician came to do routine maintenance and called Dr. Crisp when he ran into a foul-smelling body in the closet. Boy, you sure do ask a lot of questions, even for a policeman."

"Ex-policeman. I have no jurisdiction anymore," returned Paco. "But I'd like to ask a few more—about Bruce Jameson. Like, what was he doing in the basement in the first place?"

Nadine frowned with embarrassment. "I told you he fell down the basement staircase. Now that I've had time to think about it, I recall hearing it happened in Comfort Hall, all the way down from the second-floor landing to the first floor and bashed his head in. I don't know what made me think it was the basement steps in Crisp Hall. My bad."

Paco pulled out his little spiral notebook and flipped through a number of pages until he found his notes. Bruce Jameson's cause of death was listed as "trauma from fall." *Consistent*, he thought.

"Thank you, Nadine," said Paco. "You've been most helpful."

As they left the table and went their separate ways, Molly said, "There's some hockey business going on here in Guilty Gates."

Chapter 13
A Diabolical Mission

A tall man in a black sweat suit and sneakers paced back and forth like a caged tiger in its limited space. His smoky-gray eyes reflected panic as he waited for his cohort. A ceiling fixture faintly lit the room, which held a single small window at one end and a hospital-style gurney at the other end.

The window revealed a starry night crowned with a three-quarter moon. The raised gurney held an eighty-four-year-old woman covered with a flowered sheet. At one point during the man's pacing, he jerked to a stop beside the gurney. He pulled the sheet back, holding it high up in his left hand, and studied the immobile woman. She was lying on her back in a flimsy cotton hospital gown that stopped at her thighs. *Quite attractive*, he thought. *Looks twenty years younger. Trim, muscular legs like an athlete's—and so well-proportioned. I'd like to have met her thirty or forty years ago. I bet she would have been a whopping romp between the sheets. Ah me, this aging thing has certainly stolen something precious from the two of us.* He let go of the sheet and watched it fall to cover her again.

The man spun away to continue his infernal pacing. His mind wrestled with disrupting thoughts. He'd had a sexy woman like that, but she'd brought him close to financial ruin with all her foolhardy spending. They were constantly at each other's throats, especially after the medical supply company he'd founded went bankrupt.

Not long after that she threw him out. His spacious inherited home was leased out to a family of five. So, needing a place to live, he moved into Gilded Gates. From what he saw there, he thought it might be a viable cash cow to support his accustomed lifestyle.

It was pure luck that he had found another investor with deep pockets, whom he convinced to buy in on his Gilded Gates idea. The sale of the great inherited house covered his share of the venture. Together they formed a parent company, Angular Properties Management, to drain Gilded Gates of its profits. But five years running, those profits had proven too marginal, so his partner insisted they turn to more desperate means to protect her investment.

They'd been responsible for two deaths so far, and the woman on the gurney would be the third. He'd never been a religious man, but he couldn't quite erase the part about rotting in hell for his sins.

I really never wanted it this way, but I can see no other way to keep our business afloat. There are bills to be paid, always the bills. My partner in business and crime agrees with me. Or is it the other way around and I'm the one who agrees?

Noises coming from outside on the rooftop jolted his senses, the sound of a woman's heels striking concrete. The click and clack of her heels grew louder until a slightly stout woman with a stern face stepped through the double doors. She stood about five-foot-ten in sensible heels, wearing a gray-brown print shirt and beige cargo pants.

"Why are you so late?" he asked.

"None of your damn business. I do have a professional and personal life to handle."

Dressed like that? he wondered. "Sorry," he said. "I didn't mean to pry."

"Sure you did, but don't worry about it."

"Did you bring the syringe?"

"Of course," she snapped. "Why do you ask?"

"I keep thinking about what happened two weeks ago, when she woke up and made it halfway down the stairs wailing and moaning for all of Gilded Gates to hear."

"That wasn't my fault. Someone removed the last bottle from the shelf, and I had to wait 'til the next morning to get my hands on another one. No one heard her, did they?"

He shrugged. "Not that I know of."

The woman retrieved a small, thin case from one of her deep cargo pants pockets and set it on the nightstand beside the gurney. Opened, it revealed a syringe and separate needle. She picked both up and screwed the two together. From the other deep pocket, she removed a small bottle and a few alcohol wipe packets. She tore one of the packets open, swabbed the sponge-like top of the bottle, and stabbed it with the needle, before pulling back on the syringe's plunger. Satisfied with the amount, with her index finger she tapped the syringe on its glass side to get rid of any spurious air. She walked to the foot of the bed and pulled the sheet all the way back to expose the victim's entire body. Grabbing the bare right foot, she stabbed the needle between the second and third toes and sent the plunger home. The sharp pinprick and cold fluid rush elicited a moan from the victim before she faded back into oblivion.

"That should hold her for at least another twenty-four hours," said the woman.

"How much longer will we have to keep her in limbo?" he asked.

"A few days—maybe this shot will be enough," said the woman. "She has to look like she died of natural causes before we finish her off. What else is going on in this facility?" she asked.

"They've already moved the Bubbaschlufsky woman to her dorm room. That was the plan, of course. There's a couple ready to move into her suite. We just have to keep those suites filled with prompt and regular monthly fees if we're going to make any money at all. The state Medicaid subsidies just don't hack it."

"How many more residents will we have to snuff out before you're satisfied?" she asked. "This whole thing is getting pretty ghastly."

"It was your idea right at the beginning, my dear," he retorted. "That was when you first bought into Gilded Gates—perhaps a few months afterward. You started to see your investment, the whole of your inheritence from Daddy, shrink from month to month. We were both a bit naïve about the monumental expenses of running this place. We kept needing more and more of your cash infusion."

She faced him with a twisted, angry-looking mouth. "I was only joking that it would be a viable solution to our problems. You were the one who got serious about it. You were the one asking how we might get rid of some of our welfare residents. What I really had in mind was optimizing our income by moving single residents out of the suites into the dormitories, if they can't afford the full rent."

"So while you're regretting ever investing in Angular Properties, don't forget I'm losing money, too," he said. "I'm all in. I even moved into the damn place."

"You bet your ass I'm regretting I ever met you," she said. "You persuaded me this was a great investment with all those fancy arguments of yours—'latest thing for the elderly' and 'very popular.' Phooey."

"I badly needed your cash infusion," he repeated.

I know that, she thought bitterly. "It's starting to get light," she said, glancing out the little window. "We'd better pack up and get out of here."

* * * *

Behind the doors of suite 225, the LeSotos were watching the last scene of *To Have and Have Not*, based on the Ernest Hemingway novel—Bogart and Bacall motoring out to sea in a sport fishing boat, escaping from the bad guys.

"The movie's nothing like the book," grumbled Paco, as he turned off the TV set. "In the book Harry Morgan, the Bogart character, dies from tommy-gun wounds."

"You read the book?" asked Molly.

"I sure did," said Paco. "In Black Rain Corners, when I was Inspector Paco, there was plenty of free time, waiting for crimes to happen. I did a lot of reading then. I could use a good book right now to take my mind off these two baffling cases."

"I guess I do miss it," he replied. "A couple of things are bothering me about the sleepwalker. Jeff stopped to listen meticulously everywhere, even the second time, when you joined me following him."

"Maybe what he heard was on his first recounter," offered Molly. "And he was doomed to that first path ever after. Maybe his sleepwalking is so he can hear it again and find its beginnings."

"You might have something there, Mol. Come to think of it, Jeff almost said as much to us earlier."

"What was your other botherment?" asked Molly.

"As we came down the stairs to the basement, I remember Jeff stopping to listen at those shelf units on our left. Why there, of all places? I'm wondering if that point might be the rear wall of Crisp Hall. It makes no sense."

"Unless…" Molly's soprano voice perked up. "Unless there was something on those shelves he was interested in. Something we didn't notice."

"Yeah. We need to have another look at those shelves—with the lights on," said Paco. "We may have overlooked a thing or two."

"How and when do you want to do this?"

"There's no time like the present," said Paco, lifting himself out of the recliner.

"It's too close to lunch," cautioned Molly. "Carla Dobbs will be all abluster preparing lunch with her people running around like headless chickens. I don't think she'll appreciate us strolling through her kitchen right now."

"You must be hungry early, Mol. Lunch is an hour away. We're not doing anything productive right now. Maybe we should use the parlor stairs over in Comfort Hall to access the basement. Then we won't have to trouble Carla for safe passage through her precious kitchen."

Molly worried. "People in the parlor will see us. And guess what? Today's Friday the thirteenth."

Paco laughed out loud. "Since when is my beautiful wife superstitious?"

"Oh, I don't know. Since forever, prob'ly."

Paco didn't give her time to continue protesting. He was keyed up and ready. "We'll be fine, sweetheart. Let's give the parlor door a shot. Grab your penlight and saddle your Rollator. We're going to do some exploring."

Five minutes later they were in the corridor waiting for the elevator to take them to the first floor. The short ride down put them in the corridor next to Comfort Hall. The large parlor was empty, except for Peter Hunch and Edna Bush. Both were so self-preoccupied that they didn't notice the LeSotos. Peter kept wiping the drool from his chin with a tissue, and Edna was faithfully counting knits and purls; neither one looked up or around the room. Paco and Molly proceeded to the Leaping Lion tapestry and drew it back on its rail to expose the outline of a door. But there wasn't a doorknob or any sort of handle in sight—just the outline. Paco tried to get a fingernail grasp in the side crack, but other than a slight rattle, the door denied him.

"I've got longer nails," offered Molly. "Let me try."

"It won't do any good, Mol. I remember now. The lock can only be accessed from the basement steps. It's a pair of latches, one above the other that have to be lifted up at the same time. There's no way we're going to get to the basement from here. I guess we will have to sweet-talk your friend to get into the basement after all. But it's too close to lunchtime now, so we'll have to wait. Maybe later today."

Paco and Molly restored the Leaping Lion tapestry to its original position and retired to the recreation room in Fellowship Hall to wait for the cafeteria to open. They just happened to choose a table where Alice Mayport was already seated. They exchanged pleasantries before Paco attempted to bring up a sore subject.

"Alice," Paco began in a subdued tone, "we found out what happened to your so-called missing husband." He flipped through his spiral notebook to be sure he gave her the correct information.

With a blank look, she said, "I don't understand. What could you have learned so many months later?"

"Your husband died of kidney failure. He had a memorial service at the Hoover Funeral Home, and was interred at Pleasant Oaks Memorial Park."

Alice's narrow face blanched. She stared at Paco for a full minute before tilting her head. "A memorial service at a funeral home without me? Why wasn't I told? When did this happen? Where did he die? Why wasn't I a part of it all?"

"He most likely died somewhere in Gilded Gates because the funeral home picked up his body from here. I can't see any reason why you weren't informed about either his demise or his memorial service. Are you absolutely sure you didn't receive any notification from the Hoover Funeral Home?"

"Hoover? Hoover?" she repeated. "Wait! I did receive something from them. I threw it in the wastebasket, thinking it was one of those stupid advertisements pushing prepaid arrangements. Maybe I did throw it away, but for God's sake, is that any way to find out your husband is dead?"

"You have every right to be upset, Alice," said Molly. "I think you should have a pow-wow with Dr. Crisp and find out why he didn't let you know all the growsome details and how come you were left out."

"Thank you, Molly. You too, Paco. You sure are my friends."

"I see everyone's moving into the cafeteria now," said Paco. "I don't know about you guys, but I'm ready for lunch. Wanna join us, Alice?"

Their friend shook her head. "I feel too sick to eat."

Chapter 14
A Closer Look

Lunchtime had been over for an hour. All the cafeteria tables were wiped down and the floors swept clean. The dishes were washed and put away. Tall supper pots steamed on the stove. Succulent aromas wafted from the ovens. Carla Dobbs, chief cook, reigned over her domain. She now sat in a straight-backed chair flipping through her recipe book when the LeSotos stole into the room. Paco led the way, moving quietly toward the basement door. Carla's jaw dropped and was about to scold him, when she saw Molly entering the kitchen pushing her walker right behind him.

"Are you with *him*?" Carla asked.

"Oh yes, that's Paco, my husband," replied Molly, just as he had pulled the basement door open.

"And just what do you want in my basement?" asked Carla. "The only things down there are my kitchen supplies."

"We just want to look around and take some measurements," said Paco. "We won't touch any of your supplies, and we'll be out of your hair in less than half an hour."

"Don't go switching anything around," cautioned Carla. "I have to know where to find things when I need them. And how the hell are you going to get down the stairs with that contraption, anyway?"

"You watch—like this, hon," said Molly, as she collapsed the handlebars of her three-wheeled Roly and handed it to Paco to carry.

Hoisting the walker, Paco took the first step downstairs. Molly followed with her left hand on his right shoulder and her right hand clutching the railing. Together they descended to the basement floor, where he spread Roly open for her again. Flipping on the switch at the foot of the stairs bathed the entire basement in fluorescent light. A turn to the left and they faced the two sets of shelves at the rear wall directly below the kitchen. They approached the shelving units and Paco began shifting the cartons on them to the right and left, looking for anything that might have piqued the nightwalker's interest.

"What are you looking for, sweets?" asked Molly. "Carla isn't going to like you moving her things around."

"Don't worry," said Paco. "I'll put everything back the way it was. There's something behind the shelves. Part of the shelving backs up to wood and part backs up to concrete."

He moved to the right side of the shelf unit and tried to lift and drag it away from the wall. It budged a mere inch, but no further. Suddenly, he stopped moving and held his breath for almost a full minute. His face turned beet red. Slowly, he began to relax.

"Careful, Paco," said Molly. "Your heart doesn't want you to go to exscreams."

Paco returned to sliding cartons back and forth, then stopped abruptly, having arrived at a conclusion. "There's a thick, heavy wooden door in the concrete wall behind these shelves."

"A door to where?" she asked.

"I don't know," he replied. "There's a big, old-fashioned, padlock to deny our entry. With all the dust and cobwebs, I doubt that anyone's used that door in a good many years. I still wonder what's behind it, though."

"Which way is the front entrance to Crisp Hall?" asked Molly as she turned around to get her bearings.

"That way," replied Paco, pointing toward the wall opposite the shelves.

"Rapunzel!" said Molly, as she slapped her forehead with one hand.

"Rapunzel?" he repeated. "What's a darned fairytale got to do with anything?"

"I think I know where that door goes," Molly replied. "You know the story about the princess with the long hair hanging out the window of the tower?"

"Of course," he said. "But now you're confusing me even more."

"Remember when I went for a walk outside by myself the other day?"

"Yeah."

"Well, I sat down to rest on one of those park benches along the strolling path. When I looked back at Crisp Hall, I saw Rapunzel's tower with only one tiny window at the top."

"You mean like a castle turret?" he asked.

"Yup. Tall, round, and made of stone."

"How tall?" he asked.

"Taller than the building," she replied. "And I bet it's on the other side of that door."

"If that's the case, we should be able to see it from the kitchen window when we get back upstairs," said Paco. "They sure aren't entering it from here. I wonder if there's another way to get inside it from the Crisps' residence."

"Maybe we could get a quick look-see when they're not in their apartment," said Molly. "Besides, I'd love to see how fancy-shmancy they live." She ended with a wiggle of her beach-ball body.

"The only way up to their apartment is the stairs," returned Paco. "The first-floor landing is right across from Dr. Crisp's office, and that door is always locked. Plus, Ms. Irma has her desk right next to the stairs, so you'd have to get past them both to gain entry."

"Maybe I could create a reversion."

Paco grinned. He never got tired of his wife's Mollyprops. "Even so, it would still be breaking-and-entering a private residence. Entry without their permission, or an official judge's search warrant, is illegal. We could be arrested or, at the very least, tossed out of the facility on our ears."

"What about Frank Mullins?" asked Molly. "He could get us a search warrant and he doesn't have that worry. He's official."

"Just because Sergeant Frank took over the Black Rain Corners police from me doesn't mean he can get a judge's search warrant any time he pleases. He needs to take solid evidence of a wrongdoing to a judge. So far, we only have a working theory and a bunch of unanswered questions."

"So our hands have us all tied up," said Molly.

"Yeah, you might say that, Mol."

"We promised Carla we wouldn't be down here more than a half-hour. Maybe we should be getting back upstairs."

"I agree," said Paco. "There's not much we can do now. Wait! There's one more thing I'd like to take a look at before we go upstairs. Stay here. I'll be back in a minute." He half-jogged through the three basements and went up the other staircase to the door. He stopped at the top for a few seconds before retracing his steps back down to Molly.

"What was all that about?" asked Molly. "You've got me all bemuddled, dear."

"I wanted to check the locking mechanism on that other door," he replied. "I wondered why we couldn't get into the basement from the door in the parlor the other day."

"Why is that?" she asked.

"I had forgotten that the locks are arm-and-hasp latches, not at all common these days."

The LeSotos climbed the staircase to the kitchen, Paco hefting Roly, Molly clutching the banister with both hands. Carla Dobbs stood over her steaming pots, stirring and tasting. The LeSotos quickly viewed the position of the turret outside the kitchen windows. Leaning over the double sink, Paco confirmed that the locked door they found in the basement indeed led to the turret.

"You two done messing around in my supplies?" asked Carla.

"Yes, thank you, Carla," said Molly. "We won't presturb you

anymore."

"What were you doing down there anyway?" asked Carla.

"We were looking for a door to that big old castle turret out back," replied Molly.

"Did you find one?" asked Carla.

"Yeah, but it was locked," replied Molly. "We couldn't get inside."

Paco chimed in. "We appreciated you allowing us to search for it, Carla." Turning to Molly, he said, "How about a game of Ping-Pong, hon?"

Carla stared at his wife clutching Roly. *Ping-Pong? Riiiiight.*

Paco hustled Molly off before she revealed anything more of their unauthorized investigation, and steered her to the recreation room. The Ping-Pong table was free so they played three games. Paco handily won the first two, but Molly won the third. "Paco, sweetiekins, I think you gave me a handigap on that third game."

Paco smiled, but said nothing. Molly read his expression and knew she was right.

They sat down on one of the sofas to rest. Seated restlessly across the room, Alice Mayport spotted them. She bounced up and hurried her spindly body over, sinking herself down in a chair across from them. Tossing her head, her stiff, steel-gray hair fell all the way down her back. With no "Hi" or "Hello," she blurted out, "I've been looking all over for you guys. I've got something to tell you."

"Oh yeah?" Molly replied.

"I called that Gary Hoover feller over at the funeral home and asked why I wasn't notified of my husband's sudden death or even the funeral arrangements. He looked up the file and said the form sent over by Gilded Gates had a 'No' written in the space for 'Next of Kin.' He told me they used this form to know how many would be attending the service and the interment. So I cornered Dr. Crisp in his office this morning to ask him about it, and do you know what he told me?"

"No, what did he say?" Paco asked.

"He accused me of filling out the form myself," replied Alice. "Even showed me a copy. I told him I most certainly did not fill out that form. Why would I? Why would I have written No for Next of Kin when I'm his wife?" She stopped to take a few breaths.

"What did the doctor say about that?" asked Molly.

"He just shrugged and shook his head. I was so furious I called him a damn liar!"

"Wow! What happened then?" asked Molly.

"He stood up and shouted at me like a madman. The bastard threw me out of his office."

"Bodily?" asked Paco.

"No, but if I hadn't gotten the hell out of there, I wouldn't have put it past him. I left him practically foaming at the mouth, and went to find you guys. When I couldn't find you, I came in here to cool off. I'm still upset."

"I don't blame you," said Paco. Thinking aloud, he added, "I wonder whether the Next of Kin and friends were invited to the other missing residents' funeral services."

"Other missing residents?" repeated Alice, her voice querulous. "Other than my Albert? I didn't know there were others. What's that all about?"

"Nothing. It's just something a friend asked me to look into," said Paco, sorry he had mentioned the others in the first place.

"How many others were there?" pressed Alice. She pulled her unbuttoned black cardigan sweater closer around her body, clutching it in both hands like a lifeline.

"Maybe three we know about," offered Molly. Paco threw her a warning look to blab no more.

"What?" said Alice. "You mean someone is trying to eliminate all the residents in the facility?"

"Hardly that!" snapped Paco. "Molly mentioned a possibility only. Nothing for you to concern yourself about. If you like, I'll be sure to let you know if any others turn up."

Alice let out a long sigh and finally said, "That won't be necessary." She stood and slowly walked away with a confused look wrinkling up her pale brow.

"Boy, I sure let the pussycat out of the barrel on that one," whispered Molly.

"Yeah, you did. But it wasn't all your fault, sweets," said Paco. "I'm the one who mentioned the others first. It goes to show—revealing anything about an ongoing investigation can cause misinformation, and maybe even panic. We both have to be more careful what we say in front of people."

"Gee, the only thing we've got so far is a promise to go on," said Molly.

"You mean premise, Mol?"

"Yeah, that's it, honeybunches. Were only working on a vogue idea."

Paco chuckled and shook his head as they got up and started back to their suite. They rode up the elevator with Nadine Chasdane.

"Hi, Nadine, got a question for you," Paco said.

The elevator doors opened on the second floor, and the three stepped out into the hall. Nadine stood still and waited for him to speak.

"By any chance, did you happen to receive any announcements of funeral services for either Mindy Norton or Bruce Jameson?"

"Nope. Not a thing," she replied. "Why would there be a funeral if they're just missing?"

"Apparently, they both had quickie funerals and were interred locally," said Paco. "They're no longer missing, according to the funeral director."

Nadine's body stiffened. "Quickie?" she asked. "What do you mean by that?" With hands on hips she stared at him.

"There were no Next of Kins at the funeral home," explained Paco.

"I didn't know Bruce at all, except for a passing hello," said Nadine. "But I used to play cards with Mindy. I'm pretty sure she mentioned having a son and a couple of grandkids. Why wouldn't they be notified?"

Paco pulled out his little notebook and flipped through. Stopping on one particular page, he said, "According to Gary Hoover's records, there were forms saying 'No Next of Kin' for either Mindy or Bruce."

"Strange, very strange," said Nadine, shaking her curly head. "Thanks for the information." She left the LeSotos in front of their suite.

"Be well," Paco called after her.

Nadine waved in response.

"Me too," called Molly.

The LeSotos settled in for a short nap. But with all the disturbing thoughts swirling inside both their heads, neither one could sleep.

Chapter 15
Paco's Errands

Around five that afternoon Molly heard knocks on their door. Paco was in the bathroom trimming his mustache, so she tried to squirm out of her deep recliner. It took a minute or two, as she had it in the fully reclined position. The knocking continued. In her effort to hurry, barefoot, she stubbed her big left toe on the coffee table leg. Squealing "Ouch," Molly hopped toward the door.

"I'm coming, I'm coming!" she yelled. "Keep your bloomers on." She swung the door open. "Well, lookee here, it's the Amatis. Come on in. Have a seat." She pointed to the sofa and headed back to the now-upright recliner.

"Hey, Paco, we got company," she yelled over one shoulder.

In his cargo pants and Redskins sweatshirt, Paco joined them, seating himself in his favorite upholstered armchair.

Jeff sat erect and forward on the sofa, his tense body language in contrast to his faded jeans and Billy Joel T-shirt announcing "The Piano Man" concert. Maryanne jauntily kicked off her loafers and plopped down to sit cross-legged, quite at ease in her plaid pants suit and white socks decorated with teddy bears.

"Hi, Paco," Jeff began. "It's been a few days since we last talked. I wondered whether there were any new developments. Maryanne tells me my sleepwalking occurs nightly, so there's been plenty of opportunity to follow me."

"I did follow you a second time, Jeff. Molly came with me. Essentially, you kept to the same route and stopped to listen at all the same places. What amazed me most was the way you postured yourself so confidently. You rarely hesitated when you walked, and you always seemed to know where you were going."

"So, there's nothing more you can tell me?" asked Jeff.

"I didn't say that," replied Paco. "On my second trip following you in the basement, you did something that shocked the hell out of me. You stopped to listen intently at a pair of tall steel shelving units standing in front of a wall, but not nailed to it. On my first trip you didn't stop there for more than a few seconds. But this time, you stopped cold and stood there for two or three minutes. I wondered, did you actually hear something?"

Jeff shrugged. "Not that I remember."

"Think hard. Does that event trigger anything in your mind?"

Jeff frowned and tweaked his thick white mustache. "Not really. It's not that I heard anything there. It's rather that I must have *expected* to hear something. Anything on the shelves of interest?"

"No. Just a bunch of unlabeled cartons," replied Paco. "But I found something of great interest *behind* the shelves. I was just able to make out an old oak door with one of those impossible giant padlocks. But I couldn't move the shelving to get a better look."

"Oh man," said Jeff. "Maybe I *did* hear something behind that door. Do you think it's possible?"

"Sure is!" Molly chimed in. "We know what's on the other side of that door. Don't we, Paco?"

"I can't stand the suspense," said Maryanne. "Tell us."

"This afternoon," Paco began, "Molly and I went back down the basement to dig around and figure out why you stopped there. Between the two of us, we were able to move the shelf units aside only a few inches to expose the door more. We were trying to decide what it led to. We were only down there a few minutes. We made sure to push the shelving exactly back in place so no one would suspect anything." Paco crossed his right leg over his left knee and continued. "Anyway, we'd gone downstairs through the door at the back of the kitchen and came up the same way." He suppressed a smile as he said, "We kind of ambled into the kitchen. Quietly. Carla was at the stove, stirring some huge pot so she wasn't paying any attention to us. We got a good look out the window over the sink. We think the door behind the shelving connects with that stone turret you can see from the kitchen window. The turret is taller than Crisp Hall next to it. I'm guessing it's at least twenty feet across. From the best angle that we could see, there's only one tiny window near the top. Oh yeah, I forgot to mention—there were cobwebs and dust all over the door and padlock, like it hadn't been opened in years. So if the turret is being used now, there has to be another way to get to it, possibly somewhere in the upper reaches of Crisp Hall."

"Why don't we all four go exploring?" asked Jeff, his voice excited. "Now we know just where to look."

"Sounds like fun to me," said Maryanne.

"We can't," retorted Paco. "That's the Crisp residence. We could get in deep trouble with the law by invading their privacy. I used to arrest people for doing things like that."

"Don't worry, guys," said Molly. "We'll think up some other alley. Paco always does."

"One thing we *could* do," said Paco, thinking out loud. "With a little help from someone to move those heavy shelves, we might get at that padlock and get the door open."

"Sounds about right," said Jeff, ignoring the reference to 'someone.' Anyone here good at picking locks?" He looked squarely at Paco, whose lips curled up under his salt-and-pepper mustache.

"Aren't you volunteering to help, Jeff?" asked Molly, hoping to embarrass him into it.

Jeff's ruddy face turned a shade redder, and he folded his bare muscular arms across his chest.

"Of course he's volunteering," snapped Maryanne. "He's the one who started this whole damn thing—him and his craziness every night."

"Let me sleep on those thoughts," said Paco. "Maybe I'll come up with some sort of viable plan."

"I'll be sleeping on his thoughts tonight, too," said Molly. "We like to do things together."

Maryanne touched Jeff on the shoulder. "It's getting late, dear. We'd better be getting back to our own place."

"Yeah," muttered Jeff, embarrassed that he hadn't volunteered for the heavy lifting right off. After all, he was a helluva lot more muscular than Paco.

* * * *

Paco woke up the next morning from a fitful night, hardly saying anything but a grumpy "Good Morning" and a few nods responding to Molly's questions. Halfway through breakfast, she insisted on knowing what was going on inside his head. He took another bite of buttered toast and set it on his plate next to half-eaten scrambled eggs and a single slice of sausage.

"Paco, all this silence has got me *meshuga*."

Paco bolted down the last of his breakfast and said, "Molly, I've got a few errands to run in town. Do you want to tag along or not?"

"Is it too far for me to walk?"

"I planned on taking the facility's ten o'clock curtesy van, and my two stops are only three blocks apart. Is that too much for you?"

"Of course not, sweetie. I'm up for it."

Forty minutes later Paco loaded Roly into a vacant van seat and helped Molly up the steps into the van. She was wearing her new red wool dress, black jacket, and the mock pearl necklace Caitlin had given her. Three other residents climbed aboard, and the driver took off for Black Rain Corners. At Paco's request, he let the LeSotos off in front of Rayberry Florist. Paco led the way into the shop, holding the door for her and her steel steed.

"What do we need with a florist, hon?" asked Molly.

"You'll see."

"Hi, Inspector LeSoto," said the smiling salesgirl with the blue bibbed apron and a yellow ribbon in her hair.

"Just 'Paco,' Sally. I retired a few years back. Frank Mullins has the job now."

"Who's this lovely lady with you?" asked Sally.

"This is my wife, Molly. Molly, this is Sally Rayberry. Her dad and I used to go shooting together out at the gun club. He had quite a collection of antique guns. We were good buddies."

"Daddy passed away four years ago," said Sally, "and that's when I had to take over the shop. But what can I do for you today?"

"You can pick out three long-stemmed American Beauty roses for my best lady here."

"What?" Molly flushed from her neck up. "What's the occasion?"

"No occasion," said Paco. "Can't a feller buy flowers for his wife?"

Molly remained speechless.

Sally returned with the three beauties laid out on a bed of white tissue paper in a long white cardboard box. Molly took one look at the roses, turned, grabbed Paco, and pulled him to her for a massive hug and then a bus on the cheek. Sally placed the cover on the box and tied a big pink bow around its midsection.

Out on the sidewalk, a still-flushed Molly drawled, "Where to now, Inspector?"

"I thought we'd go sit in the park until lunch."

"Why don't we pick up lunch at Bubba's and take it to the park to eat at one of those benches with a built-in table?"

"Excellent idea," he said. "A nice change from the cafeteria."

Paco carried the florist's box and walked along with Molly as she pushed Roly the block and a half to Bubba's. She ordered a hot pastrami on rye for Paco and a corned beef on a kaiser roll for herself, a bag of fries to share and two sodas. As an afterthought, she added a quarter-pound square of *halvah*, a Middle Eastern treat made of *tahini* (sesame seed paste), sugar, and vanilla. She received a number and joined Paco to wait. Inwardly, he groaned as he listened to her order. His diabetic, super-chubby wife and his own heart condition. *Oh well, just this once.* He could tell she was on a bit of a high from his gift of the exquisite roses.

A dozen minutes later, the counterman shouted their number. Paco picked up the tall white bag, already spotted with a few comforting grease marks, and paid at the cash register.

"You know, we could eat here," suggested Paco. "I'm not quite through with my errands. We still need to stop in at Humboldt's Hardware."

"Is that going to be a surprise, too?" Molly asked, as she squeezed into a chair at a Formica-topped table.

"Not exactly," he replied, as he pulled up a chair and sat down next to her. "I'll be needing a tool or two, if we're going to attack that basement door."

"So…you really are going to get that door open?" she asked, while she emptied the white bag onto the table and popped several fries into her mouth.

"If I can get Jeff's help moving those shelves, I'm gonna try."

They ate quietly, relishing, with a touch of guilt, the pretty-much-forbidden food. Occasionally, Molly waved to people she recognized from a distance. When they were finished with their sandwiches and nibbling on what was left of the fries, Molly pointed to the white box sitting tall in the vinyl basket of her walker. "I'm still muddletated over you buying me flowers without any mentionable occasion. I can't get it off my brain."

"Why can't a feller buy his wife a gift without her getting suspicious?"

"Because usually it's when her feller has off-ended her, and his gift is a peace offing."

"That's a very narrow view of things, Molly. A feller can express himself spontaneously just because he feels like it. It shows he appreciates her and loves her."

"Is that the case here?" she asked.

"Well, almost," he answered. "I did have an additional purpose in buying you those roses."

"And what was that, my sweetiekins?"

Paco tossed their paper bag and garbage into a trash can and said, "You'll see when we get to the hardware store."

"Paco, I'm not going anywhere until you tell me what you have planned."

"All right, all right! It's the long white box I was after in the flower shop," he explained. "Not particularly the roses. They were purely a bonus for the woman I love. I want the box to hide the bolt cutters I intend buying at the hardware store. I can't exactly get on a bus or parade through Gilded Gates with a pair of bolt cutter handles sticking out of a brown paper bag, can I?"

Molly's cupid lips drooped. "I guess not," she said. "Sorry I doubted you, sweetie. Even if it wasn't entirely a romantic notion, it all makes sense now. Let's go see Mr. Humboldt, dear."

The trek took fifteen minutes at the speed of Molly's steps per hour. They had to stop several times so she could catch her breath. Paco didn't mind the pace. He had no other place he'd rather be, nor anyone else he'd rather be with. The door jingled and soon they were surrounded by tools, barbeque grills, garden supplies, brackets, screws, nails, and all manner of great hardware stuff.

Johannes Humboldt, a stocky man with a protruding beer belly, stepped up to greet them. He wore a Baltimore Orioles baseball cap and denim apron. "Hi there, Paco, Molly. How's retirement treating you?"

"Doing just fine, Joe," said Paco. "How are you?"

"I'm good," he replied. "How can I help you today?"

"I came in to either rent or buy a pair of bolt cutters," said Paco.

"That's a controlled item, Paco. You'll need a permit."

"Of course I know," insisted Paco. "I used to sign off on those permits. If you've got a spare form, I'll sign it for you now."

"Well, I don't know about that," mumbled Joe. "What are you going to use it for, anyway?"

"I have this thick old padlock that I've misplaced the key to," said Paco.

"It's to a trunk that's been in our basement forever," lied Molly, trying to be helpful.

"I could call Frank Mullins," argued Paco. "He's in charge of the police now."

"That won't be necessary," said Joe. "You mentioned rent or buy. Which did you want to do?"

"Well, I only have one cut in mind," said Paco. "I could have the cutters back to you in a day or two."

"Then rent it is," said Joe. "That'll be $10 a day, and I'll need a $50 deposit, please."

"I have it right here," said Paco, slipping two twenties and a ten out of his wallet. I'll pay the day fee when I return it. Can you wrap it for me?"

"Sure," said Joe as he tore off a sheet of brown paper from the large spool. He rolled the cutters several times inside the paper and stuck a piece of tape on it to hold the paper tight.

It still looks like what it is, brown paper or not, thought Paco. "Thank you," he said. "See you in a couple days."

With the cutters under one arm, he and Molly left the hardware store and turned toward the park. When they were a few doors away, Paco directed them to a curbside bench. They sat while Paco removed the roses, wrapped the long prickly stems tightly in the tissue and brown paper, then handed the bouquet to Molly.

"What am I s'posed to do with these?" she complained.

"Put them in your basket and use the box ribbon to tie them to one handlebar. You can even hold them while we're on the van." While he was explaining, he tucked the bolt cutters into the white box and shut the lid.

A few blocks later, they arrived at the pickup spot to wait for the retirement home's van, which was just pulling into a parking space. Molly was exhausted from their long treks with Roly, but she basked in the "Oohs" and "Aahs" over her stunning roses from the other residents during the ride back to Gilded Gates. All the attention was drawn away from the white box that Paco carried. The same was true as they returned to their suite. After all, it was the box from the roses. Paco grinned as he unlocked their door. *Mission accomplished.*

Chapter 16
The Inn at Gander Pointe

Gander Pointe was a long, narrow, tree-lined spit of land, goose-necking between Black Rain Creek and the Chesapeake Bay. The creek, a wide, pondlike body of sluggishly moving water, churned its shallow, muddy bottom, especially during rains. The brackish water never ran clear—just murky black. Too shallow for boating, it remained a perfect watershed for fish and fowl alike.

The Inn at Gander Pointe took advantage of the 300-degree view of nature and the bay. The distant eastern shoreline of Maryland actually melded with the horizon. Not exactly the Plaza or the Waldorf, but the inn did have a popular three-star restaurant to its credit, featuring the Chandelier Room, replete with maître d' and white linen tablecloths. The low ceiling seemed ill-fitted for the mismatched collection of crystal chandeliers. But when soft lighting danced on the prisms, even mid-morning, it created a reasonably romantic ambiance that delighted the local patrons. In keeping with the theme, a massive brass chandelier hung from the two-story ceiling of the spacious lobby, hovering above a cozy circle of overstuffed easy chairs and potted green fakery. High paneled walls and double-storied windows encircled the lobby's staircase. A wide arched passageway led to the guest rooms.

The highlight of the week was the Chandelier Room's elaborate

Sunday brunch, "Reservations encouraged." This Sunday, the eleventh of November, clusters of patrons in their Sunday best stood or sat in the lobby, waiting for their name to be called. A woman in a tan knee-length skirt and matching jacket sat off by herself in one of the armchairs. A russet-brown felt hat with a wide brim topped her clipped dark hair and brooding face. With manicured unpolished nails, she toyed with the dragonfly broach on her left lapel. Nylons covered her shapely calves, but it was difficult to tell her actual early forties age. Waiting diners were called by the maître d' and seated; others arriving took their places. The woman squirmed in her chair, turning to look with each new arrival. When a tall, gangly man in a gray pin-striped suit came through the door and approached, her facial expression turned to anger. She couldn't deny him a hug, but scolded him anyway.

"You're late. What kept you?"

"You know my time is not my own. Some unexpected business turned up. I couldn't help it."

"I'm nervous," she said. "What if someone here recognizes us together?"

"No need to worry," he said. "This place is pretty upscale. I doubt the average penny-pinching facility resident will show up here for Sunday brunch at thirty simoleons a plate."

"If you say so," she conceded. "Maybe we should put our name in to get us a table."

"Good idea," he said. "What name should we use today?"

"I like the sound of Anderson," she replied. "Say Mark Anderson."

They were seated at a table on the sundeck, a glass-enclosed anteroom that jutted out in the direction of the bay. The view was wonderful, but the distance to the sumptuous buffet table detracted from that advantage, especially if second helpings were craved.

As the couple moved through the buffet line, past the eggs Benedict and the chicken à la king, the man placed his hand on the woman's shoulder. He leaned forward and whispered in her ear, "Keep your eyes on the buffet table. I see a familiar face." She jerked toward the pan of broiled vegetables so quickly, her omelet slid to the edge of the plate.

Jeff and Maryanne Amati breezed through the buffet line, so eager to get back to their table that they skipped half the tempting entrees. They never noticed the couple that hid from them. Jeff, wearing a navy-blue Ralph Lauren polo shirt and tweed golf pants, and Maryanne, in a smart cream-colored sheath dress, were unaware of the prying eyes watching them as they began to eat with gusto and converse between bites and sips.

Meanwhile, in the buffet line, the unnamed couple was forced to move along to pancakes and French toast, all the while with their backs to the Amatis. They knew they'd have to make a separate run for dessert, if and when the coast was clear. As they filled their plates with Western omelets, bacon, and hash browns, they took the most circuitous route back to the sundeck to avoid being recognized. Neither wanted any residents to learn of their business, nor their alliance. But the woman just had to take one look backward toward the Amati table. Maryanne, with her back to the far wall, appeared to look straight at her. Tan Suit didn't turn into a pillar of salt, but she started to shake visibly and audibly with her nails clicking against the rim of her plate.

"What's wrong?" asked the man, as he slid into his place at their table.

"I think Maryanne saw me. She was looking straight at me."

"Were there any signs of recognition?" he asked.

"How the hell should I know?"

"Well, did she change her expression at all?" he asked.

"I don't know," she answered, as her nerves turned raw. She pulled her hat brim further down over her forehead, even while knowing it was too little too late.

"Calm down," he said. "Don't I always find the best solutions to things? This will work itself out, too. I assure you."

"Yeah," she mocked. "Just like you assured me the woman in the tower would die in two weeks' time if we denied her nourishment and just gave her a saline drip to keep it looking like a natural death. The damn lady is still very much alive and kicking. She was a bad selection—far too healthy a woman to start with. I heard she was quite an athlete in her heyday."

"Take it easy now," he muttered. "Sometimes these things take a little longer. She's still a good candidate—no next of kin and her signature was on a fat insurance policy with the facility as the beneficiary. Besides, we'll make sure a new resident pays full price for the dorm room she vacated."

"I don't know if all this is worth it," Tan Suit said with a disturbing shudder. "Murder is a terrible way to make a living. Murder means looking over your shoulder and lying all the time."

"Isn't holding 25 percent of the facility's shares reward enough for you?" asked the man smoothly. He reached under the table to pat her leg. "Then there's that wonderful friendship we share. Who could ask for more?"

"I know, I know," she said. "I'm just nervous that it's taking so long. Her saline bottle has to be changed again at 4:30 today, so I'll have to disguise my signature to get another one from the dispensary. If I'm caught, I'll be ruined and tied to this whole conspiracy."

"Simple," he said. "Just don't sign."

"Can't do that," she snapped. "If the signatures don't match the missing bottles, they'll start a wholesale investigation. I can't risk that. I'm in a shaky position as is. Between accounting for the bottles and hiding our tryst I'm a nervous wreck."

"Don't worry, the worst of this will be over soon, and I will take care of the rest. You can't fall apart on me now—we're almost there, woman."

"That's easy for you to say, my dear," she said. "You've got 75 percent of the ownership in your pocket and you're taking none of the risks. There's one more thing I'm awfully curious about. Why do you choose to live in Gilded Gates like any other resident?"

"I told you why. I had the family house rented out and I needed a place to stay. Besides, I like to keep a close eye on things. I can make certain adjustments when necessary. Our mutual project is just one example of this."

"Yeah, that sounds like something you'd do," Tan Suit sneered. "And why do you call yourself my friend and partner? You've made it quite clear that our relationship is purely business. You're just full of glib answers."

He shoved his empty plate aside for the waiter to take away. "You've hardly eaten anything. I should have taken you to a fast-food joint instead."

"Enough of the wisecracks already. I'm not exactly in an eating mood," she said. "I don't know how much more of this ghastly business I can stand. Getting rid of people for fun and profit is not my cup of tea, to say the least. It's a short-term solution, and until you find us a lasting one, I'm not going to be a happy camper."

He didn't answer. Avoiding her eyes and her accusations, he picked up the check and stood to leave.

* * * *

At 10:30 that evening. Gordon Lowe strode into the recreation room. The 96-year-old was still dressed in his charcoal-gray suit, white shirt with unbuttoned collar, and loosened black tie. Relieved to find the room empty, he was disgruntled—fed up with the commotion from his forever-squabbling next-door suite neighbors. He needed some peace and quiet, and it was truly quiet here in the recreation room. He picked up the evening paper from the coffee table and sat down on the sofa to read the business and sports sections. The stock market was down and the Jets lost again. But peace and quiet were not to be. Now he heard something and sensed motion somewhere. He lowered the newspaper and scanned the room.

"Who's there?" he asked, seeing nothing and wondering whether his imagination was playing tricks on him.

Gordon scanned the room again. This time he saw a mostly bald head poking up from behind an upholstered love seat. Two bland eyes stared at him.

Annoyed, Gordon did a doubletake, thinking *There goes my peace and quiet.* "Rudy Schuster? What the hell are you doing back there? Come out where I can see you."

"Shush, I'm hiding," whispered Rudy, standing up with a slight wobble from crouching too long. "I don't want to be found."

"Who are you hiding from, may I ask?"

"Edna Bush. She's a nice lady, but she's standing in front of my door, so I can't go home."

"Why in the world are you hiding from her?"

Rudy sighed. "Because I didn't go to her place for dinner tonight, and she was ordering stuffed cabbage from Bubba's Deli especially for me." He came around to the front of the love seat and sat down, looking most appealing in gray slacks, yellow shirt, and plaid tie. He was a short trim man with a smallish face and pixie-like ears and, with the exception of a thin trace of gray hair around the edges, he was bald.

"Am I missing something here?" asked Gordon. "What was wrong with going to her place for dinner?"

"I get invited to dinner a lot by all the single ladies in this joint," said Rudy. "Sometimes I get mixed up and accept two invitations for the same night. Like tonight."

Gordon was tall and skinny, with a wiry neck and an Adam's apple that bobbed visibly when he pouted. "How come you get so many invitations when I haven't gotten one lousy invite?"

Rudy couldn't help but chuckle. Gordon was known at Gilded Gates as a sourpuss. His profession as an undertaker had clung to his personality. "Well, Gordie, I'm the youngest male resident here at seventy-two. I'm a widower, still in okay shape. I'm not exactly good-looking, but the ladies find me attractive anyway. I'm the resident eligible bachelor. What can I say?"

"I'd say you're quite the ladies' man." Gordon silently admitted the little guy did have an endearing quality to him.

"That can be a nuisance sometimes," said Rudy, rolling his eyes.

"So where were you tonight when you should've been at Edna's?"

"That's the problem. I was also invited to Bella Swartz's for dinner, and she was ordering matzoh ball soup and brisket and *lokshen kugel*, Jewish noodle pudding, from the deli, especially for me."

"So you went to Bella's place instead of Edna's?" asked Gordon.

"Not exactly."

"What do you mean?"

"I went to the movies," said Rudy with an impish grin. "I couldn't decide which lady to disappoint, so I went to the picture show instead."

And disappointed both, Gordon thought with a wry smile. *Hell, I guess I just don't live right.* But then again he knew that. He'd spent his whole career as an undertaker. It was an isolating, unsocial profession. And somehow, even during all his years in retirement, he'd never shaken it off. *Oh well,* he decided, *it is what it is.*

Chapter 17
The Spiral Staircase
Monday, November 16th

Jeff and Maryanne weren't in residence all day Sunday, so Paco and Molly made a special effort to look for them at the noon meal on Monday, which was no-spice chili with or without kidney beans, a scoop of rice, and coleslaw. They picked up their lunch trays, located the Amatis in the cafeteria, and saw the two vacant chairs at their table.

"We missed you guys yesterday," said Molly once they were seated.

"Oh, we attended the morning mass," said Maryanne. "And then treated ourselves to the brunch buffet at the Inn at Gander Pointe."

"I hope you were smarter than I always am," Molly giggled. "I always overstuff myself at their scrumpturous brunch whenever Paco treats *me* to the Inn."

"We topped it off with a drive in the country and a movie last night," added Jeff.

"Hey, Jeff," said Paco, "if you're still willing to help me with the shelves, I think we now have the means to take a crack at that door downstairs."

"When?" asked Jeff.

"How about this afternoon? I'm pretty sure we can breach the door together," replied Paco. "I suggest you wear jeans or something else you don't particularly care about. From the looks of things we can expect plenty of dust and cobwebs. If you choose to go beyond the door with me, I can only caution you that we could run into violence by whomever is behind all of this."

"What about us girls?" asked Maryanne. "Are you leaving us behind?"

"Molly can't join us because I also expect plenty of stairs in a vertical turret," explained Paco. "I hesitate to bring you, Maryanne, because I don't know if we'll run into anybody on the other side. If you really want to help, you might be a good lookout in the basement."

Maryanne wrinkled her nose. "Sounds creepy. I decline."

Good, Jeff thought. "Paco, now that that's settled, where and when do you propose we meet?"

"How about 1:30 in the parlor of Comfort Hall?"

"Oh, Paco, we had trouble getting through that door before," said Molly. "Do you want to sneak through the door in the kitchen again?"

"That won't be necessary, hon. I've got the parlor door all figured out this time."

* * * *

Both men wore faded jeans and dark long-sleeved shirts when they met at the far end of the parlor. Paco was carrying the white florist's box and handed it to Jeff, who immediately sensed its unexpected weight. Luckily, there was no one else around when Paco pushed aside the Leaping Lion tapestry. He was clutching two plastic membership cards—from the Rotary and Elks clubs. Sliding his fingers along the wall, he located the crack in the wall opposite where he knew the door hinges to be, and slipped one card in, feeling for the lever of the lift latch, then the other card in the same manner. Confident that he had control of both levers, he lifted them together, and the hidden door swung inward, revealing the steps to the basement.

Making sure to arrange the Leaping Lion back in place, they shut the door behind them and descended the stairs. Weaving their way through the basements of Comfort Hall and Fellowship Hall, they arrived in the Crisp Hall basement. Paco led Jeff to the shelving units, took the box from him, and set it on the floor. Together, they took a position at the right end of the shelving unit. At Paco's count of three, they lifted and sidestepped the unit away from the wall. They repeated a like move at the other end, then manhandled the second unit in the same manner until one person would be able to comfortably fit behind the two shelf units.

Paco picked up the white box off the concrete floor. Fitting his wiry but rather creaky body between the two shelf units, he placed himself in front of the padlocked door. Jeff watched, transfixed but sweating from the suspense, even in the chilled, damp air. Paco removed the bolt cutter from the box and started toward the padlock.

Jeff instinctively saw what was coming next. "Hey, Paco, I get it. But how about letting me take over? I'm feeling useless here."

Paco gratefully handed over the heavy tool. He was actually wondering himself whether he should be tackling this nasty job. "Thanks, buddy, go for it."

Jeff's muscular biceps set to work. To get a leveraged grip, he slid his hands back one at a time on the cutter's handles, then opened and fitted the bolt cutter tightly around the rusted-steel shackle, the U-shaped part of the tarnished-brass padlock. Then he rammed the handles together with all his strength to sever the shackle. It took several new grips and repeated attempts to notch through the case-hardened steel. A snapping sound finally told him the shackle was in two. He twisted one of the remaining shackle pieces away and lifted the padlock out of the clasp eye. This enabled him to swing the hinged hasp out of the clasp eye.

A healthy tug on the oak door and it freed itself from the embedded rusted iron casing. There were rusted iron hooks on the inside of the door so that a two-by-four could bar the door from that side as well, but, fortunately, that bar lay on the floor next to the door.

"Great job!" Paco said. "But do you really want to continue on with me? It could get ugly and possibly dangerous."

"Are you kidding, man? You've got my curiosity up now. I can't stop here and miss all the fun."

"All right then."

What they faced was a spiral staircase.

Paco pulled two penlights stocked with fresh batteries from his pocket and handed one to Jeff. All at once, they confronted a massive network of cobwebs, captive dead insects, and next-to-no-light inside. Paco wound web after web around the cutter handles as he slowly moved forward and up the stairs. Periodically, he stopped—first to scrape the handles clean with the side of his shoe, and next, to grind the concentrated webs into dust with the sole of his shoe. The stale dust-filled air attacked their nostrils until they were both breathing through their mouths. Paco slowly led the way up the spiraling concrete steps, destroying cobwebs. Jeff followed close behind, providing a beam from his penlight. They kept to the outside wall, hoping to find other doors into the turret. The wall was made of mortared concrete block, revealing that the stonework outside was merely a façade.

At one point in the spiral climb to the first floor, Paco encountered a number of damaged webs, leading him to believe that someone had come this far down from somewhere above them. He had several burgeoning thoughts on who this might have been, but stored them in the back of his brain for the time being.

"Shouldn't we be past the first floor by now?" asked Jeff. "I've counted twenty-one steps already. We only had fourteen steps to the basement from the parlor."

"Right. Good thinking, Jeff. We haven't seen any doors to Crisp Hall yet either. And we're not out of cobweb-land by a long shot."

Ten seconds later, Jeff jerked to a stop. Trembling, he grabbed the banister with thick fingers to steady himself. His normally ruddy face blanched to chalky white, his blue-black eyes murky as a muddied pond. His breathing became choppy and his voice contorted. "Paco! Do you hear what I hear?"

One step above, Paco slowly turned around, balancing himself precariously. "No, what?"

"The moaning! A female voice! It's what I've been hearing every night during my sleepwalking—every time I was in the Crisp basement. Too faint to define where it was coming from, but now it's real. I didn't imagine it. I'm not crazy."

Alarmed by Jeff's demeanor, but exhilarated nonetheless, Paco placed a firm hand on Jeff's shoulder. "Take it easy, my friend, I believe you. Hold still for a minute, catch your breath. Know what? Now I'm hearing the voice, too. You're not crazy. In fact, you're a brave man. You okay to continue?"

A moment or two later, Jeff's chest stopped heaving, his breathing returned to a semblance of normalcy, and he nodded yes.

They climbed higher and higher until the cobwebs seemed less dense and the air less polluted. And when Jeff had counted thirty-two steps, they found a conventional door to what they believed was opposite the second floor of Crisp Hall. Paco tried the handle, but it was locked from the inside. The rusty hinges told them that this door had not been in recent use. Another eighteen steps brought them to another locked door. This one they believed might be to the third floor of Crisp Hall. They had left behind all but a few scattered cobwebs here and there. This access appeared to be in both frequent and recent use. It was easier breathing up here as well. The stairs continued to spiral upward, so the two men decided to follow wherever they might lead.

As they rounded the last of the spiral climb, natural light from above sprinkled into the stairwell. It came from the turret's only window—the one Molly had seen from the park bench outside. Oddly, it was open, letting in the chilling mid-November air. They had reached the top—and stopped. In front of them was a barrier: a four-panel room divider, dark brown, about six feet tall. Together they pushed the heavy divider to one side.

"Good Lord!" cried Paco.

"My God!" exclaimed Jeff.

What they had expected was an empty round room with stone walls at the top of the turret.

What they saw was a woman on a gurney, hooked up to an IV.

"She'll freeze to death up here," said Paco, "especially when it gets colder at night."

Paco cautiously stepped close and leaned over the woman. He gently pulled back the thin blanket and sheet and saw her white hospital gown clinging to an extremely thin body like another layer of skin. "She looks emaciated. There's hardly anything left of her. Wait! She's still breathing, and I'm hearing a faint wailing or moaning sound coming from deep within her throat—more like a rasping sound now. I hope we're not too late."

"The IV bottle is marked Saline Solution," noted Jeff. "I wonder who she is, and why she's in this God-awful place."

"Try the end of the bed," replied Paco. "There may be some kind of chart there."

"There is a chart," said Jeff. "It says her name is Lisa Howard and she's eighty-four."

"Good Lord! She's Nadine Chasdane's roommate—one of our missing residents," said Paco.

Jeff shuddered. "This is very strange."

"What's strange?" asked Paco.

"There's no ailment, diagnosis, or list of medications for the woman on this chart."

"This whole thing is mighty strange," said Paco. "We've got to get her to a hospital in a hurry or we're going to lose her altogether. The thing I can't figure out is how they got her and this gurney up here in the first place."

"Why don't we call on Dr. Crisp's medical expertise first?" asked Jeff.

"Jeff, we know that something is awfully wrong here, so until we find out who's responsible, I just don't trust either of the Crisps."

"How do we get her down and out of here then?" asked Jeff. "We don't have any kind of stretcher."

"They got the gurney in here somehow, so there must be a way out," said Paco. "See those double doors over on the wall?"

"Yeah." Jeff pushed down on both panic-release bar handles at once, and the double doors flew open to expose the flat rooftop of Fellowship Hall. Both men dashed onto the roof to explore a way to get Lisa Howard to the ground floor. The wide, flat roof comprised three large air-conditioning units and an array of relief pipes, vents, and elevator housings. It didn't take long before they recognized that one of the elevator housings stood a great deal taller than the other. Upon closer examination of the taller housing, they discovered another set of double doors, and alongside them, a SERVICE button.

Paco pressed the button to see if it would respond to the roof stop. Sure enough, in about half a minute the door opened to an empty carriage. Ducking inside, he pressed the STOP button and quickly examined the rest of the control panel. He saw the illuminated numbers one through three and the letter R, which he assumed meant Roof. But there was another round control key slot next to that top letter. He released the STOP button and hastily stepped outside the carriage before the doors closed again.

The two men raced back to Lisa Howard and the gurney. The IV bottle hung from a tall hook attached to the gurney. Releasing the wheel brakes freed the gurney for travel. Jeff pulled and steered from the front, while Paco pushed from the rear. Out through the turret's double doors and across the open roof to the taller elevator housing went the gurney and patient. Paco pressed the SERVICE button again. But when the door opened this time, the carriage was not empty. A skinny runt in T-shirt and grimy shorts stood there, mouth agape in surprise.

Paco recognized him as resident Vince Eden. Without saying a word, Paco grabbed Vince by his collar, yanked him out of the elevator, and deposited him on the roof out of their way.

"You are evil and you will be punished for your evil work," yelled Vince, exposing a gap of two missing front teeth in his upper jaw. Paco and Jeff looked at each other, both wondering what to do with this wacko—and why he even wanted to be on the roof.

Vince's shrill voice disturbed the patient, and she moaned weakly as the two men rolled the gurney into the elevator.

"You can't leave me here!" screamed Vince.

"Wait five minutes," said Jeff. "Then push the SERVICE button. The elevator will come back for you."

Paco sent the elevator to the first floor. As the doors opened, he peeked out and down the corridor toward the open door of Dr. Crisp's office. The office looked empty, so he and Jeff rolled the gurney out and continued pushing it to the end of the corridor, into the front hall, just opposite the exit onto the flagstone patio.

"Jeff, go find the first phone you can and call 9-1-1 for an ambulance," ordered Paco. "I'll stay with Lisa. Oh, and bring back a blanket, water, and a straw, too." Just then, Lisa released a lengthy moan, sending shivers up and down his spine.

Meanwhile, Maryanne and Molly had been sitting in the Comfort Hall parlor, anticipating that the men would exit from the basement through the tapestry-covered door. Seated opposite the corridor, Molly spotted them maneuvering the gurney through it. She and Maryanne rushed toward their husbands to see if they could be of help.

Jeff spun around, passed Dr. Crisp's open door into the dining room and then the kitchen door, returning in a few minutes carrying a glass of water. "Paco, I called 9-1-1 from the kitchen wall phone," he reported, then held the glass with the straw up to Lisa's lips. She couldn't manage the straw. Molly had another idea. Dipping her clean handkerchief into the glass and soaking it, she brushed Lisa's lips with it until they parted and permitted the wetness to caress her tongue. Her eyes opened and she moaned something unintelligible, perhaps a word of gratitude. Maryanne arrived with a floral-patterned afghan that had been draped over the back of a sofa, and gently began to cover Lisa up.

The shrill whine of a siren reverberated off in the distance—each second louder and more distinct. At last, they sighted the ambulance coming through the golden gates, flying up the driveway, circling around, and backing up to the main entrance. Two EMTs emerged and rushed to the gurney. One examined the patient, while the other looked to the gathering audience of residents for an explanation. Paco, recognizing one of the EMTs, stepped forward.

"Bob, the patient's name is Lisa Howard. Eighty-four years old. I believe she's suffering from malnutrition and possibly exposure."

"Inspector, how can that be in a house of assisted living?" asked Bob.

"Good question, Bob. It's criminal. We found her—unattended and abandoned—as you see her, in a secret stone turret at the top of Crisp Hall."

"But why in hell…Inspector?"

"I can only guess why," replied Paco, shaking his head.

The second EMT rose from his initial examination and said, "Let's transport her, stat. She needs more than we can do here." The EMTs transferred her from the house gurney to their folding gurney and loaded her into the ambulance. They reboarded up front, sped down the driveway, and out through the golden gates.

By five o'clock in the afternoon, more than a dozen anxious residents had gathered outside at the sound of the departing emergency vehicle. They stood fearful but polite, off to one side, their hearts beating fast as they watched their friend Lisa being attended to and borne away.

Suddenly, Dr. Phelix Crisp bolted out the front door and peered at the departing ambulance. He looked with annoyance at all the surrounding faces and barked, "What's going on here, and who was taken away?"

Paco stepped forward. "That was Lisa Howard, Dr. Crisp. She's extremely ill and needs hospital attention."

"Why wasn't I notified first?" asked Phelix. "Who called for an ambulance?"

"Jeff Amati did," Paco replied. "It was an emergency, and she needed a hospital Emergency Room immediately."

"But I make the medical decisions around here," shouted Phelix. "Who are you to bypass my authority?"

"Authority has nothing to do with this, Dr. Crisp," replied Paco. "As the former head of police in Black Rain Corners, I'm trained to recognize an emergency when I see one. This was an extreme case."

"I can vouch for that," said Jeff, stepping forward. "The EMTs saw it as an Emergency Room case as well."

Phelix stepped close to Paco and stared down at him menacingly. "I'm responsible for this facility. I'm not only responsible for the patients, but the finances as well. If this debacle turns out to be unnecessary, the facility will have to pay for an expensive hospital visit and stay. I might even consider charging you personally for causing it."

The crowd of residents, listening attentively, gathered behind him and began to boo softly. Dr. Crisp's angry tone started to mellow. He realized he was on dangerous ground psychologically. "What was wrong with the patient that you deemed it such a crisis?"

Paco looked up. His black crow eyes bore into the doctor's. "Where and when we found her, Lisa Howard was obviously suffering from malnutrition and exposure to the elements. She had been sedated, laid on a gurney, hooked up to an IV, and then abandoned to die—by someone. Whoever did all of that would have required some medical knowledge and also known their way around this facility pretty damn well."

"Ooooh!" The hovering residents chorused.

"How can you be so sure there's been a wrongdoing here?" asked Phelix.

"According to her roommate, Nadine Chasdane, Lisa was fit as a fiddle on the day she went missing. She left the apartment to play tennis. Does that sound like someone in need of medical attention? Nadine reported her missing that very night, yet no one ever told her where Lisa was or what happened to her."

"Are you accusing me of abusing our patients?" asked Phelix.

"Absolutely not," replied Paco. "I wouldn't think of making any accusations. I don't have the evidence to back it up."

"Then who are you accusing?" asked Phelix.

"No one at present, Doctor," replied Paco. "No one yet."

"You said before that she was abandoned," said Phelix. "Just where in my facility did you find her?"

"In the open room at the top of the stone turret, the turret that can be seen from the path around the left side of the facility or from the kitchen windows."

"Hah! No one has been in that damned old turret for years," declared Phelix.

"That may be true for the lower 90 percent of the floors," said Paco. "But the upper 10 percent? Obviously, at least one person, maybe several, have been mighty active up there as of late."

"I intend to investigate all of this," thundered Phelix for the benefit of the residents. "I'll leave no stone unturned." He spun around and pushed through the crowd. Making his way indoors to his office, he couldn't stifle his true feelings of panic and fear. He slammed the door behind him. He wanted to be alone, to think.

Chapter 18
It's Criminal
That Evening

Town Hall, a converted Victorian home, sat on a corner across the street from Black Rain Creek. The part-time mayor's office occupied the second floor, and the makeshift Hall of Records and clerk's office sprawled across the first floor. A red-brick structure next to it housed the Volunteer Fire and Police departments. The county had established a token police presence here in the early Seventies when a rash of break-ins targeted a dozen upscale homes.

The local police consisted of one full-time and one part-time officer. Oddly, against all logic, the part-time officer was in charge of the tiny force. Although the officers loosely answered to the Sheriff's Office in Annapolis, Black Rain Corners paid their salaries and created the title of inspector for the part-time officer. Paco LeSoto was the original part-time inspector. After he retired, the town put Sergeant Frank Mullins in charge. A part-time position was no longer needed, because the only crimes in Black Rain Corners seemed to be misdemeanors. Occasionally, Frank and Paco went out for a friendly beer together.

* * * *

That evening Paco mechanically gobbled up his Salisbury steak dinner in the elegant dining room. No way could he relax and enjoy it. The spiral staircase, the discovery of Lisa, rescuing her, and Phelix's baffling reaction—all too much compressed into nearly heart-stopping hours. But he wasn't done yet.

He rose and whispered a few words to Molly. She nodded, happy to stay and socialize over lemon meringue pie with her new friend, Geraldine Glazer, a former off-Broadway actress who dramatically tried to insert her former play lines into normal conversation.

Paco took the elevator upstairs and hurried into suite 225. He rushed to his desk, sat down, and picked up the phone to dial Frank Mullins. It was nearly eight o'clock and he assumed the connection would bounce to Frank's home. But he was surprised.

"Black Rain Corners Police, Sergeant Mullins."

"Frank, it's Paco. You're still in the office? I expected you'd have wrapped everything up for the day."

"Actually, Paco, I had nothing going on at home, so I stayed to catch up on paperwork. What's happening?"

"I have an urgent situation and need to see you immediately. Can I come now?"

"Of course. But how will you get here?"

Paco said, off the top of his head, "I'll ask the facility van driver to bring me. I don't want you coming here. It'll cause too much of a commotion."

Twenty minutes later, at police headquarters, Frank heard a knock. "Hey, Paco, come in and sit down." The two men took seats opposite each other at Frank's desk.

Paco wasted no time with preliminaries. "I'm here to report terrible crimes—kidnapping, cruelty, and attempted murder."

"Where did all this happen? And who was kidnapped?"

"At Gilded Gates Assisted Living Community. Where Molly and I live now, as you know. The victim was Lisa Howard, one of the residents. We found her tied to a saline bottle—isolated at the top of a turret, a stone tower-like structure at the rear of the facility. Lisa had probably not been fed a normal meal for over two weeks.

She was in such bad shape we had to send her in an ambulance to Anne Arundel Medical Center."

"When you keep saying "we" I assume you mean Molly, too," said Frank.

"No, no. I mean Jeff Amati, a friend and also a resident of the facility. He helped me in the search for Lisa."

"Have you any idea who the perpetrator is?" asked Frank.

"No, but I have some ideas—actually only a few limiting parameters to work with. Nothing specific, mind you. Which brings me to something else I'd like to take care of while I'm here."

"What would that be, Paco?"

"I'd like you to deputize me. I've already infiltrated the place by being a resident there, and deputy's credentials would give me some official status to ask a few questions here and there."

"I don't have a budget for another paycheck," said Frank. "It would have to be at no pay."

"I wouldn't have it any other way," said Paco.

Frank went to a filing cabinet, pulled out a large envelope, and dumped the contents out on his desk—a deputy badge and laminated card. He pushed both across the desk toward Paco. "Recite aloud what you see on the card with your right hand raised."

Paco complied with the recitation, establishing his official deputy status. Half an hour later, the two buddies went out for their beers.

* * * *

While Paco was out, Molly embarked on her own mission. She felt it was her duty to inform Nadine Chasdane that her roommate had been found. She knocked on the door to the double room on the second floor of Comfort Hall. At first she heard nothing, but upon continued rapping, a pattering of slippered feet shuffled to the door in response.

"Who's there?" asked a sleepy voice.

"It's Molly, Molly LeSoto. I have huge news to tell you."

"It's 9:25. I was already asleep," said Nadine. "What could you possibly want with me at this time of night?"

"I came to tell you that your roommate, Lisa Howard, has been found."

"What?" Nadine, in pajamas and hastily tied bathrobe, fumbled with the lock and opened the door "What did you just say?"

Molly felt a rare moment of puzzled silence. Nadine's hair was grayish white and thin, almost bald on top. Where were the sumptuous blonde curls?

Nadine got the message. "Busted! You're seeing the real me. My friend Winnie the Wig is standing on the dresser."

"Oh, now I remember. Good for you, Nadine," said an embarrassed Molly. She gripped Roly's handlebars tightly, wondering what to do next.

Wide awake now, Nadine said, "Good heavens, look at me leaving you out in the hall. Do come in. I want to hear everything."

With her walker, Molly stepped into the sitting room and followed Nadine to the sofa. As soon as they were seated, she began. "My Paco and Jeff Amati found Lisa."

"Thank God! But where? Is she all right? What happened to her?"

"Paco and Jeff found her in the room at the top of the stone turret."

"The stone turret?"

"Yeah. You know. It's attached to Crisp Hall and you can see it from outside."

"Oh. Of course. Sorry." Nadine's breath became shallow. "Tell me about Lisa."

"She's in real bad shape, Nadine. The ambulance took her to the hospital in Annapolis just before suppertime." Molly laced her chubby fingers together to brace herself. "Lisa was kiddynapped, subdoozed, and not fed for over two whole weeks—so she was weak and barely alive. The poor thing. All she could do was moan."

"Oh my God." Nadine's voice broke as she began to sob. "It's wonderful to know she's still alive, but like this? It's horrible. What evil-minded person did this to her? And why would anyone want to hurt her?"

"We don't know who the perforator is yet," said Molly. "My Paco is working on that and the why too."

"I'd better get dressed and go to the hospital," said Nadine.

"I wouldn't do that," suggested Molly. "Visiting hours are over, she's mostly snoozilating, and since you're not immediate family, I highly doubt you will get any information from anyone. In the morning Paco and I will be going to the hospital on official business. We'll let you know all the details when we get back."

With a deep sigh, Nadine said, "Okay. Thank you so much, Molly."

"I'll let you get back to your shutter eye now."

Nadine just nodded, too teary-eyed to speak.

* * * *

The woman with the long unpolished nails approached the door to suite 315. Dressed in a black blouse and white skin-tight jeans, she glanced up and down the hall to see if anyone was looking before gently rapping on the door.

The man inside, in a checked flannel shirt and gray slacks, welcomed her in. Once the door had closed, he pointed at the sofa, and she made herself comfortable there.

"Where'd you say you were going next week?" she asked.

"Atlanta to visit my daughter," he replied with a grin. "She's from my marriage to Hillary."

"You never mentioned you were ever married before."

"It was really none of your damn business. My late wife died thirty years ago—the big C, cancer, of course."

"Sorry, I didn't mean to pry."

"It's a good thing my daughter lives far away in Atlanta. I wouldn't want her to get mixed up in this mess. I admit I hate sneaking around like this. I don't know why you're asking about my wife."

He sat down on the sofa beside the woman and turned to face her. "Why are you sneaking in here at this hour anyway?"

"We need to talk," she replied.

"You worry too much."

146

"Worry? I take it you haven't heard the news yet," she snapped.

"What news? I haven't had the TV on all day. In fact, I haven't been out of this room since breakfast."

The woman's voice turned shrill. "Not the TV news. I mean the news about Lisa Howard. They took her away in an ambulance this afternoon."

"What? Who did?"

"That ex-policeman, Paco LeSoto, that's who. Apparently, he was snooping around—with that Amati guy, Jeff. The two of them found her, brought her down on the gurney, and shipped her off to the hospital lickety-split."

"But how did they find her? How would they have even known to look there?" he asked. "Damn it. You and I have keys to the rooftop stop on the elevator. The third elevator key is in an envelope inside Crisp's file drawers, and I doubt even he knows they're there. So how?"

"I don't know for sure, but I think I heard something about there being a basement door."

"Basement door," he repeated. "That door has been padlocked and covered over with full shelves for years and years. I can't believe they got to rescue her that way. And how did they get her downstairs and outside on that gurney?"

"They must have used the elevator," replied the woman. "You don't need any key from up there. I can't see them carrying a gurney down any kind of stairs, especially spiral stairs."

"We'll have to get rid of our elevator keys then," said the man. "Is there anything still up there that can lead them to either one of us?"

"I doubt it," she said. "We've always been careful to wear surgical gloves, so we wouldn't leave prints around. What I'm really worried about is—can the Howard woman connect you or me to the kidnapping in any way?"

"I don't know about you, but I made damned sure the Howard woman never saw my face. What about the gurney and saline bottles?" he asked. "Can they be traced?"

"I signed for the bottle with a scribble that no one can tie to me, and the gurney went missing from the Infirmary several times in the past couple of years. I seriously doubt they'll keep paying attention to it when it turned up again today."

"Well, the next question we should ask is—why did they go snooping in the first place? What in hell did we do wrong to spill the beans? What led them to that door in the basement, if that's the way they got up there to rescue her? Then there's what can we do to fix this."

"All very good questions, partner," she declared. "But I don't have any of the answers. That's really why I came to see you tonight."

* * * *

Paco arrived home near midnight with a slight glow on. His two glasses of beer with Frank were more than he'd had in years. He just wasn't used to it anymore. Frank had dropped him off at the Gilded Gates. He unlocked the door and headed for the sofa. The light was off in the bedroom, so he assumed Molly was asleep. His intent was to undress and slip into his pajamas in the sitting room so he wouldn't disturb her. But when he tried to retrieve his pajamas from under his pillow, Molly startled him. She jerked straight up and turned on her bedside light.

"Where have you been?" she scolded. "I've been lying here unasleep waiting for you. You know I can't drop asleep, unless I know you're lying right next to me."

"Sorry, I didn't realize how late it was," he said, standing there in his altogether in front of her.

"Have you been out galloping about town without me?"

"I needed to have a chat with Frank Mullins. We talked over a few beers."

"How many?"

"Just two."

"What did you two chitty-chat about?"

Paco did an about-face, walked barefoot to his desk in the sitting room, and returned with his deputy badge. "About this!" He held it where she could see it.

"Oh! You're coming out of retirement?"

"No, it's temporary. I just need some official status to get some answers."

"The Case of the Moaning Lisa?" she asked with a grin from cheek to cheek.

"Yeah. Hey, hon, it's cold standing here like this. If you'll stop this infernal interrogation, I'll put on my pajamas, and we'll both get some sleep."

"You can always come to bed, sweetiepie. I'll warm you up."

Chapter 19
The Victim

Tuesday, November 17th

At 9:30 Tuesday morning Paco made an official phone call to Anne Arundel Medical Center. Surprisingly, he learned that Lisa Howard was alert and responding to treatment, but remained on the critical list. She was presently awake, responsive, and in reasonably good spirits. Her nourishment remained strictly fluid as she needed therapy to learn how to swallow all over again. Because her voice had weakened and her throat was sore from constant moaning, Paco was cautioned to limit his interview to only the most essential questions, not to excite the patient, nor stay longer than twenty minutes. Without his deputy status, he would not have been allowed to interrogate her at all. In fact, Lisa was not allowed to have any other visitors yet.

As a deputy on an official mission, Paco had Frank's permission to drive the spare unmarked police cruiser. His driver's license was still good for another eleven months. Paco and Molly took the ten o'clock bus into Black Rain Corners to the police station. He picked up the keys from Frank, and the LeSotos drove up the road toward Annapolis.

They found a nearby parking space and walked to the main entrance. Molly and Roly trudged up the ramp that paralleled the steps to the Registration and Information desk. A matronly woman cleared Paco with a non-visiting hours badge and gave him the room number. She would not admit Molly, except to give her a pass to the second-floor waiting room.

Paco proceeded to room 215, where he found Lisa in a bed adjusted to a quarter sitting position. One intravenous line went to the back of her right hand, and another disappeared down her hospital gown. With an oxygen clip stuck up her nose and an oxygen sensor on the right middle finger, she managed a "Who are you?" look, when she first saw him enter the room.

"Ah, good, you're awake," he said. "Miss Howard, you don't know me, but I'm a friend of your roommate." Her response surprised him. Despite being ghostly pale and emaciated, Lisa had a strong face, high forehead, and dark-lashed hazel eyes. Her bright bottle-orange hair, shoulder-length, had only a few gray streaks peeking out.

"You know Nadine?" she asked, punctuating each word slowly.

"Yes. I'm Inspector Paco LeSoto. My wife and I are fairly new residents of Gilded Gates, and I'm also a Black Rain Corners police officer, a deputy, here to get your statement."

Just above a whisper, she replied, "Of course, Inspector. I'm anxious to cooperate. Please call me Lisa."

"Glad to. Have you any idea what happened to you that first night?"

"All I remember is someone grabbing me tightly from behind, then a hand coming over my left shoulder to clamp a white pad over my mouth. It smelled and tasted sweet and pungent. Then, all of a sudden, I blacked out. I never saw my abductor."

"Was there anything unique about the hand?" Paco asked. "Was it a man's hand? Calloused, hairy, smooth, large, or small?"

"I'd say it was definitely a man's hand from the sheer size of it, but I was too busy trying to fight him off to notice anything else. A lot of good *that* did."

"Lisa, do you remember anything about the surroundings where you spent those two weeks?"

"I think I spent the whole time in some kind of mechanical

bed. Wait, Inspector. I don't know if it was a dream or not. I was so groggy I couldn't see clearly. I think I was in a round room—stone block walls and floor and there were steps. I was left alone. I was still groggy, but I thought maybe I could escape from that horrid room somehow. So I struggled out of the bed and dragged myself down a few concrete steps, quite steep ones. But then too many disgusting cobwebs everywhere stopped me. I pushed some aside, but they were too thick. Then I heard a person, maybe a woman's voice. My hand was grabbed and I got woozy again. I tried to resist, but I couldn't. I was pulled back up to the room and shoved hard back on the bed. Then an IV was stuck in me. I don't remember anything more."

"You were held captive in that stone room. It's a turret that was built onto the back of Crisp Hall, a long time ago when it was a Victorian home. That's where we found you."

"*We?* Who actually found me?"

"Jeff Amati and myself. Maybe you remember Jeff and his wife, Maryanne."

"I do. Nice people. But what did Jeff have to do with this?"

"It's a complicated story. Here's what happened. Molly and I had just met them, and the four of us kind of hit it off. Jeff confessed to us that he'd been sleepwalking, and not just once. Often. Each time he heard a strange voice like moaning, but he had no idea where he was wandering or where the voice was coming from. Knowing about my police background, Jeff begged me to follow him while he was sleepwalking to figure out where the strange moanings were coming from."

Lisa's foggy eyes widened with shock and her gaunt body stiffened. "He actually heard me?" she whispered.

"Yes, that was you," Paco said. "I followed him for two nights without success. Then we decided to investigate together. We decided to explore the turret. We entered through the basement and climbed those same stairs you talked about. Up that very spiral staircase, thick with cobwebs and trapped insects, until we discovered you lying on a gurney at the very top. As soon as we saw you and the dire shape you were in, we knew we had to get you to a hospital. And we did just that. We called 9-1-1."

"God, I shudder to think what would have happened to me if you hadn't come along." Lisa's breath caught in her throat. "But what did they intend to do with me?"

Paco hesitated to spell it out, but Lisa broke in.

"Leave me there forever?"

"In a way. Lisa, I think you understand they meant to leave you there until you had passed. This was a kidnapping and cruelty. But much much worse, it was attempted murder. The problem now is to find the guilty parties and bring them to justice."

"Ahem. Sir?" said a nurse poking her head in. "Your twenty minutes are up."

"I'll be going now," said Paco. "Lisa, thank you for talking with me. If you think of anything else, please let me know." He pulled one of his old business cards from his wallet and left it on the nightstand. "Ask a nurse to call me for you."

"Oh good heavens. Inspector! Thank you and Jeff for saving my life!"

Paco located Molly in the waiting room and they took the elevator to the ground floor. She pushed Roly down the ramp all the way to the parked cruiser. He helped her into the car, hefted the walker into the trunk, and climbed into the driver's seat. Still not saying a word, he sat without starting the car. After five minutes of patiently waiting, she interrupted his trance-like mood.

"Paco, honey, you're not going to sit there like that all day and not tell me what you learned from Lisa Howard?"

"Sorry, dear. I'm just thinking about what she said, and it gave me some new food for thought."

"Paco, it's not polite to eat in front of someone and not offer them some, even if it is thought pudding."

Paco smiled. "You're right, hon. I'm afraid, our lady victim didn't reveal a great deal. Lisa was grabbed and held from behind and did not get a look at her assailant. What she claims to have seen was a man's left hand reaching over her left shoulder. Her words were 'a man's hand because of sheer size.' That hand held a small pad, most probably trichloromethane, otherwise known as chloroform. She said it smelled and tasted sweet and pungent just before she blacked out."

"Then all we really know is that the perforator is a man who might be left-handed?" Molly asked.

"No, there may be two perpetrators—possibly a man and a woman. Lisa described a hazy, dreamlike sequence where she tried to get away. She left the makeshift bed and managed a few steps down the stone staircase until she encountered a thick wall of cobwebs. She tried to push some aside, but that was all she could manage. At this point, she believes a woman in a surgical mask grabbed her hand and pulled her back to bed."

"Couldn't it be one of those mental dreams that Dr. Avi always talked about?" Molly asked.

"No, I don't believe it was a dream. Jeff and I found evidence of someone penetrating the dense maize of cobwebs near the top of the turret. I think the sequence has some credibility."

"So, what do we have to go on?" Molly asked.

"Most likely we have a female and a male involved, both with an extensive knowledge of Gilded Gates's floor plans. The male may be left-handed. I'm guessing at least one of the two is vested in a medical career."

"Why would a medical person do something like this?" Molly asked. "Don't they have to take the Hippocrassy oath not to harm anyone?"

"You're right, Mol, they do. But sometimes there are stronger motives out there, strong enough to overcome their sense of duty and humanity. If we can find out the driving motive here, we can use it to find the perpetrators. We're dealing with attempted murder."

"What if the motive is diabiblically simple, like greed, and all the psychos wants to do is kill people? We do have a list of missing people, don't we?"

"Two impulsive psychopaths on the same case—what would

their ultimate goal be? Attempted murder, the victim's death. But why? Who benefits from it and what are those actual benefits?"

"What could the motive possibly be?" Molly asked.

"Well, the usual motives are jealousy, hate, fear, revenge, and money. And I would bet on the last one, money."

"You mean you'd put your money on the money?" Delighted with her own quip, she chuckled, showing her small even teeth.

"Of course, and *who* gets the moolah in the end. Who benefits most from another person's death? All I can think of right now is the insurance money and who the beneficiary might be."

Molly added, "Well, Lisa's eighty-four, so inheritance money is a possibility, too. Remember what happened to Bertha after Schlemule died?"

"Yeah. The company has been forcing new singles like her out of the suites and into the dorms when they can't afford the full price of the suites anymore."

"Paco, this is bad. The guys running this place? They're causing exquishiating pain. First, the residents lose their beloved spousies. Then they're forced out of their nice suite where they're comfertabul. I've been thinking that Dr. Crisp is somehow plump down in the middle of this mystery."

"Now, Molly, don't you go making accusations when we don't have any real evidence to back 'em up."

Molly had had enough of this gloomy conversation. She looked at her watch. "Oh boy. It's late and we've missed lunch in the cafeteria."

"We could have lunch in downtown Annapolis. What'll it be, seafood or deli?"

"Neither," she said. "There's this little café halfway down the hill on Main Street that I've been wanting to try. I hear they make the cutest crepes filled with all sorts of things. Wanna try it?"

"I'm game." Turning on the ignition, Paco drove out of the hospital lot to West Street and then all the way to Church Circle, around to Duke of Gloucester Street, and turned left into the city parking garage. After unloading the walker, they slowly made their way through an alley to Main Street and a few doors up to Café Normandie restaurant. The narrow establishment was deep enough to provide a dozen tables that seated either two or three patrons. They found a table halfway to the kitchen, where the aroma of buttery French pancakes delighted their senses. Molly ordered a spinach and mushroom crepe. Paco craved the one stuffed with ham and cheddar cheese, but he'd promised himself to be good to his troublesome heart, so he chose the grilled chicken instead.

While they waited for their order, several patrons finished and left, opening the view all the way to the front window. There they recognized Gilded Gates residents Chester Parker, the bridge play-er, and Gordon H. Lowe III, the nose-in-the-air retired undertaker. The LeSotos picked up on the two men's body language—leaning toward each other, scowling. Gordon was flourishing his crepe-filled fork, jabbing it toward Chester, who clutched his knife and sawed away at his crepe with a force more appropriate to a tough slab of beef.

Fifteen minutes later, the two men passed close to their table on their way to the cashier.

"Hi, Chester, hi, Gordon," Paco tried. Gordon merely nodded and kept walking.

"Hey, LeSoto," Chester said. "Surprised to see *you* here." He halted at their table for a moment.

"We do leave home base occasionally." Paco smiled.

Chester said, "Paco, and you too, Molly, if you ever feel like a few friendly hands of bridge, you'd be most welcome to our little group. Do look me up. Love to have you."

"Thanks, Chester." Paco turned in Gordon's direction. "Drive carefully now," he sang out as if calling to a new teenage driver. At the door Gordon turned to look over his shoulder with a sneer.

"You shouldn't taunt the man so," whispered Molly. "He would make a terrible enemy."

"It felt good after the way he's snubbed us in the past," said Paco.

"This crepe is a yum and a half," said Molly, trying to change the subject.

"Mine's pretty good, too," he said. Silently, they had mutually agreed to pass up the sumptuous dessert crepes topped with rich sauces and whipped cream.

The two strolled, Roly and all, down to a bench on the City Dock at the foot of Main Street. There they watched the seagulls and mallard ducks, the sailboats, chugging motorboats, and the passersby. When they tired of it, they drove back to the Black Rain Corners police station to park the borrowed cruiser and turn over the keys to Frank Mullins. They caught the last bus back to Gilded Gates in time for the evening meal.

Paco mulled over the chance meetings in the Café Normandie. *What an unlikely pair to be lunching together, and so unhappy about it. I wonder why.*

Chapter 20
The Crime Scene
Wednesday, November 18th

At breakfast Wednesday Jeff steered Maryanne to the LeSotos' table. He was burning to know what Paco had learned from Lisa Howard. After the two families greeted one another, he sat down and waited. And waited. Paco sat with head lowered over a bowl of Raisin Bran, chasing down the raisins that darted in and out of the milk.

Jeff couldn't wait any longer. "Hey, Paco, how did your trip to the hospital work out? How's Lisa doing?"

Paco looked up and stopped stirring. "She was alert and talkative. Her nurse told me she was responding to treatment, but she's still critical. With a lot of therapy and TLC, she's going to recover nicely."

"TLC? What's that?"

"Now Jeff," Maryanne sniffed, "you know. Tender loving care."

"Oh, yeah," said Jeff, with a sheepish look. "So, Paco. What did Lisa actually have to tell you?"

"Not very much. She was attacked from behind and chloroformed into submission, most probably by a male. There may have been a female involved, too, but she wasn't sure. Molly and I concluded that one of the perpetrators had medical experience. Not only that, we think they both had solid knowledge of Gilded

Gates's physical layout. Otherwise, how could they have known about the turret and how to reach it? That's about it, my friend."

With a chunk of waffle tucked into one cheek, Molly piped up, "I think Dr. Crisp is behind all this nasty inhuman business. But we can't prove that yet."

Paco's black eyebrows merged in a deep frown and his mustache twitched. "Careful, Molly. I told you before—you can't go around accusing people without proof. You'll get in a heap of trouble."

"So, what's your next step, Paco?" asked Jeff. "Are you gonna grill Dr. Crisp? I'd love to be there when you do."

"First thing I'm going to do, Jeff, is go over the crime scene and see what turns up there. If you'd like to join me for that much, you may, but I can't let you in on any of my interviews. You see, I'm a deputized police officer now, and I have rules to follow." He showed Jeff his badge.

"Gee! Wow! I didn't know you were still a cop. I thought you were retired."

"I am. I'm official for this case only because I'm already embedded in the facility."

Jeff scratched his high bald forehead. "That sounds like police jargon, but I get it."

The two men finished eating breakfast first and left the women to compare thoughts on the latest shocking news over a second cup of coffee.

"When do you want to return to the scene?" asked Jeff.

"In half an hour, 8:30," said Paco. "We'll have to go in the same way we did the first time. Through that hidden door behind the tapestry in the parlor. But only if nobody else is around."

"That means old clothes again, and all those cobwebs in my face."

"You got that right. You don't have to come if you don't want to, Jeff."

"Are you kidding? I wouldn't miss it. What else is there to do around here? At least I'm doing something productive this way. I'll meet you there."

Thirty minutes later, dressed in old jeans and shirts, the men met in the parlor. It was quiet and empty. They could hear jumbled shrill voices and activity in the recreation room. Paco heaved a sigh of relief, but knew time was of the essence. Residents could start floating in at any moment. He carried a large nylon shopping bag filled with evidence bags, two pairs of surgical gloves, and other crime-scene essentials, plus a bamboo cane.

"What's the cane for?" asked Jeff.

"I can swat cobwebs a lot better with a lightweight cane than I can with a heavy pair of bolt cutters."

"By the way, did you ever return those bolt cutters to the hardware store?"

"Yup. Sunday morning on my way to the police station. Are you ready to get started?"

Paco brought along the same two Rotary and Elks Club membership cards. Now that he knew exactly where the two lift locks were, he made short work of their release. They descended into the basement of Comfort Hall and crossed the basement of Fellowship Hall, and into the basement of Crisp Hall. Under the kitchen, they found the two shelving units, still pulled away from the wall, and the turret access door still wide open. Paco reached into his shopping bag, retrieved the two penlights, and handed one to Jeff as they stepped through the turret entrance. They followed the same path along the outside rim of the spiraling staircase, up the roughly eighty steps to the top, encountering far less cobweb resistance than their first time through.

Inside the room at the top of the turret, they pulled on their surgical gloves. Paco quickly scanned the breezy room. The first thing he bagged was the saline bottle, noting the clearly written dates and the undefinable scribbled signature on its label. *Now that's intentional,* he thought. *Clear and scribbled writing together. Apparently someone didn't want to be known.*

Next, he bagged the IV apparatus, including the needle and bandage. From the shopping bag he pulled out a fingerprint kit and began to dust the few items left in the room. Pressing his lips together in disgust, he was only able to pick up one smeared, probably useless, print. He figured the perpetrators had worn gloves at all times, and the smeared print belonged either to the victim or to someone unrelated to this case. The two men began a meticulous search of the entire space. All it turned up was a torn envelope for an alcohol wipe found under where the gurney originally sat. Paco dusted that as well, but to no avail. He packed everything into the shopping bag, and the two men left. After shutting the double doors behind them, they took the roof-capable elevator to reach the ground floor.

Jeff asked Paco, "What are you going to do now?"

"First, I'm going to shower and change clothes, give myself a little more credibility. I'm beginning to stink like the musty spiral steps. Then I'm going to have a little talk with Katta about gurneys and saline bottles."

"Who's Katta?"

"Kathrine Brounell. She's an RN in charge of the Infirmary and dispensary here."

As they exited the elevator, Jeff murmured, "Good luck, man."

An hour later, Inspector Paco looked spiffy in his neatly pressed khakis, tweed sport jacket, beige shirt, and striped brown and yellow tie. He started toward Comfort Hall and, once there, he entered the rooms set aside for the more needy and ailing residents. In the common hallway between those rooms, he encountered Sonny Duster in white fatigues, one of two orderlies who cared for the more personal needs of those residents. Each orderly worked twelve-hour shifts.

Paco flipped open his police credentials, showing Sonny his deputy badge and official identification. "Is Katta in her office? I'd like a word with her."

"She's indisposed at the moment," said Sonny. "Can I help you?"

Paco sized Sonny up. Mid-thirties. His buzz-cut hair might make him a recent veteran, possibly an ex-military corpsman. He had chiseled features, sunken dark eyes, and clean-shaven cheeks.

"Thank you, no," said Paco. "It's imperative that I speak with the nurse in charge of the Infirmary. When will she be available?"

"Maybe five or ten minutes. She's just in the head, pal."

"Then I'll wait for her in the Infirmary."

"I don't know about that," rebuked Sonny. "Nobody's supposed to be in there alone. Katta will have my hide if I let you in."

"Then I'll wait here, if that's okay with you?"

"Yeah, sure. Oh, hell, here she comes now."

Paco saw a starched white nurse's uniform, from crescent cap to sensible shoes, walking toward him. As she came closer, he saw a tall woman of sturdy stature, with a wide stern face and gray-blue eyes.

"How can I help you?" she asked with a practiced, friendly tone.

"I wonder if I might have a few words with you?"

"Are you in pain? What are your symptoms?"

"None, This is not about me or my health, Miss Brounell."

"Then what is it about?"

"Is there some place we can talk privately?"

She started to say "I'm very busy…" until she saw that he was presenting his police credentials to her. "Follow me." Her tone had shifted out of officious high gear into a more guarded one.

Paco followed her into the Infirmary behind a drawn curtain hung from the ceiling. She worked her way around a large metal desk and eased into her swivel chair. Paco sat down in the patient's chair on the opposite side of the desk.

"Now, my good man, what's all this nonsense about?" By using "good" and "nonsense" in the same sentence, she hoped to throw him off his agenda.

"It's essentially about bookkeeping, Miss Brounell. Keeping track of certain items that should be under the direct control of this dispensary—where the medications and other drugs like vaccines are kept."

Her gray-blue eyes took on a steely cast. "Inspector, do you have the utter gall to accuse me of falsifying records?"

"No, no, no, nothing like that," said Paco. He reached into his nylon shopping tote and pulled out the separately bagged half-emptied saline bottle. "Miss Brounell, I have no intention of accusing you of anything. Perhaps it was my wrong choice of words. Please forgive me." Paco skillfully used his humble approach to disarm his subject and elicit the truth.

"Then what?"

"Do you keep an inventory of saline bottles?" He held up the bottle with the label facing her.

"Of course. How else would I know when to order more? I put a little check mark on each bottle up in the left corner of the label and enter the total quantity in the inventory record book—even though saline is not a controlled substance."

"Do you track the dispensed saline as well?"

"As a matter of fact, I do track everything that we actually dispense. It's the responsible thing to do. What are you asking, Inspector?"

"The bottle I'm showing you here was used during the commission of a serious crime. I would like to know who dispensed it. Who hooked it up to the victim patient? And do you recognize the initials on this label?"

"I have no idea who dispensed it. I recognize that scribble, but it's illegible. I just assumed it was one of the nurses or Ms. Irma or Dr. Crisp himself. I've seen it in my book a number of times, but I don't know who it belongs to. I can't decipher it. Every cabinet here, including that one, is kept locked at all times. However, one key fits all of them and only the doctor, Ms. Irma, and the three nurses, including myself, have keys."

"May I see that record book?" asked Paco.

"Of course, it's right here."

Katta spun her swivel chair around to the bookcase behind her. Her fingers walked three or four book spines before she selected the one she wanted. She flipped through the pages to the November entries and shoved the open book across the desk, close enough for Paco to read those entries. There they were, the same scribble recurring almost daily in the first two weeks of November.

"With all those saline bottles going out, weren't you at least curious who the patient might be?" he asked.

Katta placed both palms flat on the desk and leaned forward. "Listen here, Inspector. There are six rooms out there and four beds to a room in the Special Needs section alone. That's up to twenty-four patients demanding individual attention around the clock. Do you think I've got the time to question the staff every time an anomaly or hiccup turns up in one of my eight ledgers? Our orderlies handle the patients' basic needs, and personal ones, too. Either Dr. Crisp or Miss Irma leaves the medical orders on the bed charts. Penny Summers and Tori Nickelson, the other nurses, and I make the rounds and carry out their orders, according to each patient's bed chart. Daily saline requirements for patients receiving hydration, antibiotics, other medications, and even nutrition, meaning special menus, are going on right now out there, so it's pretty difficult to see any wrongdoing in all that."

Paco shifted to a more soothing tone. "Okay. So today I'm not going to find out who the scribbler is. Let's talk about gurneys now."

"What about the gurneys?" she asked, her tone suspicious.

"You found a gurney in the hall, unattended, last Sunday when Lisa Howard was taken to the hospital, did you not?"

"That's true," Katta said, shifting her ample bottom uneasily in her chair.

"Prior to that, weren't you missing a gurney like that one?"

"Yes. We only have two gurneys, so we spent a lot of time looking for it. It was missing for several weeks over a year ago and then it turned up again. It mysteriously disappeared and reappeared a few months ago, too. We're always so glad when it's returned. But then, for some odd reason, it got misplaced or something—again a few weeks ago."

"Don't you want to know where it was for the past two weeks?"

"Of course I do."

Paco took his time answering. His crow-black eyes bore into hers. "Lisa Howard was kidnapped, strapped to that gurney, and left to die."

Katta's body jerked upright in her chair. "Oh my God," she said.

"Kidnapped? Left to die? How could that be? Nothing like that has ever happened before in Gilded Gates."

Paco stood. "Thank you for your time, Miss Brounell. You've been very helpful." He left Katta in a stunned condition, figuring there was nothing more he could learn from her. It also occurred to him that she didn't ask him any of the normal questions on hearing the news about Lisa, like where did it happen, where is she now, and is she recovering?

As he walked briskly from the Infirmary, he sorted out his thoughts. *I'd better get all my ducks in a row before confronting the two Crisps. I need a helluva lot of information from their files—but I don't have a warrant. I need to find out which judge would be most amenable to signing for one.*

Chapter 21
Confrontation

Immediately after talking with Katta, Paco walked down the corridor to Crisp Hall and approached the doctor's office. The door was open as usual. He saw Phelix Crisp at his desk, head down, engaged in a flurry of continuous writing. Paco stood in the doorway, hesitant to disturb the doctor's concentration. A moment or two later, Phelix looked up for an inspirational thought and saw Paco, patiently awaiting just the right moment to enter.

Looking quite formal and official, the doctor straightened up in his charcoal-gray pin-striped suit and white shirt. "You again? Haven't you caused enough trouble around here? What gave you the right to invade our private property and go where no one has gone in thirty years? You're a resident of Gilded Gates—nothing more! What do you want from me?"

Paco stepped inside and strode to the front of the cluttered desk. Aware that he was not invited to sit, he deliberately remained standing to maintain his edge.

"Whoa, my good doctor. Number one, we saved a human life last Sunday. Number two, we also uncovered criminal activity in your facility. Number three, you're wrong. I am not just a resident. I also have official business here now." He held out his police credentials, but Phelix refused to look at them.

With a storm-clouded face, he ranted. "Stop your insolence

this instant! You have no official status with me. I can have you and your wife evicted—your butts thrown out of here on my word."

Paco banged his credentials down on the desk; the badge made a clunking sound. "I'm here on official police business. I have been charged with investigating the criminal wrongdoings committed at this facility."

Now Phelix had to pay attention. He leaned over and studied Paco's credentials "What the hell are you talking about, LeSoto? The Howard woman was undoubtedly trying to starve herself to death. It's quite common in the elderly, especially when they're lonely or facing terminal illness. She's the only criminal here."

Not at all intimidated, Paco chose to seat himself in the armchair for visitors in front of the desk. He never raised his voice. "Nice try, Doc, but there's a good deal of evidence to the contrary. We know that Lisa Howard was abducted in the hallway of Comfort Hall, subdued with chloroform, restrained on a gurney, and taken to the room at the top of the stone turret. She was kept sedated there against her will for three weeks without food or water. Three things kept her alive. One, she was in excellent health to start with. Two, she was kept hydrated by an intravenous saline solution. And three, she demonstrated the strongest will to live. As soon as the lab report comes back on the IV apparatus, we'll even know what was used to keep her sedated."

Phelix's bass voice countered, "How do you know she didn't conspire with another resident to do this terrible thing?"

"Get real, Doc. Who would do such a thing?" said Paco. "That person would need access to your medical supplies and equipment and know how to use them. They would also need a solid knowledge of the out-of-bounds spaces at your facility—and the know-how to access those spaces."

The doctor's stiff posture and voice remained tense. As he spoke, his Adam's apple bounced up and down against the knot in his silver and black tie. "Are you suspecting me or some member of my staff?"

"Yes, but I'm not accusing anyone just yet," replied Paco. "Every staff member at Gilded Gates had the means to commit this cold-blooded crime. Next, I have to consider opportunity—who had access to the turret. There are five ways to get to it. One, through the hidden basement door, the way Jeff Amati and I did. We found it locked and the passage loaded with cobwebs. We had to break a very old padlock to even reach the spiral staircase. Two and three, a pair of hidden doors from inside your own apartment, which gives you and your wife easy access from either the kitchen or one of the bedrooms. Four, a special elevator, the only one that can reach the roof, if someone has the right key. Five, a trapdoor leading to the fire stairs next to that elevator. However, there was enough roofing tar splashed up its sides to indicate the trapdoor hadn't been used since the last roof repair. In order to move a gurney to the turret, someone would need the key to the roof elevator. So, who has the key to that elevator that reaches the roof, Doc?"

"There are two elevator keys, both of which should be in a brown envelope in my file cabinet."

"Let's have a look, Doc."

Phelix stood and took a few steps to one of the steel four-drawer filing cabinets. Pulling out the top drawer, he thumbed his way to a particular folder, extracted the brown envelope, and carried it back to his desk, where he dumped the contents out. Only one dull-gray key fell out. He shook the envelope—nothing.

Paco noted that Phelix looked genuinely surprised. "Only one key, Doc? How can you account for that?"

"I don't know."

"Who has access to your file cabinets?" asked Paco. "Don't you keep them locked?"

"No I don't, and I don't even lock my office door because the medical files are kept in the Infirmary's dispensary. Only the residents' personal files are kept in here."

"Don't you think the residents' personal data is entitled to some kind of privacy?" asked Paco.

Phelix was no dummy. He realized his aggressive, defensive behavior could be interpreted as guilt. In a few seconds, he chose to turn compliant and cooperative. "I suppose so, when you put it like that. I guess I've been sort of lax of late on the clerical side. I'm going to make some changes in the future."

"Good idea, Doc," said Paco. "In order to protect the security of the crime scene, I will need that elevator key and the keys to your apartment's turret access doors."

"Here," Phelix said, as he handed over the elevator key. "I have the apartment's access keys on hooks next to those doors. I'll bring them to you later."

"Thank you," said Paco. He tucked the elevator key into a small leather case and stowed it in his inside jacket pocket.

"Now, I'm still working on the motive. Because we're dealing with a likeable old lady of eighty-four, I think we can eliminate hate, envy, jealousy, fear, and revenge. That leaves money. Who gains or benefits from the death of Lisa Howard? Doc, this is where you can cooperate and help me a great deal."

Behind Phelix's glasses, the creases emanating from the outer corners of his eyes seemed to deepen with anxiety.

"I want to help you all I can and prove to you that I'm innocent."

"There are four ways someone can benefit from the death of another," Paco began. "One, there's inheritance, only Lisa apparently has no next of kin. Possibly one distant niece. Two, insurance, and there we must find out who the legal beneficiaries are. Three, steal from the initial entrance payment held in reserve for the unpredictable resident's extended lifetime rents at the facility. And four, there's displacement. That's when the space the person occupies is worth more when someone more affluent occupies that space."

"I don't understand how the fourth benefit works," said Phelix.

"Don't you? It's basic accounting at Gilded Gates. I understand you have a certain number of patients here who have outlived their resources and are on state Medicaid support, a sum considerably less than the suite could produce if it were paid for by a still-affluent resident. I've witnessed cases where state-supported residents were forced out of their comfortable suites and moved into the dormitory to make room for new residents who could afford to pay the hefty full price. I've seen the letters sent to those state-supported residents. Losing those residents altogether would be one horrible step further—a criminal step, to be sure."

"That's one hell of an ugly accusation, LeSoto."

Paco suppressed his disgust and disbelief. "Doc, it's not an accusation. It's all theoretical—I'm just posturing aloud. However, I do suggest that you educate yourself on the harsh accounting procedures here because they affect many residents. One thing that would help me right now is a small peek at Lisa Howard's personal file. It might be vindicating."

"Her file is confidential," said Phelix. "In good conscience I can't let you peek at it."

"I can phone for her permission, or I can get a warrant from a judge."

"Sorry, Inspector. No."

"All I want to know at this time is who Lisa's terminal insurance beneficiary is," insisted Paco. "There's no harm in *you* taking a look, is there?"

"I suppose not," admitted Phelix, as he stood and went back to the file cabinet. He flipped through a few folders in the second drawer and returned to his desk with the Lisa Howard personal file. Thumbing through several pages, he found the one he was looking for. He studied it for a moment, then looked straight at Paco. "I don't believe what I'm seeing."

"What do you mean?"

"Gilded Gates is her beneficiary," replied Phelix. "I don't understand that either."

"Really?" asked Paco. "In that case, would you do me another favor, Doc? I'd like you to check the same information on two other residents."

"Who might they be?" asked Phelix.

"Well, to start with, Mindy Norton and Dora Ferarri," replied Paco, after consulting his little spiral notebook.

Phelix returned Lisa's file to the cabinet and came back to his desk with the Norton and Ferarri files. After flipping through the pages in the folders, he cleared his throat and hesitantly admitted, "In both cases the beneficiary was Gilded Gates."

"Is that so, Doc? Of course, you realize this makes you my number one suspect."

Tiny beads of sweat dotted Phelix's forehead. His eyes blazed as he pounded the desk with his fist. "Now, wait just a minute, Inspector. I don't own even one lousy share in Gilded Gates. True, I'm Chief Operating Officer and Chief Medical Officer, but I'm a salaried employee. I personally do not benefit in any way when Gilded Gates receives a legacy. I don't get scratch from it."

"Who is your employer then?" asked Paco.

"My direct-deposit paychecks and end-of-year tax documents are issued by the First Mechanics Bank in Annapolis. I was originally hired by a firm called Angular Properties Management Associates. I still deal with them monthly."

"I see," said Paco, as he wrote this information down in his notebook. And what happens to any profits Gilded Gates might earn?"

"After payroll and expenses, I write a check to an Angular Properties account at the same bank around the fifteenth of every month." He pulled open a drawer and took out a canceled check to show Paco.

"Uh-huh. Do you think I could borrow that canceled check for a little while?"

"I suppose so," Phelix muttered. "I've already balanced our checkbooks for the month."

"Thank you," said Paco, pocketing the check. "Now, I see the magnifying glass on your desk. Would you please take a good look at the beneficiary lines to see if there are any erasures, overwriting, or any other evidence of data-altering?"

Phelix took several minutes to peer at each document. "No overwriting that I can tell," he said. "But that's understandable, as most residents leave that line blank anyway when filling out our applications, even those with actual beneficiaries."

"I don't understand," said Paco. "Why would any resident leave that line blank? Were they instructed to? Seems to me, a blank line right in the middle of a legal contract would be an excellent opportunity for someone to insert an unauthorized beneficiary. And let me ask you this. Is there a variation in ink between the beneficiaries' line and the rest of the application?"

"Damn it, there seems to be an ever-so-slight ink variation in each one," said Phelix. "But I'm no expert at this."

"We'll leave that to the forensics people," said Paco. "It's obvious to me there's someone on the premises acting criminally on behalf of the mother company. Have you ever noticed any member of your staff spending 'no-business-to-be-here' time in your office?"

"I can't say that I have," he replied.

"Well, thank you for your cooperation, Doc," said Paco as he stood to leave.

Dr. Crisp remained at his desk, his stomach knotting up. He removed the white handkerchief square from his suit jacket pocket and mopped his sweaty brow.

Paco stepped across the entrance hall and peeked into a cubical belonging to the physician's assistant to see if Irma was there. He found her standing next to a corner clothes tree, about to don a white cardigan sweater over a flowered blouse and white slacks.

"Oh hi," she said. "I didn't realize anyone had come in. "Please have a seat while I get into this sweater. It gets so darned chilly in here whenever the main entrance door is opened."

Paco waited for her to finish and sit down at her desk opposite him.

"I see you have recovered nicely from your heart episode, Paco," said Irma. "That reminds me, I want to send Tori over to give you and Molly your flu shots this afternoon. Now, what can I do to help you? Is there something that's bothering you?"

"I'm just fine, Ms. Irma. The defibrillator is doing its job. But that's not why I'm here." Paco flipped open his police credentials for her to see. "I'm here on official police business today."

"Police business?" she repeated. "I don't understand. I thought you were retired."

"I was retired, but I've been deputized to investigate the Lisa Howard case of kidnapping and attempted murder. Since Jeff Amati and myself are the ones who discovered her, the local police thought it appropriate that I head up the investigation."

Paco reached into his little blue tote bag, retrieved the saline bottle, and set it on the desk with the label facing her. "Ms. Irma, as supervisor of nursing here, do you recognize the scribbled initials on this label? Can you tell me who they belong to?" He watched her frowning face carefully for any indication of surprise.

"I recognize the scribble all right," she replied. "I've seen it many times, but I couldn't tell you who it belongs to."

"As the supervisor of the three nurses who work here, shouldn't you be able to recognize their initials? What if one of them were stealing? How would you know who to discipline?"

"I suppose you're right," she said, her voice subdued. "I'll start an investigation myself. I'll find out."

"While you're at it, please let me know if any of them have lost or misplaced their keys to the dispensary cabinets," said Paco, as he rose to leave. "Oh, by the way, you wouldn't happen to have a key that permits the elevator to go to roof level, would you?"

"No," said Irma, "but my husband should have one." With both hands trembling, she buttoned up all eight buttons on her sweater to delay the chill creeping down her spine.

Chapter 22
"Shots" Fired
The Same Day

Paco couldn't wait to get out of his investigator-mode clothes. He tossed his sport jacket and tie onto a straight-backed chair. Undoing the top button of his Oxford shirt, he climbed into his La-Z-Boy recliner to digest not only his recent lunch, but all the facts he'd picked up that morning. He soon dozed off as his whole body relaxed and his chin dropped to allow a seesaw, snore-wheeze. Molly entered the suite and stood for almost a minute in front of him with her hands on her hips. She had done her own bit of sleuthing right after lunch, and now she was bursting to tell her hubby and exchange notes. But he was so deep into sleep that she decided she might as well join him. She plopped down on the plush sofa opposite him, rolled onto her side, and fell asleep in concert with Paco.

Forty-five minutes later a persistent knock on the door roused them both. Jolted out of a pleasant dream, an irritated Paco struggled to his feet and answered the door. He opened it to Nurse Tori Nickelson, standing there in her uniform: a pristine white tunic top and slacks, and clutching a medical kit in one hand.

"Time for your flu shots, you two," she announced in a sing-song voice as if speaking to small children. Without waiting for an invitation, she pushed her way into the sitting room. "I believe Ms.

Irma informed you that I was coming to inoculate the both of you this afternoon."

"Yes she did," Paco acknowledged. He and Molly sat down at the kitchen table.

Tori unzipped the gray kit. Open, it revealed two tiers of supplies: one small bottle, a pair of syringes, three needles, and several alcohol wipes. Molly pulled off her cable-knit cardigan and rolled the short sleeve of her blue cotton dress up over her shoulder. Paco removed his long-sleeved Oxford shirt while Tori prepared the syringes. As she administered the shots, she told the couple there might be some uncomfortable side effects, including soreness on the site for a day or two. She swiped the areas with alcohol pads, injected them both, and covered the sites with little round bandages, then zipped up her medical kit and left the suite.

Paco and Molly stayed seated at the table opposite one another.

"Now maybe you can tell me what you found out this morning," said Molly.

"Right after breakfast, at 8:30, Jeff and I went over the crime scene. We found nothing left behind but the IV apparatus and the wrapper from an alcohol swiping pad. I have them all in evidence bags in my tote. I need to get them over to Frank Mullins so he can deliver them to the forensics lab up in Baltimore. I don't think they'll help with identifying anybody in particular, but hopefully, the lab can come up with the drug used to sedate the poor girl. From the lack of prints, I assume the perps wore gloves the whole time."

"I wanted to see the crime scene myself, but I don't think I could have climbered those icky steps all the way to the top," said Molly, just as her stomach rumbled with gas. "I don't feel so good. My mouth is burning dry. I better take some of that pink Pepto Dismal."

Molly pushed herself to her feet, toddled to and from the bathroom and said, "I hope that does it." She sat down across from Paco again and asked, "What did you do next?"

"I went to see Nurse Katta Brounell in the Infirmary. She

couldn't identify the scribbled initials on the saline bottle, but admitted she'd seen it often enough in her inventory logs. What makes this tough is, five people have access to the saline cabinet: the doctor, Ms. Irma, and the three nurses. And you know what's really strange, Mol? Katta never reported the missing gurney. I left the woman feeling guilty about not investigating who Scribbles was. Oh hell! Now my stomach is rumbling too, and my mouth is dry. My sight's a little fuzzy, too."

"Wait, I'll get you some of the Dismal stuff," said Molly as she again raised herself out of the chair, pushed Roly to the bathroom medicine cabinet, and returned with the bottle. Her hand trembled as she poured the thirty-milliliter dose into the tiny plastic cup. He swallowed the thick liquid with some difficulty. "Where did you go next?"

"I went to confront Dr. Crisp. He was at his desk. When I started my interview, he got belligerent and tried to bully me to stop. He insisted that Lisa must have orchestrated her own suicide with the aid of another resident. Can you believe the *chutzpah* of the man concocting that story out of nothing? When I slammed my credentials down on the desk, he finally realized his tactic wasn't working and calmed down. I had to convince him to turn over the keys I need. He seemed surprised to find only one elevator key in the file cabinet. He didn't know who had the other one...." Paco intended to tell Molly every detail, but his voice trailed off. "Is it hot in here, Mol? I need some water."

"Me too," she mumbled.

Paco pushed his captain's chair back and wobbled to his feet. At the fridge he managed to grab the water pitcher and set it heavily down on the table. He brought out two plastic glasses and tried to lift the pitcher to pour, but his hand was shaking so violently that the water splashed onto the table instead. His entire body shuddered as he set the pitcher down with a thud, but knocked it over.

"Hey!" he yelled. Teetering, trying to grab onto the table, he crumpled to the floor.

Molly shrieked, "Sweetiekins!" Struggling to get up, she gasped for breath and collapsed, falling forward, face flat on the table.

* * * *

Twenty minutes later, Dr. Phelix Crisp stood outside the LeSotos' suite with the apartment access keys to the turret stairs that Paco had requested earlier. His knock went unanswered. He knocked again, this time harder and louder. *Maybe they're napping,* he thought. But the silence made him uneasy. He hadn't seen them in the recreation room and they weren't signed out to go into town. He decided to use his master key. He unlocked the door and found both Paco and Molly in the kitchen, unconscious. He went to their phone first and called the Infirmary for help. Then he checked to see if the two were even alive. They were both breathing rapidly. He pulled his stethoscope out of a pocket in his white coat. Listening to one heart, then the other, he found both beating a good deal faster than normal. Their foreheads were feverishly hot to the touch. Squinting as he studied the two of them, he saw no signs on either one of a physical struggle, and wondered, *Could they have been poisoned?*

Just then Nurse Penny Summers appeared in the doorway. "How can I help, Doctor?"

"Call a pair of ambulances, stat," shouted Phelix. "They both need the hospital in a hurry. It's possible they've been poisoned. They'll need their stomachs pumped or, in any case, the help of a gastroenterologist. And in Paco's case, also a cardiologist. Whatever it is, they'll need an antidote quickly. Too much time has passed already."

As soon as Penny finished the call, she hurried to the Infirmary for its two gurneys and got a hold of Katta to manipulate the second one. Phelix helped the women load both of the unconscious figures onto the gurneys. The two nurses pushed them into adjacent elevators and, on the first floor, pushed them down the corridor to the entrance hall to await the ambulances. As soon as the first one arrived, Dr. Crisp briefed the EMTs and they quickly transported Paco first because of his heart condition. Five minutes later the second ambulance transported Molly to the same hospital.

The two ambulances dropped their patients at the Emergency Room of Anne Arundel Medical Center in Annapolis. Blood samples and saliva swabs, taken during the ride, were rushed to the lab for analyses. A trauma team was put to work immediately. Apparent symptoms? Extreme trauma to the parasympathetic nervous system, which led the doctors to believe they were dealing with atropine or dihyoscyamine. Fresh needle marks in the upper arms, evidenced by the little round bandages, told the doctors the drug was injected, rather than administered orally. The drug physostigmine was injected as an antidote in both cases as a precaution. Within the hour, a toxicology report from the lab confirmed the diagnoses and the proper antidote use. Only time would tell the effectiveness of both.

Twenty-four hours later, Paco and Molly were awake and had passed the crisis points in their poisonings. No longer hooked up to IVs, they were confined to bed rest in a semiprivate room for forty-eight hours for hospital observation. Nurses checked their vitals every few hours. Paco, alert but intensely fatigued, lay in his bed with a medley of questions swirling around in his brain.

Around three o'clock, a young doctor in green scrubs came into their room. "Hello, Mr. and Mrs. LeSoto, I'm Dr. Scanlin, your hospital physician." He went immediately to their charts at the end of the bed and studied them. "How are you both feeling?"

Molly was dozing. Paco pulled himself up to a half-sitting position. "Pretty good, considering what we've been through. But Doctor, maybe you can answer a question for me. I'm totally in the dark. Do you know who called 9-1-1 and arranged for ambulances to bring us here?"

The doctor again picked up the patients' charts and scanned them. He shook his head. "There's nothing here. Normally it's not part of the chart data. Sorry about that."

"Thanks anyway."

Dr. Scanlin nodded. "Glad to see you're both recovering." He left the room.

* * * *

On Thursday, the second day of Paco and Molly's hospital confinement, they had surprise visitors. Nadine Chasdane, dressed in a paisley pantsuit, rolled Lisa Howard into their room in a hospital wheelchair. Lisa wore an oxygen nose clip and finger oxygen sensor. A small green oxygen tank rode in a side pocket to the wheelchair. The smiling glad-to-be-alive Lisa was still in hospital garb, a blue cotton gown and robe. She was a fraction of her former weight—gaunt, thin, jaundiced, and soft-spoken. Her bright orange hair with its few gray streaks was nicely brushed.

"What a delicious surprise," said Molly. "We were so worried about you."

"I'm just repaying your husband's visit to me a few days ago. They're taking good care of me here, and I'm making great progress. Everyone is so nice."

"It's a relief to hear that," said Paco. "They've been wonderful to us, too."

"All I know is that I owe the rest of my life to you," said Lisa. She blew a hand and mouth kiss in his direction. "You are my good friend forever."

"So, what happened to you guys, anyway?" asked Nadine. "All kinds of rumors are flying around the facility, and no one knows the real truth."

"We were poisoned," said Molly. "They gave us an anecdohicky here in the hospital to countertop the poison."

"It seems there was more than just the vaccine in our flu shots," explained Paco.

"That's terrible," said Nadine. "Who administered those shots, Paco? And why would anyone want to harm *you?*"

"Yeah, why would anyone want to harm *you guys?*" echoed Lisa.

"My Paco is also an official police detective investigating your case, Lisa," said Molly. "Maybe, he's getting too close to solving your case, and the purplegator wants to rub us out."

"So, how is your investigation going?" asked Nadine.

"I really can't comment on an ongoing investigation," replied Paco.

"If it's not too much of a secret, when are they going to let you guys come home?" asked Nadine.

"I don't see why we can't bail out of here some time tomorrow morning," replied Paco. "That is, if the doctors don't find some excuse to keep us here another day or so."

"You both look great to me," said Nadine.

"Before I forget, Lisa, there's one question I wanted to ask you. How sure are you that there was a man *and* a woman involved in your kidnapping?"

"The more I think about it, *very* sure."

"Thank you."

"I can't wait to get out of here," said Molly, "They've got me on all this nasty diet food. I'll never eat broccoli and Jell-O again. And, if I have a problem with my figure, it's none of their crummy business. Besides, Paco says there's just more of me to love." She blushed and giggled.

* * * *

Dr. Crisp was dictating a medical report on one of his resident patients when he heard a knock on his door. He kept it closed only when he used the Dictaphone. He turned off the machine. "Yes, come on in."

His wife stood on the threshold. "Sorry to disturb your dictating, dear." In a severe beige pants outfit covered by a white examining coat, Irma walked to the desk and sat down heavily in the walnut armchair across from him. "I have a problem, Phelix. Well, more than one, in a way. I'm still reeling from the news about the LeSotos. Any idea how they're doing?"

Phelix hesitated. "No. I suppose I should be checking with the hospital. So, what's up, Irma?"

His wife murmured, "Phelix, I know I sound like a real shithead saying it, but a crisis like this is bad for business." Then, squaring her shoulders, she said, "My immediate problem is we're short one nurse. Tori Nickelson hasn't shown up for work the second day in a row and she left early on Tuesday. I sent her to give the flu shots to the LeSotos, but no one has seen her since. I tried calling her at

180

home, but no one answers the phone. It doesn't even go to voice mail. Something bad is going on here."

"Oh shit, that's all we need right now. Do you suppose she's responsible for poisoning the two LeSotos? And now she's on the run from the law?"

"It certainly looks that way," said Irma. "Why else would she go into hiding?"

"Check her personnel file in that cabinet over there and see if you have all the correct contact information," suggested Phelix. He waited while Irma opened the cabinet drawer and flipped through Tori's folder.

"Yeah, it's the same phone number and address that I have on her," said Irma.

"Then call the agency and have them send us a temporary nurse until we get this thing figured out."

"I will," Irma said. Then, in a rare show of genuine emotion, she shook her head. "And I trusted Tori."

Chapter 23
Homecoming
Friday, November 20th

In the little town of Black Rain Corners, secrets were almost impossible to keep. Late Wednesday afternoon, Sergeant Frank Mullins had called Paco to discuss their ongoing case, the suspicious deaths at Gilded Gates. He left messages, but Paco never called back. *Not like him*, Frank decided. He called the retirement home office and learned the bad news: that the LeSotos were both in the hospital.

* * * *

On Friday morning, a number of medical precautions and prescriptions accompanied the LeSotos' discharge from the hospital. They were feeling surprisingly chipper, fully recovered from the poisoning. Sergeant Frank, anxious for details about their medical crisis, finally reached Paco and volunteered to drive them back to Gilded Gates. Paco sat up front to tell his "boss" all he could. Frank absorbed every detail. When the debriefing drew to a close and silence became uncomfortable, they heard from Molly in the back seat.

"We're headed back to Gilded Gates, but at least it's not the Pearly Gates," she jested. "Thank God for that."

"You bet. We were truly fortunate to have dodged death," agreed Paco in a vague voice.

Frank drove through the gold gates, up to the entrance, and turned off the ignition. He sat still, waiting. Instinctively, he felt that Paco had more to say and that it would be something important for him to hear.

He was right. Paco made no attempt to open the police car door to get out. Instead, he unbuckled his seatbelt and twisted his body to the left so he could face his wife in the back seat. "I don't want to scare you, Mol, but the fact that someone tried to kill us means they might try again. Hopefully, our perpetrators left some additional clues in their failed attempt."

Exactly what Frank expected to hear—and what had crossed his own mind.

Molly shuddered at the thought. "What do you intend to do first now that we're back? Remember, sweetiekins, we're not s'posed to overdo ourselves for the next bunch of days."

"I plan to have a nice little talk with each of the nurses. Maybe I should start with Tori Nickelson. She administered our shots." Paco paused. "What's the matter? You look like you just remembered something."

"I did," said Molly. "I wanted to tell you about it, but you were still sleeping, shnorting away just before Tori came with our shots. I was in the Infirmary, shambling through the special needs rooms, looking at the clipboards at the foot of each bed. I wanted to see the salty bottle records with the initials. I found goodly readable initials for each nurse and Ms. Irma. But not the scribbly one."

"Ah. Well, then, we know for sure that one of the four has something to hide, and I plan to find out which one." Paco opened the door and half-slid out. "Frank, thanks for the ride."

Frank nodded. "Glad I could do it. And thank *you* for the update." He climbed out, opened the door for Molly, and handed her the two canes on the back seat that the hospital had lent her. "Be careful you two."

Paco and Molly watched him drive around the circle and head down the driveway through the gates. As they stepped into the entrance hall, Dr. Crisp saw them from his office and called out,

"Good morning, Mr. and Mrs. LeSoto. Come on in." Motioning them to two chairs, he said, "You both look like you've recovered nicely. I'm so pleased." He then launched into a speech that he assumed would be welcome, relieving Paco of the need to ask.

"Who knows what would have happened if I hadn't knocked on your door when I did? I wanted to give you the apartment's keys to the turret steps' doors that I've kept on hooks next to them. I'd seen Tori come out of your suite, so I knew at least someone was at home. I used my master key to get in when you didn't respond. I figured something was wrong and I found the two of you in a nonresponsive state. Once I sensed poisoning, I had Penny call for two ambulances right away. We're not equipped to handle anything like that here."

"We wondered how we got to the hospital," said Paco. "Thank you for rescuing us. Have you talked to Tori yet, or at least found out how atropine got into the flu shot sera?"

The doctor remained silent for a moment. His strong face betrayed discomfort, with wrinkles forming on his high forehead and worry lines extending from the corners of his mouth and eyes.

"That's just it," he replied. "Tori hasn't shown up for work for the last few days, and she's not answering her phone. In fact, we have a temp nurse coming in tomorrow. As for the needle, syringe, and flu sera vial—that whole medical kit—there's no sign of it anywhere here."

"Do you have a home address for Tori?" asked Paco.

"Of course," said Phelix. Quite aware that he was now speaking to the police investigator, he added, "Let me get it for you."

His search in a file cabinet yielded an address in the Eastport section of Annapolis, just over the Spa Creek bridge. Paco copied the address into his little spiral notebook that had even gone to the hospital and back in his jacket pocket.

"I'll be sending someone to the house to check on her," said Paco. "And I'll be talking to the other nurses in the meanwhile."

As they were leaving the doctor's office, Molly turned to Phelix and said, "Doctor, we owe you a debt of grabitude. You liberally saved our lives."

"Yes, thank you again," said Paco, as they walked out into the entrance hall.

At the elevator, Paco said, "Okay, hon, I'm on my way to the Infirmary. See you back at our place. Be careful with those canes. They're not all that stable."

"Sure thing, sweetie," Molly said. But she had something else in mind. First, she did stop at their suite. Tossing the hospital's canes in the hall closet, she happily grabbed her trusted Roly and left for a chat with Bertha Bubbachlufsky. She found Bertha sitting alone on the side of her bed in a large room that was also home to five other roommates.

"Hi, Bertha, how are you?" asked Molly.

"Oh, I'm still kicking, but that's about all."

"What's wrong, Bertha? Are you sick?"

"No, no," she replied. "Just too many roommates. I got one that's *meshuga* altogether, another with a mouth full of filth, a third that's a highfalutin' snob, and a frothing-at-the-mouth bitch. The other one, Hilda, she's nice and easy to talk with. But enough about my *tsuriss*, how are you, my dear?"

"I'm okay now, but I did have to spend a couple days in the hospital."

"Was it take-out?" Bertha asked.

"Take-out? What do you mean?"

"Whenever anybody around here needs an operation, they take something out."

"No, nothing like that," replied Molly. "I had a little poisoning, and they gave me an anecdoodle that made it all better."

"Oh my," Bertha said, with some doubt.

"Do you still have that eviction letter that kicked you out of the suites?" asked Molly. "It's one of the reasons I'm here calling on you."

"Sure I do," said Bertha. "It's in my top drawer. I take it out every so often, so I can spit at it."

"Do you really spit on the paper?" asked Molly, her chubby face scrunching up.

Bertha grinned. "Oh, it doesn't really get wet. I make my lips like this and go pooh. It's nothing but hot air that comes out of my mouth. The rotten letter's fine."

"Oh good. Could I borrow the rotten letter for a little while?"

"As long as you like, dearie."

Bertha retrieved the villainous letter from the top drawer of her dresser and handed it over. Molly tucked it into a pocket of her flowered dress and embraced her friend in a tight squeeze. They separated when one of Bertha's roommates entered the room.

"You'll come see us for a cuppa coffee real soon, Bertha," said Molly, as she eased herself and Roly out into the hall.

* * * *

On the floor below Bertha's room, Paco walked through the hall, passing the special needs residents' rooms on his way to the Infirmary. Sonny Duster stood in the hall just ahead of him. Not a word was exchanged between them, but the orderly signaled, with a wave-on and a pointed finger, that his boss was in the Infirmary. Assuming Sonny's signaling also meant Katta wasn't busy, Paco knocked twice, didn't wait for a response, and barged through the door. His first sight was the bulbous white tush of Wilma Adams, bent over a chair ready to receive an allergy shot. Her shriek "Get outta here" sent Paco into an about-face through the door and back into the hall. Already red-faced, he caught sight of Sonny grinning like Lewis Carroll's Cheshire Cat. He darted into one of the rooms, leaving Paco to bathe in his own anger and embarrassment. To make matters worse, when Wilma walked out the Infirmary door, she gave Paco an evil eye worthy of Satan himself. He figured he'd have to live with that relationship going forward.

Now he had to face Katta Brounell, registered nurse and practiced disciplinarian. This time he knocked and waited for permission to enter.

"Come!" said the powerful voice.

Paco opened the door and found Katta at her desk. "I apologize, but Sonny waved me on through. I didn't think he'd do that if you were with a patient."

"Sonny thinks that's a big joke," she said. "It's the third time this month he's pulled that kind of infantile behavior. I really need to have a stern talk with him. Wilma Adams wasn't too happy."

"Obviously. Please convey my apologies to her."

"I will. So, what's missing now, Inspector?" she asked.

"Exactly to the point, Miss Katta. Tori Nickelson gave my wife and myself flu shots last Wednesday afternoon. I'd like to know who signed out the vaccine bottle, needle, and syringe for those shots."

Katta's eyes turned dark. "Why would you want to know that? They were simple flu shots."

"That's just it, they weren't simple flu shots." Paco frowned. "You hadn't heard?"

Katta cocked her head and her cheeks colored. "Heard what?"

"Somehow, atropine found its way into the vaccine, and it sent Molly and me to the hospital for two days."

Katta gasped. "Oh my God. No, I hadn't heard. That's terrible. Are you both okay now?"

"Yes. But what I need to know is, who signed for those things?"

Katta spun her chair around to the bookshelf behind her desk and selected one of the log books, then thumbed her way to the correct page and entry. "Without having the exact serial number on the vial or bottle, my best guess would be Ms. Irma. She also signed out a needle and syringe on Tuesday morning."

"I assume those bottles contain enough flu vaccine for more than just two shots," said Paco. "So, who's in possession of that bottle now? Was it returned to the Infirmary?"

"No, it wasn't returned here," said Katta. "Of course, it should have been. I think you'll have to ask Ms. Irma why not."

"I'll do that. By the way, have you found out who the scribbler is yet?" asked Paco.

"No. The other nurses and Ms. Irma have already denied ownership. I'll let you know if I make any progress there."

"Then I'll be on my way," said Paco. "Thank you for your assistance."

With a smile, Katta called after him, "No surprises next time. And do take care, both of you."

He waved and left the Infirmary thinking, *Either there's a serious lack of communication in this place or Katta was putting on a good act.* Heading across Fellowship Hall to Crisp Hall, he arrived at Irma's cubicle. Wearing blue scrubs and carrying a leather folder under one arm, she was about to head out when he appeared in her doorway. He held up his hand and said, "I'll only keep you a moment, Ms. Irma." He watched as she returned to her desk chair. She did not invite him to sit.

"What's it all about this time, Inspector?" she asked.

Paco studied her sharp-featured face. *What an odd way to address me. So cold, so rude. It's impossible that Phelix hasn't informed her of our flu shots and the hospital.* Shifting into his soft-spoken interrogating mode, he said, "Last week you told me that Molly and I needed to get our flu shots. I just now spoke to Nurse Katta. She said that last Tuesday afternoon you signed out the medical kit containing the vaccine bottle, the needles, and the syringes. I assume you sent Nurse Tori Nickelson to give us the shots. Somewhere between the dispensary refrigerator and our upper arms someone injected atropine into that bottle. I'd like to know if anyone else handled those materials in the interim."

Irma was quick to respond. "Phelix told me what happened to the two of you. I'm sorry you were poisoned. Does that make me a suspect?"

No remorse, no sympathy. "Of course. You're one of several suspects. I'm not accusing anyone yet."

Irma crossed her arms over her chest in a defensive move, as if to prevent herself from saying too much. "I gave the kit containing the flu supplies to Tori. What she did with the bottle afterward, I have no way of knowing. She's probably the one you're looking for. Unfortunately, she hasn't shown up for work in days."

"I'm well aware of that," said Paco. "While the vaccine was in your possession, was it left unguarded for any period of time?"

"The vaccine was locked in the Infirmary's dispensary refrigerator," said Irma. "But I was in and out all morning, as usual. Anyone with a key could have tampered with it. I assume the used needles and syringes wound up in a Sharps disposal receptacle, but which receptacle and which of the many needles inside? It would be like looking for a needle in a haystack, only in this case there are at least three haystacks and nearly three weeks' worth in each one."

"Who else knew the shots were intended for Molly and me?" asked Paco.

"Just Katta and Tori," said Irma. "Now if you'll excuse me, I need to check on one of our special needs patients. She ushered Paco out without a word.

Chapter 24
Do Nurses Lie?
Same Day

The Anne Arundel County police cruiser from Black Rain Corners arrived in Annapolis at around 10 a.m. Sergeant Frank Mullins drove to the City Dock and over the drawbridge to the waterfront community of Eastport. Six blocks later, he pulled up to the curb in front of a three-story apartment building of red brick with white trim, surrounded by neatly clipped shrubbery. After checking the written address that Paco had given him, he stepped out of the cruiser and proceeded to the front door. Inside, he read the names of the apartment renters on their mailboxes and pressed the call button below Tori Nickelson's name.

"Who's there?" a female voice answered.

"Sergeant Frank Mullins, county police. I need to speak with Miss Nickelson."

"Miss Nickelson is indisposed," said the voice. "She's not speaking with *anyone* just now."

"I need to insist. This is urgent police business. I must speak with her."

The inner door lock began buzzing, granting him access to a wide hall and a first-floor apartment. The door to 1C was already open. A blonde thirtyish woman in blue pants, white tank top, and sneakers stood there waiting for him. He showed her his police creds, and she stepped aside, allowing him to enter. The apartment looked neat and spacious, with Ikea-type Swedish-modern furnishings.

"Miss Nickelson?" asked Frank.

"No, I'm Amy Westmoreland, her roommate." With anguish covering her small face, she said, "Tori has locked herself in her bedroom and won't speak to me. She's been in there since Tuesday." Near tears, Amy said. "I can hear her sobbing, but she refuses to tell me what's wrong. She hasn't even come out for meals. She's deliberately starving herself. And she's a nurse! She's been so happy in her job, and then suddenly this. She does have her own bathroom, so she has water to drink, if she wants it. But I wonder if she even brushes her teeth. I'm so worried about her. This is not at all like her. In a way, I'm glad you're here—maybe *you* can convince her to come out."

Frank walked across the sitting room and down the hall leading to the two bedrooms. The open-door bedroom was obviously Amy's. He rapped on the closed door.

"Hello, Ms. Tori. I'm Sergeant Mullins from the county police. I'm not here to arrest you. All I'm here for is the answers to a couple of questions. Can you hear me?" No response, not even the sobbing Amy spoke of. "Miss Tori, if you don't respond to me, I will assume you cannot respond, which means I will have to force my way into the room. Are you sick? Are you hurt?" Silence. "If you won't respond, I will have to take down this door. I'm sure you don't want that. Now, if you are able to, please open the door and show Amy and me that you are okay." He put his ear to the door and listened. This time he did hear movement in the room, but neither a response nor a door opening. "I am now going to count down from ten to zero. When I reach zero I will force the door open." He listened again without a sound. "Ten... nine...eight... seven...six...five..." The lock clicked, and the door swung into the bedroom before the count of four.

Tori Nickelson stood barefoot by the door, her hand still on the knob. She was African-American, of medium height, with a well-proportioned figure, an intelligent oval face and café-au-lait complexion. A wide pretty mouth. A fluffy cloud of black hair encircled her head, stopping at her ears. There were deep bags from lack of sleep under her hooded lids. She was visibly shaken, disheveled, and appeared to be quite weak. She still wore her pastel nurse's uniform, although it was completely wrinkled and twisted about. Amy rushed past Frank and took Tori in her arms, embracing her fully, head-to-head, whispering rapidly, consoling her.

"Thank you for coming out," said Frank "Tori, I'll be patient with you, if you'll let Amy get some drink and nourishment into you."

Avoiding Frank's eyes, Tori gave a weak nod and allowed Amy to lead her into their small kitchen, while Frank waited in the sitting room on a maple rocker. He waited a full forty-five minutes before appearing at the threshold to the kitchen and noting that Tori's plate and glass of milk were empty. "Tori, I think it's time for me to ask my questions and be on my way. Why don't you come and sit down where you'll be more comfortable?" He motioned to the sitting room.

Amy helped Tori stand up, settled her carefully in the wing chair, and sat down in a far corner. Frank seated himself in a side chair across from her.

"My only purpose in being here," he said, gently, "is to talk to you about the flu vaccine bottle, which now belongs in the evidence chain. Exactly how did you acquire that particular vaccine bottle?"

Tori's hunched body suddenly stiffened, alert. The dejected, defeated stance was gone. Her keen gray eyes looked steadily into Frank's. "Ms. Irma called me into the Infirmary and walked over to the dispensary. She opened the refrigerator door and handed me the bottle with instructions to administer flu shots to Mr. and Mrs. Paco LeSoto. I put the bottle, the syringes, the needles, and alcohol wipes in our gray medical kit, the way I always do."

"Did you initial or sign anything when you took possession of that bottle?" asked Frank.

"No."

"Aren't you required to sign out for a vaccine bottle?"

Tori shrugged. A slight blush appeared on her gaunt cheekbones. "I guess we should have a requirement like that, but maybe we're a little too easygoing in this facility on some matters."

Frank pressed on. "Was that bottle left unguarded at any time during your caretaking?"

"No sir. Well, before I went up to the LeSotos' suite I did leave the kit on the bathroom sink while I took care of personal business. It was less than two minutes."

"I see. After you administered the flu shots to the LeSotos, what happened to that vaccine bottle?"

"I put everything—the bottle, needles, syringes, alcohol wipes—back in the medical kit and returned to the Infirmary. As soon as I got there I wrote 'Minus 2' on the bottle's label. Katta Brounell was in the dispensary, so I handed the bottle to her. I watched her open the refrigerator and put it on a shelf. Then I dumped the syringes and used wipes in the proper waste disposal bins, and the needles in the Sharps containers mounted along the back wall."

"I have to ask this next question," said Frank. "Did you alter the contents of that vaccine bottle at all?"

Anger flashed in Tori's eyes. "Sergeant, I did not *alter* the contents of that bottle. I took enough out for two flu shots, one for Molly and one for Paco. But I didn't put anything into it. I hadn't even met the LeSotos before last Tuesday."

"I see. If that was the case, why did you leave Gilded Gates and go into hiding? You didn't show up at work for three days. You didn't even call your boss to say where you were."

Tori's shoulders slumped. "To tell you the truth, I freaked. When I heard that the LeSotos were taken to the hospital for suspected poisoning, I thought I would be the primary suspect. I just couldn't face that. I've never intentionally harmed anyone. I have an excellent record as a nurse. I don't know how anything foreign got in the vaccine. Sergeant, I'm a suspect, aren't I?"

"Yes, you are," replied Frank, "but so is all the rest of the staff at Gilded Gates. We're still looking for motives—to find out who would gain from such a horrific act."

He stood to leave. Looking down at Tori he said, "Thank you for being so forthright. You've been very helpful. And please take care of yourself, get your health back. Thank you, too, Amy. I'll see myself out."

When he reached the cruiser at the curb and climbed in, he picked up his car phone and dialed Paco. His original intention was to merely inform Paco of Tori Nickelson's responses, but when he heard that both he and Molly had new findings pertinent to the case, he suggested, "Let's have supper together. I know this great place on Route 301. It's called Ripping Good Steak House."

"Sounds terrific to me," said Paco. "I've had my fill of institutional food lately."

"I'll pick you both up in a half-hour out front at Gilded Gates," said Frank.

"Molly wants to know if it's dressy-up or causual."

"Tell her it's casual, a truck stop," answered Frank. "And truckers know good food, value, and friendly service when they find it."

* * * *

The Ripping Good Steak House pulsated with rustic charm: wagon-wheel chandeliers and log-cabin décor, with captains' chairs at round wood tables and roomy red-vinyl booths. Molly collapsed Roly, wedged herself into a booth, and sank in, to her delight. Paco followed. Frank settled in opposite them. Frank chose the Texas-cut, bone-in prime rib; Paco the standard prime rib; and Molly the filet mignon. All the orders included a fully dressed baked potato and robust salad bar. Frank also ordered draught beer for the Le-Sotos and iced tea for himself; after all, he was driving. While they waited for their orders, Paco and Frank visited the salad bar and Paco returned with Molly's salad per her instructions: Caesar salad, heavy on the croutons. They spoke between bites and sips. Paco launched the discussion.

"I would say that three people are currently suspected of tampering with the vaccine bottle. I've traced the fresh, unused bottle of vaccine from Nurse Katta and her dispensary fridge to Ms. Irma and then to Nurse Tori Nickelson. I do not believe that someone tampered with the vaccine before it left the fridge. For one thing, there wasn't any specific target, and second, several flu vaccine bottles were stored there. All three of these staff members had keys to the cabinet, as did Dr. Crisp and Nurse Penny Summers. So, five suspects at the outside. The motive for targeting Molly and me would have to lie in the idea that we knew too much about the plot to kill Lisa Howard. It looks like the vaccine trail ended with Tori Nickelson. She gave us the actual shots. What happened to the bottle containing the unused shots is a mystery to me."

"I think I have the answer to that," said Frank. "I was able to interview Nurse Tori this afternoon. But it wasn't easy. When I arrived, her roommate told me Tori had locked herself in her bedroom for three days. I tried talking to her through the closed door. Finally, I threatened to break the door down if she didn't come out. That worked. She was a mess—dehydrated, weak, so bad that her roommate had to get some nourishment into her before I could even talk with her. That took forty-five minutes. Finally, Tori sat down with me. She said she did not initial the label on the vaccine bottle. She merely wrote on it "Minus 2." She told me, rather embarrassed, that there was no requirement for the nurses to initial the vaccine bottles either before or after use." She said she returned the bottle of unused flu doses to Katta and even watched her put it back in the fridge. This happened hours before she learned about the LeSotos being poisoned. When she did learn about it, she was so upset she fled the facility and locked herself in her room for several days without food. She seemed honest to me in everything she said. Either she's as innocent as a baby or she's an awfully good actress."

Chomping on a warm hunk of buttered French bread, Paco said, "When I questioned Katta, she claimed the vaccine bottle was *not* returned to her in the dispensary. That means either Tori or Katta is lying. He paused and scowled. "Oh boy, I missed the boat on that one. Right then and there I should have asked to see what was in the fridge. Was the vaccine bottle in there or not? Sorry about that, Frank. As far as suspects go, does that mean we now have only two? Maybe. Is there another explanation?"

Their steaming feast arrived on foot-long oval platters. Frank's Texas prime rib lapped the plate on three quadrants and the bone stuck out on the fourth.

"What about the male counterpatsy in all this?" asked Molly, sinking her teeth into the first slice of the rare filet mignon and savoring the flavor.

"The orderly Sonny Duster doesn't seem to be an active party in the poisoning," said Paco. "But he's a herky young guy. We shouldn't lose sight of his possible role in the original crime. He could have been the one who pushed the gurney carrying Lisa into the turret tower. There's no evidence, but at least he has the strength to push one of those things around."

Paco dug into his baked potato topped with sour cream, bacon bits, and chives. He had already decided to throw caution to the winds at this terrific restaurant. *I'll get back to my heart-healthy diet tomorrow. At least there's a side of broccoli here.*

"I hate to admit it," Paco added, "but we're at a dead end, for now anyway, on who put the atropine in our flu shots—and when."

"What about Dr. Crisp?" asked Frank. "He runs the damn place. He certainly knows his way around. Wouldn't he fit the bill? Wouldn't he be the one to benefit most from a more successful facility?" Frank had surgically extracted the bone from the huge T-bone and set it aside before feeding his face with one enjoyable bite after another.

Paco set his fork down, eager to explain. "Frank, I've interviewed Phelix in depth. He told me that he and Irma are salaried and don't own any part of Gilded Gates. That, of course, is easy enough to check out. So, unless he receives illegal, under-the-table pay-back bonuses, he's not our man. He claims that he writes a monthly profits-only check to Angular Properties Management Associates, care of the First Mechanics Bank in Annapolis. I do need to find out more about this management firm."

"I have Bertha's eviction letter with me," Molly said, rummaging around in her purse. She waved it in front of the men and unfolded it. "I've been muddletating on it. See, it's signed by a Jonathan R. Witherton, Jr., CFO. That's the financial honcho, isn't it? Shouldn't it be signed by a boss or their president? And look at the letterhead. Just the name of the firm—no address, no telephone, no email. Not a blooming thing. I wonder if it even exists, except maybe on a piece of paper."

"Good thought, Mol," said Paco. "In that case we'll just follow the money and go directly to the bank. They might be able to tell us something about this Mr. Jonathan R. Witherton and whoever else has access to this particular bank account."

"You'll need a search warrant to get that kind of information," said Frank. "I don't think it'll be a problem. I should be able to help with that."

"Go ahead. Get a warrant if you can," said Paco. "You have more pull than I do these days."

They finished their dinner with a round of apple pie a la mode. It was after ten when Frank dropped them off at Gilded Gates. They were all stuffed—but clear-eyed and clear-headed, like Broadway performers ready for the next act.

Chapter 25
Angular Properties
Monday, Thanksgiving Week

Sergeant Frank Mullins chose to avoid the two night-court judges available over the weekend and waited until the Anne Arundel County courts opened on Monday morning. This way, he was able to select the judge who might take the least bit of convincing to sign off on his warrant application. His plea to Judge Michael Lione took less than twenty minutes. Paco was waiting in the passenger seat of the cruiser out front when his boss came skipping down the courthouse steps. From Frank's body language, Paco knew he'd secured the necessary warrant. The next stop was the First Mechanics Bank in Annapolis. Twenty minutes later they left the cruiser in the parking lot and entered the bank's lobby.

A young woman in a ponytail saw them hesitating and greeted them near the desks area. When Paco asked to speak with the manager, she said, "The manager has an off-site office. May I ask what this is all about?"

"Our business is about one of your accounts," said Paco. "A confidential matter to be sure." Both men flashed their police credentials.

"Then I think you should be speaking with Mrs. Dwyer, our on-site assistant manager. If you'll have a seat over there. I'm sure she'll be with you shortly."

Paco peered across the open space to the brass placard noting where Mrs. Dorothy C. Dwyer sat. The pony-tailed woman whispered something to her, and Mrs. Dwyer nodded twice. She was busy exchanging pages with an elderly man sitting across from her, signing document pages one by one. Ten minutes later, her customer left, and she motioned for Paco and Frank to approach. They took seats in the chairs across from her. Paco figured Mrs. Dwyer to be in her late forties, with a plain face and frizzy brown hair that stopped just above pearl stud earrings. She wore a sky-blue suit and prim, high-necked white blouse.

"Please sit down, gentlemen. I understand you're from the police. How can I help you?"

She acknowledged their police creds with a positive nod. Paco handed her a canceled check from the Gilded Gates account made out to Angular Properties Management Associates.

"What is this about?" she asked, once she had perused the check.

"We're investigating the recipient parties to this account," said Paco. "We would like to learn all we can about them—their identities and contact information."

"Our customer information is confidential," said Mrs. Dwyer. "I can't release any of it to you without a court order."

"I believe this document will help," said Frank as he handed her the judge's warrant, ordering her to release the account's background information.

Mrs. Dwyer studied the document with pressed lips, and when she finished, she took the check and leaned it against her computer monitor stand. Her fingers flew over the keyboard in a flurry of taps. She read to herself for a spell, scrolling periodically to expand her search. When she was done, she turned back to them.

"I can see where sums between forty and fifty thousand are deposited regularly mid-month, and these amounts are regularly withdrawn by check a few days later, always leaving a consistent balance of two thousand dollars."

"Can you tell me who is making the withdrawals?" asked Paco.

"Consistently, it's a Mr. Jonathan R. Witherton." But after a few more keyboard taps and a short scroll, she added, "This is odd. There's no address on the checks, just his name."

"Would there be any other way to come up with his contact information?"

"Well, there should be more information on his original application to open this account," said Mrs. Dwyer. Back at the keyboard, she brought up a new information screen. "Ah, here it is. The address is 325 East Marquardt Street, Baltimore, Maryland 21203. The telephone number is (410) 543-1103."

Paco wrote the information in his little notebook as she spoke. Then he looked up and asked, "Is there any chance that a paper copy of this application still exists?"

"I can check our files," said Mrs. Dwyer as she rose to her feet.

"Wait!" said Frank. "Ma'am, before you handle it, would you mind wearing these cotton gloves? It's possible the man's fingerprints might still be on the paper." He handed her the forensic gloves he'd taken from his pocket.

"I don't mind at all." She slipped into the gloves as she walked toward the wall where a line of eight filing cabinets stood erect like soldiers waiting inspection. Paco watched her examine one drawer, then the one below it. A minute later she extracted a file folder, brought it back to her desk, and opened it wide for them to see. It contained the same information they'd just acquired digitally.

"By any chance would there be anyone here who could describe Jonathan Witherton?" asked Paco.

"That would take a miracle," said Mrs. Dwyer. "The application is dated 1993. That's five years ago."

"I just thought there might have been some anomaly in his looks, the way he dressed, or the way he spoke that would trigger someone's memory today."

"I wouldn't know who or where to start," she said. "We've had such a turnover in the last two years."

"May we take this document with us?" Paco asked.

She hesitated and squinted while thinking it over.

Paco got the message. "Of course I'll sign a receipt for it."

Mrs. Dwyer nodded. "In that case, yes, you may take it. But please treat it carefully. This is the original. We do have a photocopy of it."

"Excellent. You wouldn't happen to have a protecting envelope for this document, would you?" asked Paco.

She tucked the original document into a letter-sized envelope and handed it to Frank, then slipped off the cotton gloves and handed them back to him. They thanked Mrs. Dwyer and left the bank building.

"We're doing great, it's only ten o'clock," said Paco. "We have two more stops to make. We need to drop this application off at the crime lab in Baltimore and then attempt to find this Baltimore address."

"You got it," said Frank. "We should be there in about half an hour." He drove them from the bank to the Baltimore Police Department's Forensic Science and Evidence Services Division. Frank went inside, turned over the envelope with the document inside, and filled out the necessary form requesting that they lift the latent prints from the document and run them through both the FBI's fingerprint service and Interpol's Automatic Fingerprint Identification System (AFIS).

While Frank was inside, Paco waited in the car. He used the car phone to dial Witherton's phone number, and an automated message replied: "The number you have dialed is not in service." Using operator information, he finally reached a police precinct within the zip code 21203 after three tries. He reached the duty desk sergeant and identified himself. Paco asked, "Do you have a complete street map of your precinct handy?"

"Sure, on the wall behind me," answered the desk sergeant.

"Can you locate a Marquardt Street for me?" asked Paco. He spelled it out for the sergeant.

"What's it near?" asked the desk sergeant.

"All I know is 325 East Marquardt Street, Baltimore and the zip code is 21203," said Paco.

"I need to put you on hold, Detective. Maybe ten minutes."

"No problem," said Paco.

Closer to fifteen minutes later, the desk sergeant said, "Sorry, it took longer than I expected. I can't find any address like that in our precinct. I even looked it up on the computer. In fact, there's no such street, avenue, lane, or location in our zip code. Someone's pulling your leg, sir."

"I suspected as much, but I had to be sure," said Paco. "Thanks a lot, Sergeant." He hung up. Minutes later, Frank came down the steps and climbed into the car. Paco briefed him on his futile attempt to find the address and also told him about the phony telephone number. They decided there was nothing more they could do that day.

The air had turned heavy. The sun had gone on vacation. A gray blanket covered the sky. Silence reigned in the car as Frank negotiated roads clogged with Thanksgiving week shoppers, stop-and-go on the Baltimore Beltway, and lanes closed from accidents. Navigating the traffic congestion struck Paco that their case was becoming more of an entangled web every day. An hour and a half later, Frank dropped him off at Gilded Gates.

Chapter 26
Rendezvous in the Rain
That Night

At nine o'clock that night, a white Infinity Q-50 sedan rolled up to the far end of the Gilded Gates parking lot—far enough from the building so that its two occupants would not be recognized. Not that it mattered. The lot was empty. As if sheer distance were not enough, the near-winter clouds, heavily burdened with impending precipitation, cast another layer of isolation for the man and woman sitting in the front seat. Still, the woman's nerves reflected her doubts openly. She shifted her car into Park.

"Are you sure it's wise for us to be meeting like this?" she asked, shivering in her olive-green rain jacket.

"You're the one who asked for this meet," retorted the man. "What on earth is bothering you, anyway?"

"That busybody LeSoto couple. They're too smart for their own good. They messed up the whole deal for us. We needed to get them off our backs."

Heavy drops of rain fell on the windshield, as if triggering his response.

"You caused this mess, lady. Poisoning their flu shots? What the hell were you thinking?"

"It seemed like such a good idea at the time."

"A good idea? For chrissake, think about it. What you did was actually narrow the field of suspects. How close to fingering us is this retired cop?"

"Damn close," she replied, her voice trembling.

"Are you likely to be found out?"

"Yes, and I'm scared. I think he's narrowed it down to the three of us, if I read him correctly. He knows one of us three put the atropine in the flu vaccine bottle."

As their discussion heated up, so did the inside of the closed car, fogging the windshield and making her begin to feel a bit clammy. She unzipped her jacket and opened it wide.

Just then a single bolt of lightning struck a broken-up mound of asphalt in the middle of the empty parking lot, illuminating the entire area with a strange lingering brightness. A boom of thunder followed. Both the man and woman sat up straight with shock at the closeness of the strike. They remained silent for minutes, their minds churning with sinister thoughts. The man spoke first.

"My dear partner, I know there's only a very small chance of either of us being arrested, but if either one of us is arrested, shouldn't we pledge to protect each other's identity, and not trade it for a lesser sentence?"

"Uh…I don't know," she lied. "I haven't given it much thought. I guess so…out of loyalty to each other. Yeah, okay."

He leaned over to the driver's side and patted her right cheek. "I knew you'd see it my way, my dear." His voice had grown softer, almost tender.

She turned toward him, believing he was actually going to kiss her. Now both of his gloved hands cupped her cheeks, holding her face to his. Her eyes were closed, so she couldn't see that his eyes were wide open and intense. Slowly, his gloved hands slipped down her cheeks until they encompassed her longish neck. The fingers began to tighten into a stranglehold. Her eyes suddenly popped open and saw her impending fate in his eyes. She managed the single scratchy word "No!" The grip tightened even more, so the ensuing words were completely stifled and the airways squeezed off. Behind the steering wheel, her pushing hands and kicking feet were powerless. And then it didn't matter anymore. Precious breath had been denied for much too long.

When at last he dragged his hands away from her, she started to fall forward toward the car's horn. He gave her a little sideways push and her head came to rest between the driver's door and the rim of the steering wheel. He felt drained and only a little regretful. *I had to kill her. She would have given me up in a flash. I suppose I would have given her up as well to save my own ass from a few years in stir. It was a matter of me taking the initiative first.*

He wanted to leave the Infinity, but about a hundred yards of pounding, freezing rain separated her car from the entrance to Gilded Gates. He checked under the front seat and found her umbrella. Unsnapping the nylon cover, he slid it off. The umbrella was bright pink strewn with fuchsia butterflies. *Better than nothing*, he thought as he shoved the cover under the seat. He opened the passenger door and pulled the hood of his windbreaker over his head. After popping open the umbrella, he stepped out under it. Horizontal raindrops beat against his pants legs. He quick-stepped through sloshing puddles all the way to the entrance. Once inside, he jerked his head left and right. *Where can I get rid of this damned thing?* He saw a cylindrical umbrella stand just outside Irma Crisp's office and headed straight for it. With his right hand still groping for the button to collapse the umbrella, he didn't see the LeSotos emerge from Movie Night in the dining room.

Pushing her walker, Molly slowed down just before they turned into the corridor opposite Fellowship Hall. "Fancy-shmancy umbrella you got there, fella." She couldn't get a good look at the hooded man, and soon thought no more about it as they continued to their suite.

Chapter 27
It's Murder

The punishing rain stopped just after midnight, replaced by snow flurries. An hour later, the flurries turned aggressive until a thick carpet of fresh snow covered the Gilded Gates parking lot and the lone car at the far end. Tuesday arrived raw, cold, and forbidding.

At 6:30 a.m. Cecil Williams, a local farmer, drove his tractor with its snowplow rig up Spring Drive and through the snow-covered gilded gates. He had been seasonally contracted to clear any and all substantial snowfall before employees and visitors arrived. The snow had stopped. The sunrise was struggling through dense clouds. Cecil cleared the circle at the main entrance and the handicapped spaces before turning into the spacious parking lot. He didn't notice the Infinity parked at the end of the lot. The white sedan was almost camouflaged until he rolled up to it through a mound of snow and slush. He normally pushed such a mound to the edge of the lot before turning around and plowing the other direction. But not this time.

What the hell? Cecil slammed on his brake, dismounted the tractor, and approached the snow-smothered car. In the icy air he was glad he'd put on his down parka. Using his mittened hand, he brushed away the snow from the driver's-side windshield. He needed to identify the owner so he could have the car moved. Because of the early hour and stress of the storm, he had started by clearing the windshield instead of the license plates. At first, Cecil saw the empty passenger seat. Then he saw the slumped-over figure. Seeing no visible foul play, just someone in need of help, he pulled open the driver's-side door.

A body fell toward him—head first, doubled over. "Aaah!" Cecil roared in shock. He caught the body in his arms, lifted it up, and set it back on the seat. A woman with short dark hair and an open green rain jacket. Her head flopped to one side. It was at that moment that he noted black and blue marks on both sides of her neck and the deathly glare on her face. The farmer's stomach spasmed. He shrank back and slammed the door shut, shaking most of the snow off it. He had never met a dead body before.

Cecil Williams climbed aboard his tractor and slammed into reverse to back away from the snow mound. He lifted his plow attachment, turned around, and churned on the packed snow to the building entrance. Arriving there, he dismounted the tractor and entered the building. He found Dr. Crisp's office door locked, but found a phone in Ms. Irma's double cubicle. Dialing 9-1-1, he reached the Black Rain Corners Police. Incoming calls after hours were redirected to Sergeant Frank Mullins at home.

"Sergeant Mullins," he answered with a yawn.

"There's a freakin' dead body in a car out in the Gilded Gates's parking lot," said Cecil. "She's in the front seat with black and blue marks all over her neck."

"Who are *you?*"

"I'm Cecil Williams. I got that old tobacco farm off Route 2 near Lothian. I'm the snow-plow contractor for Gilded Gates."

"Thanks for calling. Don't leave," said Frank. "I'll be on my way there in a few minutes."

Frank pulled on his clothes and drove to the new crime scene in twenty minutes. Meanwhile, Cecil had cleared more of the lot. As soon as he saw the cruiser, he cleared another strip right up to the crime scene car. He tooted the tractor's horn. Sticking his left arm out the window, he waved to the cruiser. Frank responded and drove down the cleared strip to the Infinity. The two men exchanged greetings.

Frank made an initial, no-touch inspection of the body and the rest of the car and immediately phoned the mobile forensics unit to come to the scene. He noted that his victim wore a pastel nurse's uniform under her open unzipped jacket, so he figured Paco could provide an initial identification. He looked at his watch and saw that it was almost 7:30.

Paco was sipping his morning coffee when the call came. He arrived outside at the front entrance ten minutes later, wearing an L.L. Bean hooded jacket, winter boots, and black wool cap. Frank waved him to the Infinity.

Peering inside, Paco stood motionless for a whole minute, breathing hard, his breath emitting puffs of frosty air. "Good God! It's Nurse Katta Brounell!"

"Who?" asked Frank. "Don't you mean Kitty or Kathy?"

"No, she goes by the nickname Katta," said Paco. "Her full name is Kathrine Brounell. She was in charge of the Infirmary and dispensary here at Gilded Gates. I guess that narrows down my suspects to one in our flu vaccine poisoning."

"How do you figure?" Frank asked, shifting from one foot to the other, wishing he'd worn his heavy-duty parka.

"Katta was one of the two nurses I suspected of lying about the ultimate disposal of the bottle," replied Paco. "One said she returned it, and the other denied returning it. I figured one or the other injected the poison into the flu vaccine." Beginning to sniffle in the cold, he pressed on. "I also suspect that Katta was a party to the attempted murder of Lisa Howard. I believe poisoning Molly and me was intended to keep us off their trail. And now I believe Katta was murdered to protect the identity of the mastermind of these horrific schemes."

They heard a vehicle slipping and sliding on the parking lot, shortcutting across the sun-sloppy snow. It was the mobile forensics team in a pickup truck, with a walk-in box in its cargo bed, providing special tool storage, including cabinets, shelves, and drawers. It pulled up to the Infinity and three forensic-collection technicians stepped out of the cab. A tall, sallow-cheeked man in a black pea coat approached Frank. "I'm Skip Allen, the team leader." After a short briefing by Frank and Paco, the team began their examination of the crime scene vehicle.

"Not much we can do until they're finished, Frank," said Paco. "Come on inside and maybe we can scare up some breakfast."

"Good idea," said Frank. "It's freakin' cold out here."

"We'll be in the cafeteria at one of the tables just inside the entrance," said Paco. "We'd appreciate a quickie rundown on anything you find, so we can jump-start our investigation."

"Sure thing, pal," said Skip.

Frank left the cruiser where it was, and he and Paco trudged across the cleared portion of the lot all the way to the entrance. Just as they reached the door, a second crime lab vehicle arrived, a morgue hearse, and parked next to the Infinity Q-50.

Using a house-only wall phone inside the cafeteria, Paco called Molly and invited her to join them for breakfast. As he'd intended, Paco selected a table near the entrance. While they waited for Molly, Dr. Crisp approached their table, unshaven and in an open-collared shirt.

Without so much as a "Good Morning," Phelix barked, "Paco, what the devil is all the commotion out on the parking lot? Why are the police here?" Facing Frank, he demanded, "And you are?"

Unintimidated, Frank stood, eye to eye with Phelix. "Sergeant Mullins in charge of the Black Rain Corners police force. I'm here with the forensics team to investigate a murder."

"What the devil? Murder investigation?" asked Phelix. "Who was murdered? Oh, no, not one of our residents."

"No, not a resident, Doctor, one of your nurses," replied Paco. "Katta Brounell was found dead in her car by Cecil Williams when he was plowing the parking lot early this morning."

"Oh no! How did Katta die?"

Paco said vaguely, "We don't know for sure yet. I can't tell you any more—it's an ongoing investigation."

"This is terrible. Keep me posted, Paco," said Phelix. He slunk off toward his office shaking his head every few steps. He didn't feel any sympathy for the woman. Instead, he was wondering how he was going to care for the needy residents in the Infirmary with Katta gone. And he didn't even get his breakfast. He passed Molly just entering the cafeteria and ignored her cheerful greeting as she passed him. She stopped, turned, and when he was out of earshot, gave him the raspberry. She found their table and sat down.

"What's with the good doctor?" she asked. "His mind is all up in a tootsie."

"Oh, he was upset about the body found out in the parking lot this morning," said Paco.

"A body!" she repeated. "Anybody we know?"

"Yeah, Nurse Katta from the Infirmary," said Paco. "My guess is she was murdered sometime last evening, during the heavy rainstorm."

"How can you say that? Paco?" asked Frank. "We don't even have the medical examiner's report yet."

"There was only one set of tracks in the snow leading up to the driver's door and none leading up to the passenger's door," replied Paco. "The one set of toes-in tracks belonged to Cecil. So, it had to be some time before much of the snow arrived."

"Good show, Paco," said Frank. "I missed that. Must have been the early hour."

"That's horrible. How'd she die, Frank?" asked Molly.

"The black and blue marks surrounding her neck say strangulation," he replied. "At least that was my first impression. I also noticed that the marks on her neck didn't seem to define any fingers, so I assume the killer wore gloves."

"Suffercating succotash! Does that mean she was the one who wanted to poison us?"

"Maybe, hon," said Paco. "But I don't think she was working alone. If she was in cahoots with someone, there's another dangerous person still out there who thinks we're getting a mite too close to uncovering his identity. We have to be extra careful going forward, especially now that he—or she—killed off a cohort to protect his identity."

The three were silent throughout the rest of breakfast, deep in their own thoughts. Frank wondered whether the fingerprint report had come in yet back at the police station and where that information might lead him. Paco began to speculate who among his fellow residents might have been cold-blooded and cruel enough to commit these crimes. Molly began conjuring up ideas on how to trap the killer, then deciding each plan had some basic fallacy.

Frank spotted the forensics team leader in the doorway. "Over here!" he called.

Skip Allen approached carrying a large notebook and sat down in the empty chair next to Frank. His eyes in wire-rimmed glasses darted about, sizing up the situation.

Paco and Skip nodded to each other, already professionally acquainted, and Paco introduced him to Molly.

"So, Skip," said Frank, "What've you got?"

"There's not much new to report. It's death by strangulation—most likely by gloved hands. My estimated time of death eight to twelve hours. We collected dozens of solid prints, most of which were the victim's. Our search inside the car resulted in..." Skip flipped his notebook open and read: "Her tan leather purse was on the floor of the front seat. From the wallet in her purse we learned that she was Kathrine Brounell, RN. Current driver's license, credit cards, nothing unusual. The contents of her purse—one Milky Way candy bar, a packet of tissues, a small bottle of Extra-Strength Tylenol, and a cosmetics case containing lipstick, compact, a mini-toothbrush, and toothpaste tube. Under the front passenger seat we found a pink umbrella cover, no umbrella. The glove box held a flashlight, a ballpoint pen, the Infinity car manual, and a brown envelope containing her car registration. On the floor in the back, we found a pair of black size-eight, high-heeled shoes and some recent issues of the *Annapolis Journal-Gazette*. The trunk was clean and empty except for a jack and donut tire. That's all I can tell you now. We'll have a complete report for you in a few days."

"Thank you, Skip, good work," said Frank, offering his hand for a shake.

He nodded. "See ya now. Frank, Inspector, Mrs. LeSoto." Skip bounced up out of his chair and left.

"I'd better be off now, too," said Frank. "I'm anxious to see if the fingerprints report is in on Jonathan Witherton's bank application." He strode to the door and disappeared.

"So, Mol, that just leaves us," said Paco. "This has all been quite a shock. What's going on with you?"

"I'm just muddletating on an idea I got," replied Molly. "Say, when do those four guys play their bridge game?"

"Every day around two o'clock in the recreation room. Why, what did you have in mind?"

"You'll see, sweetie," she replied. "Maybe we should be playing a game of Ping-Pong around that time."

"Okay." Paco didn't ask for an explanation. He knew Molly was enjoying her own secret plot.

* * * *

It was 2:30 when the LeSotos arrived at the Ping-Pong table. The bridge game hadn't started yet. They looked over at the foursome just sitting down. A brand-new deck of cards was being undressed from its clear cellophane wrap and taken from its blue Bicycle-brand box.

As always, the LeSotos were totally unmatched. Paco racked up a pile of points in a row. Molly played her usual game holding onto one handlebar of Roly with her left hand and whacking the ball with her right. But today she was distracted by the bridge game going on a few card tables away. Her head turned every few shots and she hit the middle of the net or overshot the table. Suddenly, she turned to her left and lifted her paddle in a smart underhand tap, sending the little white ball in the direction of the bridge game. It flew through the air in a high arc, bounced squarely in the middle of the table, and bounced once more, landing in Happy Harry Lightfoot's lap.

"Oops oops oops!" cried Molly, as she angled around another

card table with Roly and came up between Gordon Lowe facing left and Chester Parker facing right. "I must have hit a ferocious ball over here. So sorreee."

Harry held the ball out to her. Steadying herself on her walker, Molly leaned forward, placing her left palm down over Chester's discard pile and her right hand out to receive the ball from Harry's fingers. None of the players noticed Molly's left hand perfectly palming the top playing card from the discard pile. All eyes, including those of the fourth player, Mark Tomlinson, were on Molly's stocky right arm stretching across the table. Molly slyly pocketed the playing card in the waist pocket of her dress with minimal handling, and returned to Paco and their unfinished Ping-Pong game.

They played several more games with Molly actually winning one. Paco was surprised that her game had improved so much. When plain fatigue caused the ball to land on the floor more often than not, it was time to quit and wash up for lunch.

Chapter 28
Prints

Secure in their suite, Molly carefully removed the filched playing card from the waist pocket of her dress and laid it on the kitchen table atop a fresh Kleenex tissue.

"What do you have there, Mol?" asked Paco.

"Maybe an answer or three to who's the percolator."

"Just how are you going to determine the perpetrator, dear?"

"When four people play cards there's a celebrity of fingerprints all over them," she clarified.

Paco's bushy eyebrows shot north. "You're kidding me. You actually suspect one of those four gentlemen of being our killer?"

"Sweetiekins, when we were shlepping out of the dining room on Movie Night, I'm pretty sure I saw one of them in front of Ms. Irma's office. There's a brella-stand next to the door. This guy was standing there holding a pink umbrella with butterflies on it. He was trying to close it."

"What's that got to do with anything?"

Molly's face beamed as she explained. "First of all, that's a ladies' umbrella. You wouldn't be caught alive under one of those. And don't you remember at breakfast the forensics man said he found a pink umbrella sack under the front seat? Pink umbrella and empty pink umbrella sack—They crunch together like peanut butter and jelly. Don't you see the conniption?"

"Of course, but I don't see how this playing card helps us," said Paco. "We don't have any prints from the crime scenes to compare it with. We don't have any prints from the turret room and the vaccine bottle, and now none from the car, according to that forensics team."

"But we do have Mr. Witherton's prints coming from the bank-account application," she pointed out.

"True, but right now that's only a possibility," warned Paco. "Even if it does prove fruitful, we won't know which of the four bridge players is the killer. There's no way to separate all the prints on the playing card."

"But if the prints are fruity, four goodly suspects are better to have than a whole houseful of fuzzy suspects, aren't they?"

Paco squinted as he thought about it. "Yeah, I guess that makes sense. We'll just have to wait and see, won't we?"

* * * *

Right after the evening meal the LeSotos returned to their suite to hear the phone ringing. It was Frank calling to let them know that the fingerprint report from the lab had just come in over the teletype.

"What did it say?" asked Paco.

"They raised two sets of clear prints from the bank document, but neither set was in the system," said Frank. "They gave us numerical identifications for each set for future reference. Oh, and they believe that one set might be female and the other male. Other than that, we have nothing."

"One female and one male? Hey, that's something. Don't get discouraged, Frank," said Paco. "Thanks to Molly, we now have something to compare those prints to. She has a hunch that our man may be one of four guys who play bridge almost every day in our recreation room. Would you believe, this afternoon she managed to swipe one of the cards, the three of diamonds, from the deck they were playing with. It should be full of fingerprints for us to compare to your first sets. It should narrow our list of suspects to four, and if any of them is in the system, we might narrow that list down even further."

"Sounds good. I can stop by first thing in the morning and take the playing card to the lab," offered Frank. "I have to pick up the application from there and return it to the bank like we promised."

"Excellent," replied Paco. "What time are you coming by?"

"How's 8:30?"

"Fine. I'll meet you down at the entrance," said Paco.

"See you then." Frank hung up.

Paco looked at Molly for a minute or two as though there were some unfinished business between them. Then he remembered. "You never did tell me who you saw with the pink umbrella."

"Now that I think about it I'm not so sure who I saw," Molly admitted. "I only glanced over there for a teensy second. He was standing at the brella-stand in front of Ms. Irma's office and I saw the back of his head as he was trying to close the umbrella. He was wearing a rain jacket with the hood up over his noggin. But my mental said it was one of those bridge guys. All four of them kinda look alike from the rear. You wait and see, I'll be right about this."

"Uh-huh," mumbled Paco, remembering how many cases he'd solved on mere hunches.

* * * *

Early Wednesday morning, the day before Thanksgiving, Frank intended to keep his word, but it took two hours longer than he expected. He hadn't taken into account the glut of traffic, even worse than on Monday—a bunch of last-minute shoppers, bumper-to-bumper, through wet, slushy streets. But at least the sky was clear and the sun was trying to make its appearance. Finally, he picked up the three of diamonds playing card in an evidence bag, and dropped it off at the lab in Baltimore. He also collected the Witherton checking account application and returned it to the First Mechanics Bank in Annapolis as he'd promised. When he returned to his office in Black Rain Corners, he called Paco.

"I dropped off the playing card," Frank reported. "But the crime lab technician told me they had a serious backlog. They're closed tomorrow, of course, and, due to holiday staffing over the Thanksgiving weekend, we won't see any search results until sometime Monday. It's a matter of priorities."

"I doubt it will matter much," admitted Paco. "I don't see the killer as a runner. I believe he's too attached to this place to give it up so easily."

"Well, have a Happy Thanksgiving then," said Frank, about to hang up.

"Wait! Molly has something she wants to ask you." He handed her the phone.

"I want to invite you to spend the day with us tomorrow, Frank. As our guest. There's a brunch from nine to ten-thirty and turkey dinner from one-thirty to four with all the holiday trimmings."

"Thank you, Molly," Frank replied. "But are you sure you want someone like me around who will talk shop with Paco on the holiday?"

"Sure we do, Frank. You can keep Paco company while he watches football all day, even if the Redskinnies aren't playing. You got a better offer than that?"

Frank hesitated for only a few seconds. As a divorced sixty-year-old with no family in Maryland, his social life was nonexistent—and especially bleak on the holidays. "Now there's an offer I can't refuse. Of course, I'll come. Thank you very much. See you tomorrow. I'll be there for brunch around nine."

* * * *

Thanksgiving weekend found Paco recovering from overeating and over-thinking about Katta's murder. But Sunday night gave him a welcome distraction. The Washington Redskins defeated the Oakland Raiders 37 to 6.

On Monday morning, the last day of November, the phone rang twice. Drowsy but awake, Paco leaned over a still-sleeping Molly to answer it. Sliding out of the sheet and comforter, he held the stretched-out phone cord high as he walked around to the other side of the bed.

"It's 6:45, for God's sake," he whispered into the phone. "Who the heck is this?"

217

"Sorry, ole buddy, it's Frank. I got the report back on the play-ing card prints. It was on the teletype as soon as I walked into the office. I thought you'd want to know right away."

"I do. What's it say?" asked Paco.

"Lots of good prints. One of the four playing card prints is a sixteen-point match with the male prints on the bank application. Two of the playing card prints are in the system from their military service. One is Colonel Mark Tomlinson, U.S. Army, Retired. The other one is Corporal Gordon H. Lowe, III. Neither of these two match the bank application."

"That leaves us with two suspects," said Paco. "Our killer is ei-ther Chester Parker or Harry Lightfoot."

"Looks like we're getting close to an arrest," said Frank. "Good work. Talk to you later."

As soon as Paco put the phone down Molly sat up in bed. She'd been listening intently and asked, "How can you deliminate Mark and Gordon from the list of suspects? What's going on, anyway?" She rubbed her eyelids with her fists, slid her feet off the bed into fake-leopard slippers, and padded across the floor toward the bath-room. She hesitated outside for the answer to her question.

"The lab report on the playing card prints is back," Paco yelled. "We eliminated Mark and Gordon because we have their military service prints and neither one of them matches Witherton's. But we do have lots of good prints, including a match with Witherton's."

"Oh goodie," said Molly, as she disappeared into the bathroom.

A few minutes later Paco heard a flushing and faucet running. Molly appeared in the doorway with a pensive look on her face. She stood there for a moment, running a hand through her tight pearly-gray curls. He could almost imagine the wheels turning in her head. "What?" he asked, knowing his wife was about to make a major pronouncement.

"Chester Parker has got to be our killer," said Molly.

"Hey, Mol, wait a minute. Chester was nice to me the day we moved in, got me a luggage cart. Sure, he's a snobby Englishman, and he's not friendly to us 'cuz we don't play bridge, but that doesn't automatically make him a killer," scolded Paco. "What makes you think we can eliminate Happy Harry so easily?"

"I remember that Happy Harry added Dora Ferarri to our missing persons list. Why would he tell us that—help us, if he was the same person that made them disappear?"

"Maybe Happy Harry just cooperated with us to throw us off the track. We still don't have enough to nail either him or Chester."

"What else do we know about those two guys?" asked Molly.

"Other than a pretty good guess of their ages and the fact that they like to play the sophisticated game of bridge—absolutely nothing."

"But we do have Jonathan R. Witherton's fingerprints," said Molly. "I need to get more fingerprints."

Oh-oh. Paco scowled and his mustache twitched. *My wife's on a roll and that could be bad.*

"What we need now is get to breakfast before they stop serving," he said. "Even if we use prints to positively eliminate one or the other of the two men, the only crime so far is tax fraud. I want the man for kidnapping, murder, and attempted murder. And…I don't want you taking any more risks, Molly. I mean it. It's downright dangerous."

When they finished washing and dressing, they left the suite for the cafeteria. The menu that morning was waffles with jam, sausages, and beverage. It was Molly's favorite breakfast here, so when she finished her portion, she went back for seconds, despite Paco casting her an annoyed look. While waiting in line, she noticed some of the residents carrying their trays to the Drop-off window, and this gave her an idea—but only after her own breakfast. She looked around the room and spied Chester and Harry eating at their separate tables.

A third waffle and sausage were doled out onto Molly's tray, and she returned to her chair across from a frowning Paco. She ate quickly, with her eyes darting between the two suspects, waiting for either one to get up with his tray.

Munching his bagel, Paco knew his wife was up to something,

but he couldn't comprehend what, which made him extra-nervous.

Minutes later, one of the two suspects got up and headed for the Drop-off window. Molly swallowed the last bite of sausage, set her tray down on Roly's bag, which was nestled between the handlebars, and toddled toward the Drop-off window. Paco's mouth dropped open. His wife had left the table without so much as an "Excuse me." It wasn't like her. He was even more startled when she managed to get in line right behind one of the suspects.

The man laid his tray on the sill, turned, and started to walk away. Molly didn't wait for his tray to be whisked away. Instead, she placed her tray on top of his and palmed the butter knife from his tray, clutching it by the buttery blade. As a result, her tray was taken away first and the suspect's next. The kitchen helper on the other side of the window grumbled a comment—indistinguishable, yet heard as a grunt, a sound that caused the suspect to turn for a second and look back. But did he see Molly slip his butter knife into her dress pocket?

She returned to the table and waited for Paco to finish his breakfast. He wiped his chin with a napkin, stood up, and without a word, carried his tray to the Drop-off window. He knew she'd been engaged in some kind of risky stealth maneuver because she was humming a little tune as they walked back to their suite.

"What the devil are you up to now, Mol?" he asked.

"I may have some fresh prints for you, sweetie," she whispered.

"I've told you how dangerous your meddling can be, and you stuck your neck out anyway."

She giggled. "You never complained about our necking before this."

Chapter 29
Gone Missing

The first day of December arrived with a weak sun struggling to melt the dirty snow still lingering from recent storms. Molly was restless, looking for something to do. She had heard that Bertha Bubbaschlufsky wasn't feeling well and decided to pay her a visit at one o'clock in the afternoon. She knew that Bertha was now installed unwillingly in one of the dormitory rooms.

Molly pushed Roly to the nearest elevator and pressed the DOWN button. Just as it arrived, a tall, wiry man stepped out of the stairwell door and followed her into the otherwise empty elevator. She recognized him, but couldn't face him. He frightened her, so she turned her back—definitely a wrong move. Something smelled sweet all of a sudden. The next thing she knew, a gauze pad had been slapped across her mouth and nose. She struggled to no avail. He was too rough. Soon the smell became even sweeter and stronger until she couldn't sense anything and slumped to the floor.

Her abductor removed a key from his pocket and placed it in the key slot. He turned the key and pressed UP. The elevator skipped two floors and zoomed directly to the roof. When the doors opened, the man locked the elevator in place, removed and pocketed the key, and dragged heavy Molly out onto the roof. Leaving her lying there for a few seconds, he stepped into the elevator, turned it back on, and pressed the button for the first floor, leaving Roly inside. He ducked out, allowing the unit to function normally, down and up, excluding the roof stop. He had no intention of bringing the Rollator walker into the turret.

The kidnapper dragged Molly across the roof and through the double doors to the room at the top of the turret. Inside, he hefted her onto a long work table that was covered with a cheap cotton blanket, and laid her flat on her back. Wearing a black nylon bag strapped diagonally over one shoulder, he unzipped it and pulled out an already-prepped syringe. He pushed the left sleeve of Molly's flowered dress up to her shoulder and injected a long-term sedative into her fleshy upper arm, then studied her for several minutes to be sure she was deeply zonked from the combination of chloroform and sedative. He smiled grimly. *I'll remove her from the facility under cover of darkness tonight. I can't take a chance with her now. She's the cop's snooping wife, and she saw me with the pink umbrella. That damned thing will surely connect me to Nurse Katta's murder.*

* * * *

Inside the LeSoto suite, Paco had been reading Dickens's *Great Expectations* for several hours when he heard the heavy padding of feet outside the door. *Maybe it's Molly returning from her visit to Bertha.* When the sound subsided and the door didn't open, he decided it wasn't her. He tore his attention away from Pip's London exploits to the clock on the wall. *Four-thirty. She should be back by now.* His concern grew. At 5:30 the last straw broke, and he reached for the in-house telephone directory. Paco found Bertha's number and quickly dialed it.

"Bertha, it's Paco. Can I speak with Molly, please?"

"Molly isn't here, Paco. This morning she called me to say she was coming to spend the afternoon with me, but she never showed up. I even bought her favorite noodle kugel with raisins. Is she sick? Is there something wrong?"

"I don't know," replied Paco. "She left here at one o'clock with every intent of visiting you. The dining room opens in another half-hour, and you know Molly when it comes to missing a meal.

I'm going out to try and find her now."

Paco slipped into his shoes and a jacket and left the suite. When she wasn't to be found in the recreation room, the exercise room, or the pool, he tried the dining room and the busy kitchen with equally negative results. Neither Dr. Crisp nor Ms. Irma had seen her all afternoon. Outside the front door, he found Jeff Amati and a friend tossing a baseball back and forth. They hadn't seen Molly either.

A terrifying thought mushroomed in his mind, a thought he'd been attempting to suppress for the last hour. He hurried back into the dining room, this time seeking out the two remaining suspects. He knew where each of them usually sat because there were assigned tables for evening meals, which were sit-down, catered, and waitressed. Both seats were unoccupied. He retreated into Ms. Irma's empty office, picked up the phone on her desk, and dialed Frank at the police station.

"Black Rain Corners Police, Sergeant Mullins."

"Frank, it's Paco. Molly's missing, and I believe the murderer has kidnapped her. I need your help. How soon can you get over here?"

"I'll leave now," said Frank. "Be there in fifteen minutes."

Paco's stomach lurched as he set the receiver down, visualizing Molly as a prisoner up in the room at the top of the turret. He considered all the ways he might get to her. The first one that came to mind was the way they'd entered the first time—from the secret door in the basement. *Maybe I can sneak up on the murderer that way.* But entering the basement through the kitchen was out of the question during mealtime with Carla and her assistant cooks buzzing around, so he rushed down the corridor to the parlor.

Oh crap! In the parlor, he found at least five residents lounging about—chatting, reading, watching TV. His heart began to race with frustration. *How can I do this without everybody seeing me?* Luck was with him. Everyone was just marking time before going in to dinner. Five minutes later, they all drifted out of the parlor, down the hall, and into the dining room. No one noticed that Paco wasn't joining them.

He approached the Leaping Lion tapestry on the back wall and moved the right bottom corner to one side. At the seam in the paneled wall, he used his two membership cards to lift the two latch handles up. The secret door leading to the basement swung open. Once it was open, he flew down the stairs, at least that was his intention. At eighty-seven, flying wasn't an option. He gripped the railing with his right hand and focused on each concrete step to keep from falling. He discovered that the two shelving units were still standing away from the wall, exposing the secret door. He lifted the broken padlock from its hasp and tugged on the door handle. The door wouldn't budge. He shook it a number of times, then tried forcing it with all his strength. No deal. The door had obviously been secured from the inside, most likely barred.

He climbed back up to the first floor, rushed out of the parlor, and continued along the long corridor in front of Fellowship Hall until he found himself in front of the special roof elevator. He recognized it all right, but the damned thing made noise—he wouldn't be able to surprise the culprit. *If I can't surprise the sonofabitch kidnapper, I'd better be armed. I'll need the elevator key as well.* He rode the elevator to the second floor of Fellowship Hall, and entered the LeSoto suite.

Heart hammering, Paco strode to the bedroom and his bureau. Yanking open the deep top drawer, he pushed aside the pile of rolled-up socks and grabbed the large metal box hiding in the back. With a key from the ring in his khaki pants pocket, he unlocked the box and lifted up the lid, exposing a bulky oil-soaked rag. He carefully unwrapped it to reveal two handguns: a Colt .45 and a Glock 9mm, both semiautomatic pistols—all that were left of his former gun collection. He selected the Glock. While he loaded the eight-round magazine, he noticed a pair of keys in the bottom of the box. The flat key he knew was the one to the turret stairs from the Crisp apartment. The unique barrel shape reminded him that this was the second elevator key he had confiscated from Dr. Crisp's files.

Paco slipped the loaded Glock into his waistband and the keys into his pants pocket, then shut the box, shoved it behind the pile of socks, and slammed the drawer shut. He felt beads of cold sweat under his armpits. This wasn't a routine chase. It was his precious wife. As he left the suite, he heard a police cruiser siren wind down outside the main entrance. He got to the first floor in time to meet Frank opposite Dr. Crisp's office.

"Thank God you're here," said Paco. "I'm pretty sure he's got her in that room at the top of the turret."

"Is he armed?" asked Frank.

"There's no way of telling until we actually confront him. But I'm armed."

"Okay. How do we get up there? Can't we just take the stairs?"

"No," said Paco. "The public stairs for the residents don't go all the way up to the roof. Follow me."

Paco led the way down the corridor in front of Fellowship Hall and into the special elevator. "My God!" cried Paco. "Molly's walker! Now I'm sure she's up there." With shaking hand, he inserted the barrel key in the keyhole marked ROOF. On one clockwise twist of that key, the doors closed, the elevator car hummed loudly and rose three floors. The two men's weapons were drawn when they opened the door to the roof. They stepped out and tiptoed toward the steel double doors of the turret, their eyes and guns ever turning this way and that, wary of surprise from some other part of the roof. When they arrived at the steel doors, Frank was the first to notice that the handles had been removed.

"We can't get in. Now what?"

"At least we now know for sure that they're inside," said Paco.

"Do we have a plan B?" asked Frank.

"Maybe. Frank, you stay here to make sure he doesn't break out this way. I'm going to try another way in."

"Paco, you said there was no other way short of breaking down doors."

"That's right," Paco said. "I'm going to get into the turret steps from the second-floor door of the Crisps' kitchen. I've got the key in my pocket."

Frank frowned, thinking *How the hell can he get into the Crisps' apartment?* But not wanting to shame his old-man deputy, he merely said, "Good luck, man."

Actually, Paco had no idea how he was going to do it. He took the elevator back to the first floor, ran down the corridor, and approached the Crisps' private apartment door. He eyed the big red fire extinguisher cylinder sitting on a wall hook a few feet away. He took it down and was ready to smash it through one of the smaller cherrywood door panels when he heard someone behind him.

"Whoa there, LeSoto!" yelled Phelix. "What the hell are you trying to do, break my door down?"

"Actually, yeah. The murderer is holding my Molly hostage in the turret room, and there's no other way to get there except through your apartment—the doors to the turret stairs."

"What about the elevator to the roof or the basement door?" asked Phelix.

"They're both locked—barricaded." Paco's voice trembled. "I planned to pay for the damages to your door anyway."

"Here, let me unlock our door for you," said Phelix. A few seconds later he had the residence door open. "Go up the stairs, straight down the hall to our kitchen and then to your left. The second key I gave you is for both the kitchen and bedroom access doors."

"I know," said Paco. "I have it right here in my pocket."

Paco climbed up the stairs and followed Phelix's directions to the kitchen. But it wasn't until he reached the turret door that he realized his heart was also racing, hammering hard against his chest like it was planning its own escape. Then he felt the terrible shock, the internal device alarm. He dropped onto a kitchen chair for a couple minutes until his defibrillator corrected the messed-up beat. It was a mean warning, but he had to press on—his Molly was in danger, and Molly was his life and love. He rubbed his sore chest with his left hand and unlocked the door to the turret with his right. Just as he opened it Phelix appeared in the kitchen behind him.

"You okay?" asked Phelix. "You don't look so well."

"I'm good," replied Paco with clipped breath. "Stay here. Lock the door behind me."

Paco heard the lock fall into place as he started the agonizing climb up the spiral steps. His heart began to pound again, but nowhere near like before. He imagined his footsteps were much louder than they were. He heard no movement, nor any sounds emanating from the room above. He knew the layout up there, but not what to expect from the murderer. Occasionally, he heard a faint familiar moaning, like Molly awakening from a deep sleep, and he tried to find some comfort in it—she was still alive! He moved slowly, and when the landing finally came into view, he withdrew the Glock from his waistband and held it out in front of him. As he mounted the last few steps, he felt a gust of wind from the one window rush across his face. He was there! In the turret room!

The moment Paco stepped inside, a fist came crashing into the side of his head. The stunning blow sent the small man to the floor on his back, his gun in another direction. His attacker retrieved the Glock, loomed over him, and held him down with a foot across his chest. Paco stared hard into the semidarkness surrounding the man's face, but he still couldn't identify his enemy, only the business end of his own lost Glock. Frank couldn't be of any help—he was locked on the other side of the two steel doors.

Chapter 30
Pure Grit

Paco lay on his back, helpless to move under the shoe pressing down on his stomach. He did his damnedest to counter the pressure by pushing on the man's ankle with his bare hands, but they weren't enough. All he could do was lie there, endure the painful pressure, and stare into the surrounding semidarkness until he made out the barrel of his Glock close to his face. As soon as the man made sure that Paco had seen the gun in his possession, he removed his foot and stepped out of the shadows into what little remained of the day's twilight. From his current position, Paco saw a tall, skinny man with a narrow, clean-shaven chin. *Not Chester Parker by a long shot*, he thought.

"Get up. Get your ass over to the window and sit down on the floor so I can keep an eye on you," growled the man.

Paco's knees wobbled as he stood up and did as he was told, lowering himself onto the floor under the window. He had been listening intently. The voice was familiar, someone he knew. Sitting under the window gave him a different perspective of the man. The full head of red hair flecked with gray streaks. But the cowlick over the forehead and drooping over one eye clinched it. The man was Happy Harry Lightfoot.

"You won't get away with this, Harry," said Paco. "Sergeant Frank Mullins is on the other side of those double doors. He and others already know that you are Jonathan R. Witherton."

"And he can't get in here, can he?" said Harry with a leer. "It's our party—yours and mine. And without women who whine and interfere, throwing emotional monkey wrenches into my plans."

Paco gasped. "God in heaven, Harry, you killed Katta Brounell!"

"So? That bitch deserved it. She was about to betray me."

An inflamed Paco was about to respond when he heard a weak sound, something between a moan and a yawn. He struggled to his feet, not caring what Harry might do about it. He saw the four-panel room-divider and lurched forward to push it aside. His captor did not stop him. What he saw was a motionless Molly lying on a worktable on her back with her eyes shut, emanating slight snores, her chest heaving and falling. Paco felt his heart skip a beat with indescribable gratitude finding that she was indeed alive.

Worried that Paco might make a move on him, even in his weakened state, Harry quickly turned his attention back to his newest prisoner. Meanwhile, Paco continued to stare at his wife, wondering what to do next. He was afraid to waken her too suddenly, but couldn't bear to see her lying there so helpless. And he didn't want to get shot either.

A quarter of an hour passed before her eyelids began to flutter, then opened to the world around her. She rolled on her side to see better. Her eyes widened with fright as she saw Happy Harry standing there with a gun trained on Paco. Molly dared not speak. She kept her silence and slid her bulk slowly off the table where she'd been held until her sneakered feet touched the concrete floor. Fully conscious now, she furtively glanced about for a weapon of her own and decided the empty glass water pitcher sitting on the side table might be just the thing. But it dawned on her: *Hells bells, no Roly, no canes.* She steadied herself by grabbing a corner of the long table, a chair, anything within reach. Shuffling behind Harry, she yelled "Hey!" knowing he couldn't keep his eyes on both Paco and his prisoner at the same time.

Swinging the glass pitcher from her hip, she clobbered Harry up the side of his head. The staggering blow sent him two steps forward and face down. The gun flew out of his hand, slid forward to the edge of the stairs, then over the edge and out of sight. Although Molly had delivered her most stunning blow, Harry was still stirring, attempting to get to his feet.

Paco seized the moment by jumping on top of him. The two men rolled about on the concrete floor, wrestling for optimal position, neither man able to stay atop the other long enough to throw a decent punch—only harmless short jabs. But Molly could see that Harry was a head taller than Paco and at least ten years younger. Wobbling in her flowered dress, she struggled to follow them around the floor, looking for an opportunity to strike again with her pitcher, but a clear opening never came. Still weak and slightly woozy from her captivity and the drugs injected into her, she had to be careful not to be pulled down into their desperate, drawn-out struggle. Finally, Harry's hands went for Paco's throat, and the small detective couldn't pull them away. He balled up both fists and swung at Harry just below the ribs with all the strength he had. Harry let go of his throat and sat up straight long enough to muster a roundhouse to Paco's chin.

Molly shrieked when she saw Paco's body collapse, out cold. While Harry was trying to stand up, she thumped toward him and head-butted him squarely in the stomach, ramming him down onto his backside. She intended to kick him in the solar plexus while he was still vulnerable, but he managed to bring his skinny body to his feet. Seeing Molly's intention, he took two steps backward—one too many—and teetered on the top step of the concrete stairwell. He attempted to stabilize himself by grabbing the wall and stepping down one step. But that one move put his foot directly on the spot where the Glock had landed. Seeing his plight, Molly straightened up and shuffled closer. Harry tried to fall forward, but she placed her hand on his chest and gave him the slightest shove, a mere tap, toppling him backwards into the depths of the spiral staircase. He tumbled around the natural curve and out of sight. His bellowing and screeching were short lived. Molly heard his nonstop tumbling for a few more seconds, hoping he'd fallen all the way to the bottom. She continued to listen keenly in case there were any more movements below, but heard only silence.

"Ooh! Ooh!" moaned Paco, regaining consciousness on the cold concrete floor.

Molly shuffle-rushed over to him. "My poor sweetie, are you okay? Where do you hurt?"

"My head," Paco groaned. "It feels like I'm gonna have a knot the size of a golf ball by tomorrow. But where the hell is Harry?"

"Nowhere. Are you cussioned? Do you know who you are and where we are?"

"Of course I do," he replied. "Do I have to tell you that I'm Paco and you're Molly and we're up in the top of the stone turret."

"Thank God, but you will still have to see a fishishion tomorrow."

"I will. My jaw feels like mush where he hit me." He put his hand in his mouth and retrieved a bloody tooth. He was about to throw it aside.

"No no, keep it," said Molly. "Maybe the dentist can glue it back."

"Now will you tell me what happened to Unhappy Harry?" asked Paco.

"He tripped on your gun and fell down the steps," she said, "and I haven't heard from him since."

"Maybe we should check on the sonofabitch," said Paco. He started toward the stairs.

"Careful, don't trip, hon," she said. "That gun is still on the steps somewhere."

Paco found his Glock and was about to descend the stairs, when they heard a banging on the steel double doors.

"It's Frank outside," said Paco. "I forgot all about him being out there. Look, the door handles, they're on the floor. That's why Frank and I couldn't get in that way."

Paco pressed down on the inside bars to release the doors, and they both swung open. Frank stepped inside the turret. He swung around with his gun in hand, quickly scanning the room.

"Well, where the hell is he?" yelled Frank. "Did he get away?"

"He fell way down the spinning stairwell," said Molly, glowing with an imaginary halo above her head. "We haven't seen him since."

"I was about to go down and see whether Harry actually survived the fall," Paco blurted out. "Not likely, though."

"Harry?" repeated Frank. "I thought you said the killer's name was Chester."

"No. I said he was one of the two possible killers," said Paco, with a shrug of his shoulders. "Molly was convinced it was Chester."

"You needn't go down the stairs, Paco," said Frank. "I'll check him out, and you two can go back to your suite. Molly, thank the good Lord you're alive and okay. You guys have had enough trauma for today."

He studied the two of them, first searching Paco's drawn, weary face, then Molly's. "Hey, would you like me to call 9-1-1? Get an ambulance to take you both to the hospital to get checked out?"

"No no no," the LeSotos protested in unison. "But thanks for the offer," added Paco.

As Frank started down the spiral staircase, Paco, still his wiry, strong self, supported Molly and pressed the roof elevator button. The doors opened. She shrieked, "Roly! Boy-o-boy, am I glad to see you!" She plunged inside and grabbed the handlebars. On the second floor she vigorously pushed her walker alongside Paco and into their suite.

"Hon, did Harry give you anything to eat?"

"You kiddin'?"

"We both haven't eaten since lunch, darlin'," said Paco. "And the dining room closed hours ago."

"Sit down, sweetiekins. I'll fix us some peanut butter and jelly sandwiches and a glass of milk. Then my hero can tell me all about how he rescued me."

Seated at the small kitchen table across from each other, Paco told her the story of his relentless search for her, his call for Frank's help, and finding her walker in the elevator. It was then that he knew she'd been kidnapped and was being held in the room at the top of the turret. He was sure she was in there when he and Frank were stopped by the double doors with their handles removed. When he told her of his trip through the second floor of the Crisp residence, he began to rub his chest unconsciously, and Molly took notice.

"What happened to you in the Crisp residence?" she asked. "Did you have another heart attack?"

"I don't think so…well, maybe. More like a warning," he replied, face pale and unshaven. "The alarm went off in my defib, and it gave me one hell of a shock. I had to sit down for a few minutes until my strength came back. Then I was okay, so I continued up the stairs. Harry knew I was coming for him. He lay in wait for me at the top of the stairs and hid behind the wall. He knocked the gun out of my hand and we wrestled for a bit until he landed a good one to my chin. I hit the back of my head hard and I was out of it for a few minutes, so I don't know what happened after that."

"You poor darling," said Molly. "We'll get you to a doctor for a checking-up first thing in the morning." She got up from the table. At the refrigerator, she opened the small freezer compartment and grabbed a bag of frozen peas. "Here, hold this on the back of your head where it hurts. It will help the swelling go down."

"What did happen while I was out, anyway, hon?" he asked.

"I head-butted him once and when I came at him the second time, he was already teetering on the edge of the stairs. It only took a little tap on his chest to send him on his way."

"So, you helped him over the edge then?"

"Just a teensy bit," she said, her cupid lips in a crooked grin.

A knock on the door to the suite disrupted their conversation. Molly let Frank in.

"Big news, guys. I just wanted to tell you that Mr. Lightfoot has met his end—a broken neck. He wound up on the second-floor landing right by the door. An ambulance is on its way to pick up the body. I took a few pictures to document his fall. That's about it. Now I'll leave you two in peace. And a few days from now, when you've fully recovered, Paco, you can write me up a complete report."

"You better believe it," Paco said with a weak smile.

"Thank you, Frank," said Molly. "And now you can disembowel Paco from being your deputy, so he can go back into retirement. Permanent this time. I don't want his filibuster alarm going off anymore."

THE END

Larry grew up in New Haven, Connecticut, and served in the U.S. Navy during the Korean War. After earning a BS in Information Systems Management from American U., he became a field engineer riding Navy ships for RCA. He spent most of his career at Honeywell/Alliant Techsystems, designing electronic equipment for the U.S. Government. Larry feels fortunate to have wed two terrific ladies. Losing Hannah to leukemia in 1986, he married Rosemary some time later. Together they launched their career coauthoring mystery, suspense, and fantasy fiction in their Honolulu condo overlooking the Pacific Ocean.

Rosemary, a Smith College graduate and former *Harper's* assistant editor, also writes personal essays, many published in the *Washington Post, Baltimore Sun, Chess Life*, and elsewhere. She was divorced when she met Larry on a blind date. He told her, "When I retire, I'm going to write a novel and I want you to help me." She knew he was Mr. Right, so she chirped, "Okay!" Twenty-two books later, Larry still conjures up their mysterious plots while Rosemary adds the pizzazz. And they haven't killed each other yet!

Email the Milds at:
roselarry@magicile.com
Visit them at www.magicile.com

The Paco and Molly Mystery Series (#1)

Locks and Cream Cheese—In scandal-ridden Black Rain Corners, a Chesapeake Bay mansion harbors locked rooms and deadly secrets. A wily detective and a gourmet cook tackle the case.

The Paco and Molly Mystery Series (#2)

Hot Grudge Sunday—Bank robbers and conspirators derail the sleuths' blissful honeymoon at the Grand Canyon. Can they nail the suspects after they themselves become targets?

The Paco and Molly Mystery Series (#3)

Boston Scream Pie—A teenage girl's nightmare triggers a sinister tale of twins, two feuding families, and a blonde bombshell who hates being called "Mom."

Available on Amazon.com and all e-readers.

Kent and Katcha: *Espionage, Spycraft, Romance*—Novice American spy Kent Brukner is sent on a mission to Russia where he meets passionate Katcha. Together they face Major Dmitri Federov and his crafty colleague Sasha. Based on Larry's association with former secret operatives.

Kauai Spies and Big Lies—New adventures of Kent and Katcha that take them to the Hawaiian Islands to fight domestic spies and probate fraud.

Coming Next Year

On the Rails, *The Adventures of Boxcar Bertie*—What's a young teacher to do when she is unemployed and homeless in 1936—the middle of the Great Depression? Bertie Patchet dresses as a male, takes to the rails, and rides boxcars into the dangerous unknown.

Available on Amazon.com and all e-readers.

The Dan and Rivka Sherman Mystery Series (#1)

Death Goes Postal—Rare 15th-century typesetting artifacts journey through time, leaving a horrifying imprint in their wake. Dan and Rivka risk life and limb to locate the treasures and unmask the murderer. Not quite what they expected when they bought the Olde Victorian Bookstore. **(Also available as an Amazon Audible Audiobook)**

The Dan and Rivka Sherman Mystery Series (#2)

Death Takes A Mistress—A young Englishwoman is murdered by her lover. Years later her daughter, seeking revenge, journeys from London to Annapolis, MD to find her father. But to which family does he belong? Dan and Rivka set out to expose the true villain.

The Dan and Rivka Sherman Mystery Series (#3)

Death Steals A Holy Book—Dan and Rivka inherit a rare Yiddish translation of a 14th-century holy book, but it is stolen and their book restorer is murdered. Can they recover the book and nail the culprit? Our story is based on an actual rare volume inherited by author Larry.

Available on Amazon.com and all e-readers.

The Dan and Rivka Sherman Mystery Series (#4)

Death Rules the Night—All the copies of an important book are missing from the bookstore, local libraries, and the author's bookshelves. Who is trying to hide the book's secrets and what are they? Can stalking, threats, and murder keep Dan from solving this mystery? Rivka fears for their lives.

Cry O'hana, Adventure and Suspense in Hawai'i—A car accident, blackmail, and murder tear apart a Hawaiian o'hana (family). Teenager Kekoa witnesses the murder and is forced to live a life on the run. Danger erupts at a Filipino wedding, a Maui resort, and the Big Island's volcanic steam vents. Can the family reunite and bring down the killer?

Honolulu Heat—Leilani and Alex Wong anguish over their son, Noah, an idealistic teenager who teeters on both sides of the law. He meets his dream girl, but they share horrific secrets. Noah finds himself immersed in a bloody feud between a Chinatown protection racketeer and a crimeland don.

Available on Amazon.com and all e-readers.

Unto the Third Generation—Two young people, each unaware of the other, volunteer to become cryonauts—physically frozen in a life suspension experiment. A steelworker and a waitress postpone their destinies for untold generations. But two world-shaking events put their lives in jeopardy.

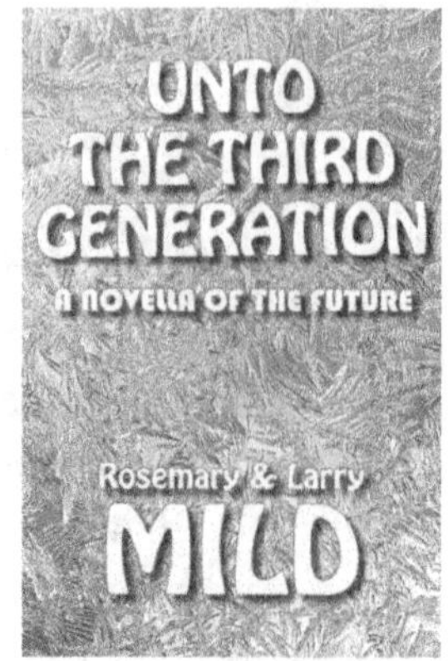

Charley and the Magic Jug and Other Stories—Climb the mountain to the secret cave with Charley. Watch three brothers face a sweet but certain death. Learn how a tiny pill can threaten lives. Get away through time with thieves. See what the tide reveals in "Tsunami." Follow Casey as he chases the ladies. And so much more.

ALSO BY LARRY

No Place To Be But Here—It is not only Larry's own story, but that of his family. Join him as he tells how his two wives, three children, and five grandchildren have shaped his life as much as he has molded theirs. Tragedy is certainly no stranger as he deals with death, cancer, murder, and global terrorism, not only on the written page, but in his own life.

Available on Amazon.com and all e-readers.

Murder, Fantasy, and Weird Tales—Delve into tales of the brave, the foolhardy, and the wicked on their journeys to the unknown in Hawai'i, Japan, Cambodia, Italy and elsewhere. Art lovers, a hit woman, a vampire, and others reveal their secret compulsions.

The Misadventures of Slim O. Wittz, Soft-Boiled Detective—"If you're looking for a truly bumbling gumshoe, you want me, Slim. I'm frequently behind the eight ball and seldom paid. In eight complete mystery stories I always bump into criminals. And you're right: my case record is remarkably shaky."

Copper and Goldie • 13 Tails of Mystery and Suspense in Hawai'i—Sam, a disabled cop now a PI, and his canine sidekick, Goldie, ply the streets of Honolulu's dark side in a Checker Cab, stalking bank robbers, kidnappers, and killers.

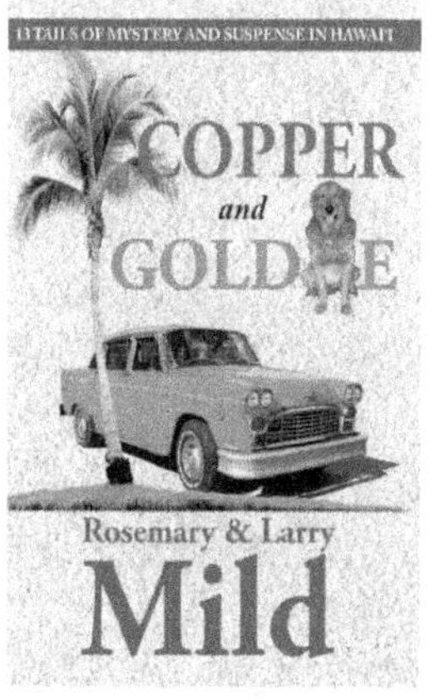

Available on Amazon.com and all e-readers.

Miriam's World—and Mine—Miriam Luby Wolfe, a junior at Syracuse U., spent her fall semester in London exploring her talents: singing, dancing, acting, and writing. But she never made it home. A terrorist bomb destroyed her plane over Lockerbie, Scotland. Learn about Miriam, the Pan Am families, the bombers, and the political fallout.

Love! Laugh! Panic! Life with My Mother—Don't we all have mixed emotions about our mothers? Rosemary's mom was super-achieving, but tough to live with. Luby Pollack was a journalist, popular book author, and psychiatrist's wife. Always the heroine and sometimes the villain, from the viewpoint of her loving but ornery daughter.

In My Next Life I'll Get It Right—A collection of personal essays ranging from the hilarious to the serious—keen, sometimes wicked, observations on everyday life. See how Rosemary views her two marriages. Join her as she takes on sailing, skating, Jazzercise, football, and more—and feel for a mother's heart-wrenching loss.

Available on Amazon.com and all e-readers.